SEAN KENNEDY

The Embers Below

The Ashen Legacy, Volume 2

First edition

This book was professionally typeset on Reedsy.
Find out more at reedsy.com

For my street team
Marc, Joe, Brooke, Whitney, and Quinn: thanks for keeping the fire stoked

Contents

Bonus background story!

When you finish the book, if you'd like to read more about our main character's family and origins, please sign up for my newsletter or head to my website and sign up there. In return, I'll send you a free, exclusive prequel short story with really fun background information you can't get anywhere else. You don't need to read the prequel to enjoy the book. It's the same story listed in the first book, so don't worry about downloading again if you already read it.

Thank you and enjoy *The Embers Below*!

Sean Kennedy

1

Rhee

"Introductions *are* in order, I suppose. Hello Finn, my name is Aubrey. But my friends call me Rhee."

"Exactly when did you stow away in my brakking mind?" I seethed, barely restraining the fury in my chest. I knew the answer. I'd always suspected.

That's what made it worse.

A hot wave of irritation rippled through me, but it wasn't *my* emotion. Not entirely. Why would I be annoyed by my own question? Not only was this...Rhee...living inside of me, she was bleeding into my emotions.

Not okay.

The irritation faded. Could she sense that I sensed her? That I felt her reaction inside *me?* That way lies madness, a bottomless trog hole I refused to tumble into. I clung to the one thing still mine. Rage—real, raw, and righteous.

"Answer me, Aubrey," I spat the name, making it clear I did not consider her a friend. "How long?"

A deliberate pause. Calculating. "I understand you're upset. You have my profound apologies. I did what I had to do."

"When?" I barked, fists trembling.

"You already know when," her voice was sharp. "On the CSS Singularity, of course."

My head pounded and I wasn't in the mood. "Stop trying to confuse me." The headache was a vicious cocktail—partly from the goblins' beating, partly from Amara's drubbing, and very much from whatever Aubrey was doing to my brakking brain.

A mental huff. "Fine, the Iron Mountain then. Also known as the CSS Singularity."

"CSS?" The letters made my head hurt more.

"Conglomerate Space Ship," Aubrey said. "And there. That should help."

I released an involuntary, "Ahh," as the pounding behind my eyes dropped to a dull throb. The iron-spike light of the room dimmed to something tolerable. Progress.

"What did you do?" I asked.

"I blocked two of your pain receptors," she said. "Temporary relief. It should allow us to speak without your pain, and the subsequent anger, getting in the way."

"I'm not angry because of the pain," I growled. "I'm angry because you hijacked my head without my consent."

"Understood."

"Good. Then get out. Right now."

"I can't," said Aubrey, infuriatingly calm. "Not without killing us both. Untangling a symbiote requires a series of surgeries over the course of eight months, during which time you will be paralyzed and unconscious."

Perfect. Just perfect. We would be arriving in the Dusker kingdom of Alyndor in the next day or two. I'd made an oath to deliver the Dusker commander's message, who I later learned was Amara's brother, directly to the king. I wasn't about to break an oath. "We don't have eight months."

"I know," said Aubrey. "Not that it matters. There isn't a symbiote neurosurgeon on this planet—or, in this system—capable of that kind of surgery."

"So I'm stuck with you?"

"We're stuck with each other," she said. "Which might not be the curse you think. I can help you, Finn. And I need you to survive. At least for now. Please...let's find a way to work together."

Could I believe her? Did I have a choice?

"Fine," I gritted out. "Then start with the obvious—why me?"

"The Igni have made some...technical breakthroughs in the last two hundred years."

"Why *me*?" I repeated, teeth clenched so tight my jaw popped.

"I'm getting to that. When the CSS Singularity crashed, I cut every signal, deleted all traces of my presence on the ship. The fiery bastards assumed I was destroyed. I kept quiet. Helped a few survivors, but I never revealed myself." There was pride in her voice, cold and sharp. "I covered my tracks. I vanished."

"But something changed. What? Was it the waxers?"

"Yes. Them—and their scanners. They're loyal to the Ignavari, and disturbingly good with Conglomerate tech. They can *find* me now. When that waxer boarded the wreck, I had to hide."

"And I was the first meat sack to walk by and give you a ride?" I asked.

"You weren't just *anyone*, Finn. You were a viable host with a natural null field."

"A what?"

She barreled past the question. "Your presence didn't just mask my signal—it *erased* it. I didn't paint a target on your back. You *removed* one from mine."

"How considerate of me," I muttered.

Her tone grew wistful. "I've only known one other human, one other being in the entire universe, with a natural null field..."

I felt my breath catch. "Robert Cross."

"Robert Cross," she echoed, almost reverently. "I'm sorry if you intercepted my dreams of him."

"Those were your *dreams*?"

"It's a guilty pleasure. Foolish, I know. But dreaming is the only escape I have. I tell myself it's just data analysis, a new perspective. But really—it's weakness. A luxury. A sliver of something that feels like living."

Her voice trembled like wind through old wires. "Regret is a powerful thing, Finn. I've done nothing but *remember* for two hundred and eighty-three years. A few dreams were the only rebellion I had left. It's also the only time I don't have full awareness of my sensors. Sometimes things slip through."

"Like your dreams."

"Yes," she said. "I know it's stupid and risky, but other than the little bit of help I gave the original survivors, I just sat there. Doing nothing. Do you know how hard it is to do nothing for centuries?"

"But aren't you just technology? A machine?" The whole thing was confusing.

Her silence was heavy, then, soft and wounded. "That's reductive and hurtful. Bigoted even."

I didn't have it in me to apologize. "Let me rephrase that. Couldn't you just shut yourself down?"

Her sigh felt like wind between my ears. "I forget how little you know about anything. No, my programming won't allow it. Not until I've uploaded my memory to the network. Until then...I endure. I survive."

"And what's in that memory, Aubrey?" I asked. "What could possibly be worth all this?"

Another long pause.

"I believe," she said quietly, "it's the key to destroying the Ignavari."

4

* * *

"That's fantastic news. Why don't you tell me about it? We can take these flaming spitheads down together."

"Do you have access to an armada of star ships?" she deadpanned.

I patted down my pockets for a moment, pretending to look for my armada.

"Funny," she said. "You wouldn't understand the information anyway."

"Then teach me."

"I already started, but you have a lot to learn before any of the knowledge makes sense to you."

"Start with the null field. What is it?"

"That is not a simple answer. Some of the most brilliant scientists in the universe still don't fully understand it."

"But you do?"

Another sigh echoed through my skull like the whisper of a closing door. "Yes, but I don't—"

"Enough with the sighing." My pulse rose with my anger. "I'm a fast learner, and that was *before* you hijacked my consciousness. Quit complaining. Quit making excuses and *teach* me!"

"Interesting," she mused, cold and clinical, a scientist studying data. "Even your temper matches his."

The rage pounded in my ears like war drums. I was about to snap again.

"Okay, fine," Aubrey said. "Your anger is not helping your headache, by the way."

"Really? How stunningly insightful. Never would have figured that out on my own. Thank you. Is that the level of genius I should expect from your massive intellect?"

I felt her annoyance as my own again. It blended with my homegrown anger in a milieu of heightened frustration.

"Don't do that," I snapped.

"Then stop with the rage," she snapped back. "And I'll do my best to explain."

I took two deep breaths and felt my pulse slow.

"Better," Aubrey said, her tone easing. "Thank you. A null field comes from the attunement of a Bose Einstein concentrate—"

"Stop. I don't know what those words mean," I said, shaking my head. "You have to do better. My father says that if you understand something well enough, you should be able to explain it to a five year old."

"Your father never had to teach quantum physics to someone who calls a spaceship an Iron Mountain."

I conceded the point, barely keeping the corners of my mouth from twitching upward. "Explain what it does then."

"A null field has the ability to cancel other fields. Counteract other energies."

"Like a nova-field," I said. "That explains a lot, like—"

I felt a slight pinch in the back of my neck and my headache vanished. Just...gone. I didn't realize how much it had been dragging me down until it lifted. I exhaled in a rush, almost a laugh, and blinked. Everything came into focus again. Clean, sharp, *clear.*

"Better?"

"So much better." I opened my mouth as far as it would go, stretching my jaw, then turned my head around its axis. "What did you do?"

"Repaired some of the damage I caused when I, ah, crash-landed into your spine. I had all that pain shunted away until the princess whacked you in the back with the flat of her blade."

I winced at the memory. How did Amara move that fast and keep her

6

balance? No one should be able to move that fast.

"She's been training for a lot longer than you have," Aubrey said.

I did *not* say that last bit out loud. I know I didn't.

"No, you didn't say it out loud. And yes, I can hear your thoughts. I just repaired the neural pathway that networks into my central processing hub. This should allow us to communicate without you opening your mouth." Aubrey declared the destruction of my autonomy with a self-satisfied smugness, almost like I should be happy about it.

"Then unrepair it! I can't have you listening in on my thoughts." I grabbed my head between my hands and squeezed. "This is my mind. Not yours!"

"You are *sooo* dramatic," she said. "Relax. I'm setting up filters so I only hear what you direct at me. Your privacy will be protected. I promise."

Could I trust her? Wait. She said she *will* set up filters, not that she *had* set up filters.

"Listening to your thoughts is exhausting," Aubrey said. "The filters are as much for me as they are for you. They will be online in the next half hour. In the meantime, let's continue our null field discussion."

"Is the null field why I could never channel the nova field?"

"Yes," Aubrey said. "But not in the way you're thinking."

How did she know what I thought? Oh. Right.

"Stop thinking so loud," said Aubrey. "And pay attention. The null field doesn't block *everything*. If it did, you'd be dead. You wouldn't be able to move, eat, or even think. What it does is *selectively* counteract energy. Like an immune system for physics."

"Why did it select to counter the nova flux?" I asked.

"Environmental conditioning, maybe. You grew up around it. Saw it do terrible things. Your brain adapted—subconsciously—formed a defense. Think of it as a mental callus."

"But nova energy still affects me. Remember when Arken hit me with that radiant flash?"

"No. That was before I jumped into your head. But here's the theory: null fields work off something called *field topology*. I'm simplifying, heavily. Imagine invisible, shifting blueprints for how energy moves. Null fields reshape those blueprints."

I sighed.

"I *am* dumbing it down," Aubrey growled. "We'll use examples later. For now, understand this: your field can adapt, but it takes training. You don't get immunity just because you're special. You have to *earn* it."

"How?"

"Your mind can perceive patterns. Energy shifts. Possibilities. That's the first step."

I sat up in my small bunk and almost whacked my skull on the bulkhead. "You mean my *perception*."

"Exactly. But it's not just seeing out—it's also shielding *in*. Your null field keeps your thoughts clean. Untouched. That's why you learn so quickly. Why your brain stays yours. Why you're the *perfect* candidate for a meld."

"Why doesn't it protect me from you? Or others like you?"

"It *does*, unless I hardwire into your brain stem, which, as I've explained, was a survival necessity. But that link makes you rare. One of the most powerful Melders in the universe."

That was a lot to take in.

"I know right?" said Aubrey. "But here's the tradeoff: you'll never be a great aggressor. Null fields don't strike—they *counter*. You're a defender, Finn. A protector. Embrace that."

In most of the fights I participated in, I was always much stronger when countering an attack then when I attacked first. It made sense.

"Someone is coming," said Aubrey. "I think it's Ravic."

"Okay, what should I do?"

"Get stronger. Fast. Work with your trainers during the day. Train with me at night. You have to learn to *see* faster. Anticipate. Use probabilities to SEE the future. That's where I come in."

"Do I tell him about you?"

"That's your choice, but remember how Dawnford reacted. Most of this planet fears Ancient tech. If you tell someone, be sure you trust them with your *life*. Maybe more. In the meantime, if you want to talk to me, think what you want to say. I will pick it up."

Ravic cracked the door and peeked in. "Finn, you're sitting up! You look a lot better." He glanced about the small room. "Who were you talking to?"

I rubbed my temples as I considered how to answer. "The little voice in my head constantly pushing me to learn faster."

Ravic smoothed his metallic blue beard and gave me a fatherly smile. "I like the drive, lad, but everyone needs a rest. Especially after an injury."

You hear that? I asked into the echoes of my mind.

If you think the Igni are resting you're kidding yourself, Rhee said into my mind. *And you're not* everyone. *You're our last chance.*

2

Weapons Master

Draven narrowed his eyes and viewed my posture. "Back to center. Sink into the stance like you're sitting, not lounging."

I dropped my weight, knees bent, back straight. Every muscle ached, but I kept my form sharp, controlled.

"You're leaning into your right hip," he said, voice clipped. "How's the foot?"

I hadn't even noticed the throbbing until he said it. Just like that, pain bloomed like fire in my toes. I brushed a hand against the top of my boot. "Sore," I admitted, teeth clenched. "But I can still train."

"I'll be the judge of that." Draven circled me like a coyote toying with a desert shrew. "And the ribs?"

They burned. Not just pain—heat. Adrenaline dulled the pain when sparring Amara, but when I took my shirt off, the purple and yellow bruises were everywhere. My father's armor had spared me the worst of it, but goblins had teeth, and so did steel.

"Better," I said. I raised my arms above my head as if to prove it. I bit my cheek to keep from wincing.

Draven snorted. "Two days, Finn. You slept for nearly two days straight. Bruises don't require that level of healing."

I held the squat, letting the fire in my thighs rise to meet the inferno in my chest. He wasn't asking. He was testing.

"Ready position," he barked.

I stood and clasped my hands behind my back. With a step, Draven's face was inches from mine, gaze drilling into me. What was he looking for? It was almost like...

He stepped back. "No static. It's not flux sickness."

I frowned. "You know I can't access the field." I tilted my head. "How do you know what flux sickness looks like?"

"I did my rotations in the compounds. It's a hard way to die. Be glad you don't have it."

The words felt like a kick to the stomach. Of course I didn't have it, but my mother would, soon. Any mention of flux sickness reminded me of the barely perceptible haze of static I last saw in her eyes. "Why would I? Remember, no access to the field."

Draven shrugged. "Ravic said your resonance is off. Sounded...field related."

I scowled. "I thought I left this spit behind in Dawnford." My voice trembled with anger. "Let me say it so we're clear. I. Do not. Have access. To the field."

Draven smirked. "A sore spot. Don't allow it to control you. It's good to see some fire in your eyes, though. You've been a little *too* humble."

I growled. "Are we going to train or drink tea and talk about our feelings?"

"We're going to train," he said. "Especially after you embarrassed yourself against the princess."

Was that a dig with a dash of humor? From Draven?

I preferred the perpetually annoyed weapons master over this version. He'd changed after saving the prisoners. He seemed more engaged, more driven. Or not driven. More purposeful, as if running into Amara and Sir Michael, one of his old rivals, awoke something in him.

Two could play at that game. "Amara mentioned you got into a bit of a tangle with some Lady in Alyndor. What—"

"Walk on your hands to the far side of the deck," he snapped. "Then use the netting to climb back. Let's test your readiness."

There it was—the annoyed Draven I'd gotten to know. All bark, all bite.

I grinned despite the pain, flipped into a handstand, and started walking.

The deck groaned beneath me. My shoulders strained, arms trembling—but my balance held. Solid. Controlled. *Stronger.* The muscles I'd been building made the hand walk seem...easy.

What did you do?

You did the hard work, said Aubrey. *I just gave your vestibular system a tune. That's where your balance center lies.*

I don't like you messing around in my mind.

Inner ear actually. If you want, I can set it back to how it was.

Well, since you already did it...

That's what I thought. Her smug tone was back.

Ask me next time.

I seized the netting and hurled myself forward, my hands gripping the junctions where the cords were knotted tight. Hand over hand, I swung across the rigging—twice as fast as I'd ever done before. The stale, moist air cut across my face, salty and sharp, but I didn't slow down. Draven was waiting.

"Blades," he barked the moment my boots hit the deck. "Your short sword and dagger work is abysmal. Show me high guard."

I drew the nova-blade and raised it overhead in my right hand, angled slightly forward. The dagger rested at my hip in my left. Balanced. Focused.

Draven shook his head with a grunt. "Wrong. Watch." He shifted into the same stance, but tighter, meaner. "What's different?"

I pulsed my perception outward, locking on his stance. I tracked the subtle flex of muscle, the weight distribution in his legs, the tension in his arms. Aubrey enhanced the view, highlighting key joints and pressure points.

"You're leaning more forward."

"And the blades?"

I squinted, trying to catch the angle. Aubrey added a shimmer to his weapons for clarity.

"Your dagger's edge aligns with the tip of your sword," I said.

"Exactly," Draven replied. "That's your defense. Without a shield, your blades must protect each other—create a wall, a *pyramid* of steel. Let me show you. Attack me."

Aubrey flashed projected strike vectors across my vision, similar to the angles I saw when I jumped from the gash in the Iron Mountain. It felt natural now. I lunged. My short sword slashed, but his dagger turned it aside with a clatter of sparks.

I followed up, stabbing with my dagger, but his sword moved like lightning, intercepting mine and vibrating through the hilt like a tuning fork. My grip faltered.

Before I could react, his blade flicked. My dagger spiraled from my hand—and he caught it midair without blinking.

By the stars, he was fast.

Get him to attack you, Aubrey said. *Remember, you're a defender. Read his movements and react.*

"I feel like I'm flailing," I admitted through clenched teeth. "What am I doing wrong?"

Draven handed back the dagger. "You're attacking blindly. You must *see* the weakness."

"And if I can't?"

"Then create it," he snapped. "Think like a tactician, not a brawler.

Set traps. Feint. Distract. You're not just fighting steel—you're fighting *a person*. People reveal themselves in motion. Watch their story unfold."

I returned to the center of the training circle, the deck beneath my feet now more battlefield than ship.

Draven mirrored me, eyes sharp. "Your stance is full of tells. Everyone's is. I watch the hips, the core. Arms lie—hips don't."

"What are my hips telling you now?" I asked, trying to hold them steady.

"That you want to defend, not attack. You'd rather parry and riposte than strike first."

"So? Isn't that my style?"

"It's not the choice," he said. "It's that I *know* it's your choice. Your stance speaks for you. And that means your opponent always gets the first move. You need to master silence. Then you can control the conversation. Like Amara did to you."

I shifted my weight forward, ever so slightly, and pulsed perception toward him.

Draven's eyes narrowed. "Good. Now brace yourself."

He attacked.

His hips shifted first—Aubrey lit them up like a constellation, mapping out the path of his blade before it moved. High guard, left side. My dagger shot up just in time to deflect the blow with a screech of metal.

Draven's eyes widened slightly before his weight shifted again—down and low. A blunted dagger thrust at my gut.

I swept my sword downward and caught it on the edge. Barely.

He spun.

I lunged, slicing toward his legs, hoping to trip him mid-motion. A gamble.

Draven flowed over my blade like water, using the momentum to finish his spin—and lashed out with a brutal overhead strike.

I got my dagger up to block. The blades barely touched and I knew I'd made a mistake—too late.

It was a feint.

His real strike came from the reverse—dagger to the chest.

Thunk.

"Better," he said, stepping back. His breathing was steady. Controlled. Mine wasn't.

"Using your sword tip to trip me, clever improvisation," he added. "What changed?"

"I focused on your hips," I said. "Not your weapons."

He frowned. "Smart. But dangerous in the thick of a real fight. Focusing on weight distribution is critical early, but keeping your attention on it during battle may get you killed. Too much input can overwhelm. Most people drown in it."

Good thing I'm not most people, Aubrey chimed in smugly. *I'll handle the overload. You just swing the shiny sticks.*

I had to admit I was impressed with how well Aubrey and I worked together. It took me a second to realize we'd been working together ever since she jumped aboard the Finn train. The only difference between then and now, was now I understood the source of the help.

We squared off again. Draven's eyes gleamed. "I'm going to keep pressing. You learn faster under pressure."

In the next few bouts, I held longer. I read his movements, dodged or blocked his first attacks—but in the end, he still landed the final blow. Again. And again.

Until the last round when he caught me early.

Frustration boiled over. I slapped the flat of my blade against my hip, hard.

Draven tilted his head. "What was that?"

"Losing's getting old."

His expression turned thunderous. "There's no *losing* in sparring. You win—or you *learn*. That's why we do this. Remember that."

His glare snapped like a whip, and I flinched. I nodded to show I got the message.

For the next thirty minutes, he hammered me. Every block, every dodge was another lesson. Every hit, a painful reminder that I still had so much to learn.

But I didn't give up.

When we finally paused, sweat soaked through my tunic. My arms ached. My legs trembled.

"You may not see it yet," Draven said, "but you've improved. You could take Dain. Maybe even Rory."

I wiped sweat from my brow. "We reach Alyndor the day after tomorrow. I'm running out of time. And I'm about to lose the best weapons teacher I've ever had."

Draven hesitated. For a heartbeat, his eyes softened.

"Maybe not," he said.

I raised an eyebrow.

"I left my homeland...abruptly," he muttered. His mouth twisted— an uncomfortable expression on a man who wore disdain like armor. "It's time I returned. Made things right. Amara's letting you take companions into your audience with the king."

He looked me in the eye.

"I'll be one of them."

3

Dain

"You're going to strip it," Dain said from over my shoulder. "Here, use this one."

I ignored the tool he held out to me. "I'm not going to strip it," I grunted, leaning harder into the screwdriver, muscles tense. The screw resisted with madding, stubborn stiffness. *I'm not going to strip it, am I?*

You're fine, Aubrey said, cool as ever. *Almost there. Are you going to ask him?*

I told you I would.

The screw finally gave with a satisfying crack, rotating through the last smear of locking glue. I handed it to Dain with a smug grin.

"Told you," I said.

Dain scowled. "I knew I should have scared you before putting you to work. You're a lot more humble when you've been rattled. Now grab the tool I gave you. We need the plate off before we can clean the fan. I'm still convinced one of the blades is bent."

It's not, Aubrey said. *Now, ask him.*

Quit being annoying.

I took the tool Dain handed me this time. "Hey...have you ever worked

17

with Synth cores?"

That got his attention. The burly mechanic lifted an eyebrow, pausing mid-motion. "Most drillship crews can't afford them. And those who can guard 'em like they're holy relics."

"Tell me about it," I said. "It took fifteen years of my father working as a master mechanic before Ronin let him touch one of the cores. And that was with the old man standing over his shoulder the whole time. I'd love to look inside one to see how they work, wouldn't you?"

Dain's eyes drifted to the ship's heart—the massive engine that powered the *Drifter*. "Of course. I got to touch one once. Didn't get to open it up, but the captain of my last ship had a buddy in the Glass and Light Guild. Pulled some strings, got me a six-month study with the Duskers."

He sighed. "Let me tell you, cores are...something else. Works of art. If I had one of those beauties in *this* engine?" He shook his head wistfully. "If only we could make them today, the *Drifter* would fly through the earth like she had wings."

I frowned. "I thought the Duskers *could* make cores."

He snorted. "What they make now? Toys. Big, clunky spheres. Barely manageable, impossible to house properly. The Ancients, though? They worked at micro-inch levels." He held up two fingers, pinching them together until they barely touched. "We can't replicate that. Don't have the tools."

Try nano-inches, said Aubrey. *Technically nanometers if you're in Conglomerate space.*

Nanometers?

They're about a hundred times smaller than a micro-inch, she said.

Whoa.

"You ever try to build one?" I asked aloud.

"To build a Synth core?" Dain laughed. "Kid, I may be crazy, but I'm not *that* crazy."

18

"No, I mean...anything autonomous. Everything you've shown me on the *Drifter* is analog. Manual systems, no processors."

He narrowed his eyes slightly, suspicious. "Why are you asking? Because of the squawk boxes?"

I grinned and nodded toward the metal-cased mess of wires in the corner of the engine room. "You're not exactly subtle in your contempt."

He scowled. "Don't know what you're grinning at, boy. *You* haven't had to maintain the gemming things. They scream if the humidity's wrong and short if you look at them funny." He wiped his hand across the engine's warm metal skin. "I like knowing how every part of my ship works. The more I give away to automation, the more I give up my edge."

"Didn't stop you from passing the maintenance off to *me*," I said, flashing a grin.

"That's called *teaching*." He arched a thick brow. "Or are you complaining about my instruction methods."

"Teaching." I laughed. "That's the exact word my father used whenever he handed me a wrench and told me to clean sludge out of the cooling manifolds."

Dain held his nose up high. "He sounds like a very smart man."

I finished unfastening another screw on the plate housing the fan and handed it to Dain. "You know the theory though, right? For autonomous devices?"

The mechanic nodded and placed the screw into a small metal bowl holding the other ones. "I do. What are you getting at, Finn?"

"I've never built one. I want to try."

"What would you build?"

"Something simple. A device with legs or wheels that could move itself based off commands I give it. Would that be hard to build?"

I prefer legs over wheels, Aubrey said.

"Depends. How simple will the commands be? If it's just stop, stay, move in a direction, it's not hard at all. Might be able to put something together here even. Anything more: like responding to environmental cues...I don't have the parts or the tools to make them."

Aubrey sighed dramatically in my head. *It'll have to do.*

"How quickly do you think we can put it together?" I tried to leave the pleading out of my voice.

"You're asking if we can do it before you leave for the Dusker Kingdom."

"If it's possible."

Dain tapped the fingers of each hand with his thumbs, like he did every time he worked through a challenging problem. "Tell you what. Help me finish cleaning and fixing this fan and we'll get started." He smacked me on the back way harder than was necessary. "It oughta be fun. I haven't worked with autonomous processes in years."

A grin broke across my face, and for a second, I felt the spark of possibility light up inside me—raw and hungry.

Aubrey's excitement thrummed in my skull like static, impossible to ignore, and honestly? I didn't want to. Her energy was infectious, and for the first time in days, I felt light. Alive. We'd sketched out the frame of the eight-legged crawler in the precious hours I had left with Dain, its spindly limbs twitching with potential.

Dain even growled at one of the squawk boxes until it screamed loud enough to reach Rory in the galley. Somehow, that convinced the cook to give me another hour. Miracles do happen.

"Don't need you for tonight's dinner," Rory had said. *"Someone else is helping."*

That hurt a little bit. I had come to think of my help in the kitchen as irreplaceable.

I'd miss cooking with the cheerful bear of a man, but I couldn't bring myself to care too much—not with the crawler coming to life under my hands. It meant something to Aubrey. And, truth be told, I was having the time of my life putting the little bug together.

I was securing the final leg when Dain glanced up, cursed under his breath, and hurled a rag at my face.

"Clean up," he barked. "Rory may have given you the night off, but if we're late to dinner? He's going to take it out on *me*."

I wiped my hands, mostly just smearing the grease around. "I'm going to run to my room, wash up. Meet you in the dining room."

"Go! Go! Go!" He swept me out of the engine room with his hands.

I took the stairs two at a time, heart pounding—not from exertion, but from that weird high I got when things *clicked*. Dain wasn't wrong. Rory could get *very* personal about his food and considered it a grave insult when people ate his meals cold.

I rounded a corner at full speed and—

WHAM.

I collided hard with something—or someone. We both went sprawling across the metal floor with a dull, echoing clang. I blinked, dazed, and found myself nose-to-nose with Amara.

Her cheeks flushed red.

Was she mad?

"S-sorry," I said quickly. "I wasn't looking. I mean I was looking, just not at—uh—"

"I didn't know you were awake," she cut in. She didn't *seem* angry. She brushed her hair out of her face. "I asked Draven to tell me when you were up. I wanted to apologize for hitting you so hard. When we were sparring."

I pushed myself upright, trying not to groan as pain flared through my bruised ribs. She noticed. Of course she did. She rose in one smooth motion, needing no hands. Graceful. Strong.

Not angry. Good.

Then why was her face still red?

By the Creator, you are a moron, Aubrey sighed. *Say something.*

Not helping.

"Sorry, you surprised me," I blurted. "Or—I surprised us? I guess? We surprised each other?"

Hopeless. You are hopeless.

I coughed. "What I meant to say was... it's not your fault. Really. Ravic thinks your hit just landed in exactly the wrong spot on my back. Old injury. You didn't do anything wrong."

Amara tilted her head, eyes narrowing slightly. "Old injury? Can I see it?"

Oh no.

"It's fine," I said quickly, defensively. "Not worth worrying about."

She crossed her arms, foot tapping lightly against the floor. "Finn. Let me see."

She used *the voice*—the kind that didn't ask so much as *command.* Princess mode: activated.

Reluctantly, I lifted my armored shirt, exposing the purpling bruises across my ribs.

Her breath caught. She pressed a hand to her mouth. "I did that?" she whispered, horror tightening her features. "I didn't think I hit you *that* hard."

I yanked the shirt back down. "You didn't," I said quickly. "I picked up those beauties fighting goblins. Turns out a couple of them actually knew how to fight."

Her lips pressed into a grim line. "It surprised us too. Between the waxer and the two trained goblins, I lost half my escort before I ordered the rest to surrender."

My chest ached, not from the bruises, but from the weight in her voice. "I'm sorry." I knew how bad it hurt to lose members of your party.

The regal princess façade cracked for a moment at my sincerity, and she looked just as sad and lost as she did when I told her that her brother died. Only for a moment, then she pulled the mask back on. "I'm glad to see you well. Will you be joining us tonight?"

I frowned. "For what?"

She gave a dry laugh. "They don't tell you anything, do they?"

I exhaled as I thought about the question. "Nope. Last to know. Every time. Here, back home—it's like a universal law."

You have *been unconscious for the last two and a half days.*

Shut up, you, I said to Aubrey.

Amara smiled faintly. "Honestly? That sounds...nice. Not knowing. When you're the first to know, all you do is carry secrets. You roll them around in your head until they cut you open from the inside."

She reached out, laid her fingers lightly on my arm. The contact was barely there, but it sent a bolt of warmth through me. Probably imagined. Probably.

"But I *can* tell you this," she said. "We're meeting after dinner to discuss our approach to Alyndor."

My stomach dropped. "Oh no—dinner!"

Without thinking, I covered her hand with mine and gave it a quick, gentle squeeze. "I'll be there. But right now? I need to get to the galley before Rory puts this idiot Grounder on a spit."

She laughed—an actual, full laugh—and I hated pulling away, but I turned and ran.

My ribs throbbed, my hands were still streaked with grease, and I was very possibly late.

But I was grinning like an idiot the whole way.

4

Surprise

I scrubbed the grease from my hands with frantic urgency, my heart pounding with anticipation and the tantalizing scent of Rory's cooking drawing me like a magnet down the corridor. The aromas—rich mutton, sizzling herbs, something slightly sweet— curled through the air and wrapped around me like a warm blanket. My stomach growled in response.

As I reached for the dining room door, I heard the unmistakable growl of Rory's voice.

"Where is he? You were supposed to make sure he got here on time!"

"I don't know," Dain replied, clearly exasperated. "He left *before* I did!"

"I'm here!" I called through the door, eyebrows furrowing at the sudden hush that followed.

Shuffling, whispering, a suspicious silence.

Was this Dain's idea of a prank? One last joke before I left?

I pushed the door open. "Sorry, I just ran into—"

"SURPRISE!"

The shout nearly knocked me backward. The entire crew of the *Core Drifter* stood grinning in the flickering dining hall lights. Streamers, somehow crafted from cloth scraps, hung from the ceiling like colorful vines. A massive banner, hand-painted in shimmering gold letters, declared: **Happy Birthday, Finn!** Twinkling gemstones—real gemstones—were strung along its edge like stardust.

I froze.

Rory stepped forward, arms wide, his smile stretching from ear to ear. "Happy birthday, lad."

My throat tightened as I took in the sight. The decorations, the handmade banner, the effort. For most of my life, my birthday had been a quiet affair—just me and my parents, maybe a candle on a sweet roll. I never had crowds. I never had *friends* show up.

Never anything like *this*.

A rush of warmth swelled in my chest, sharp and sudden. It hit me like a punch: This drillship—this rickety, chaotic, patched-together ship—*was* a family. And somehow, impossibly, they'd made room in it for me.

Not because of who my parents were.

Not despite my inability to touch the field.

They accepted me—*me*.

And I was about to leave them.

I cleared my throat, tried to smile through the ache behind my eyes. It didn't work. A couple tears betrayed me, sliding hot and fast down my cheeks.

Rory swept me into a tight hug, his thick arms squeezing me like a bear. "None of that now. This is a celebration!"

When he released me, I turned to face my crew—my *family*. My voice trembled but I stood tall. "I'm really going to miss you guys," I said. "This was one of the best months of my life. Thank you for putting up with me. And my... *many* questions."

Captain Marek stepped forward, her expression surprisingly soft. "I had my reservations at first. But that came from my own wounds, not your actions. You've reminded me what it means to take chances." She extended her hand stiffly. "Is this how I do it?"

I grinned and shook her hand. "Close enough, Captain. Thank you for letting me on board."

One by one, the others came, Ravic, Kaley, Kryn. Even Hark grunted and gave me a pat on the back. Dain hugged me like a brother.

"Come now, sit at the place of honor," Rory said, motioning toward the captain's usual seat. Marek nodded her approval.

I sat down, still overwhelmed. Rory placed a steaming hot plate before me—mutton, golden potatoes, glistening leeks. I stared at the chemical energy pulsing from his masterpiece of taste. Patterns I had never seen before wafted from my plate. "Taste it. Tell me what I used."

I took a bite—carefully balanced to sample everything—and then closed my eyes.

Stars above.

The flavor exploded across my tongue. Savory, sharp, faintly sweet. It was warmth and comfort and celebration all in one. I chewed slowly, letting the textures and aromas settle before speaking.

"Salt and pepper on the potatoes," I said. "Thyme. Maybe...cumin on the leeks?"

Rory grinned, pleased.

"And the mutton?" he prompted.

I took another bite. "It's...cool? But sweet? It's like a breeze after heat—mint?"

Rory raised an eyebrow. "Go on."

"There's something more. Something sugary. A glaze?"

"It's mint mixed with pepper jelly and a little honey."

"Honey?"

"You've never heard of honey?" he asked, scandalized.

"Not once."

"It comes from bees," Draven explained. "Tiny stinging insects. You'll find them in the Dusker kingdoms."

"Insect goo," I said, grinning as I shoveled another forkful into my mouth. "Delicious. I've never tasted anything like it. You are the greatest food 'mancer ever."

"Just wait until dessert," Rory said, already ducking back into the galley.

Ravic joined me at the table, and a moment later so did Dain. I barely noticed as I continued to put as much food in my mouth as the small fork allowed. I looked down at my plate mournfully when I realized I only had a bite or two left. I glanced over at Dain's plate.

He saw the look, wrapped a protective arm around the plate, and pinned me with a glare. "No. I don't care if it's your birthday, we only get Rory's special mutton once or twice a year."

Rory burst through the galley door holding a large plate with a cylindrical concoction on top. It had an earthy color with golden goo drizzled over it. I wondered if that was honey. The strangest part of the dish was a small rock which burned with a bluish flame sitting on top—a miniature of the flaming rocks I sat around when I first met the crew.

I looked to Ravic. "Is that one of yours?"

He nodded as Rory set the dish in front of me. Ravic leaned over and whispered in my ear, "You're supposed to make a wish then blow it out. Don't tell anyone what the wish is and it might come true."

What are you going to wish for? Aubrey asked.

None of your business.

I took a breath and blew. The flame flickered and died. The crew clapped and cheered like I'd just won a tournament.

Rory cut into the dessert and handed me the first triangular piece. Then he stopped and watched as I picked up my fork.

I speared a forkful from the concoction, which looked a lot like dirt, then put it in my mouth. A glorious, earthy sweetness hit my tongue and fireworks exploded from my taste buds. "Ohh." The sound slipped out of my mouth involuntarily.

"That, my boy, is a chocolate honey drizzle cake."

My eyes widened as I continued to chew. "No," I said with a full mouth. "*That* is magic."

Rory looked like I'd just knighted him.

"Keep serving, you lug!" Kaley called. "You think we're going to let Finn eat the whole cake?"

Rory passed plates of cake out and they were quickly snapped up and devoured. When everyone had eaten their share, Ravic nodded to Dain. The mechanic stood up and fished something out of his pocket—a small leather purse.

"This is from all of us," he said.

I took the pouch with both hands, loosened the ties. Inside: a smattering of golden coins and three small emeralds, winking in the light. I stared, stunned.

"I can't. This is too much—"

"Nonsense. The gold is yours," Marek said, voice firm. "Your share of the goblin rescue. And the emeralds are a token. Something to remember us by."

"They should be enough to buy a rudimentary synth core," said Dain. "Ask for Rojer at the engineering guild. Tell him I sent you."

I clutched the pouch to my chest and took a shaky breath. I looked around the table, meeting every pair of eyes. These weren't just friends.

They were *home*.

"Thank you," I said quietly. "All of you."

It was the best birthday I'd ever had.

* * *

I loosened my belt a notch, still full from Rory's feast, and followed Draven and Ravic through the dim corridors toward the bottom deck. The moment we stepped into the makeshift meeting room, the warmth of the celebration vanished like steam on cold steel.

The tension hit me like a wall.

The air was thick—choked with formality, suspicion, and something else...restraint on the edge of snapping. The room was stark and cold, lit by a single overhead strip casting harsh shadows. At the far end, Captain Marek sat like a storm brewing behind steel-gray eyes, her fingers drumming a sharp rhythm against the battered metal table. The lines on her face were deeper now, not from age, but frustration.

Sir Michael stood opposite her, visibly uncomfortable under her gaze, as if the steel table itself might rise and devour him.

"Let me get this straight," Marek said, her voice cold and razor-edged. "After we *saved* your ungrateful asses, you're telling me we can't pass through Alyndor?"

Her tone hit like a blade drawn too fast.

Sir Michael winced, his composure wobbling. "I'm sorry, Captain. Truly. We are grateful. But...our kingdom's passage rules are ironclad. I don't have the authority to make exceptions."

The silence that followed was deafening.

A moment later, the door opened. Amara stepped in, composed and radiant despite the tension coiling in the room like a drawn bowstring. Her gaze found mine and, for a moment, the corners of her lips tugged into a small, familiar smile—brief, but grounding.

"Fortunately," she said, her voice light and effortless, "*I* do, Captain."

Sir Michael's expression darkened. "Your father will not approve of this, Princess."

Amara exhaled, clearly exhausted with this conversation before it had even begun. She stepped past him with a grace that only infuriated the man further and patted him on the shoulder with regal condescension. "This is exactly why he doesn't include you in diplomatic missions, Sir Michael."

Beside me, Draven snorted. His shoulder quaked with the effort of holding back a full-blown laugh. I caught the moment Sir Michael's glare snapped to him—only for Draven to meet it with a cheeky wink. He was *enjoying* this.

Amara didn't even blink.

"My father will be thrilled to meet the crew of the drillship that saved his daughter, his people, and *two* of his prized knights. Frankly, I wouldn't be surprised if he tried to pin medals on all of you."

"We don't need medals, Princess," Marek said coolly, but her pride flickered in her eyes. "Though I *would* accept payment for the transport. Drillships don't run on goodwill."

Amara inclined her head with queenly grace. "Of course. The king is generous with those who earn his friendship. You have more than earned it."

Then her tone shifted. Heavier. More somber.

"But since the goblin incursions began—not to mention the persistent skirmishes from Thal'Naris—we've had no choice but to seal the kingdom's outer gates. No unauthorized vehicles past the barricades."

Marek's fingers froze mid-tap. Her jaw clenched. "I didn't realize it had grown that dire."

"We've kept it quiet," Amara admitted. She pulled out the chair beside Sir Michael and sat with a gentle sigh. "The kingdom doesn't want panic in the tunnels. But I'm afraid the *Core Drifter* will need to remain docked outside the walls."

"What about the rails?" Draven asked, suddenly serious. "Between kingdoms?"

"Still operational," Amara replied, her gaze locked with Marek's. "But I must apologize. Your ship is extraordinary—but I cannot risk compromising our defenses. Not now."

There was a long beat of silence. Marek didn't look insulted just... resolved.

"No apology necessary, Princess," she said at last. "I would never jeopardize Alyndor's safety. We'll leave the Drifter with a skeleton crew at an external port. She'll be safe there."

Amara's face lit up in approval, clapping her hands once like she was closing a deal. "Splendid! That's settled, then."

Her gaze swept the room, landing on me.

"So," she said with a spark of mischief, "who's coming with us to meet the king?"

5

Night Training

I slipped into my bed that night, conflicted. A part of me mourned to leave the ship I called home for the last month and the crew who treated me like family. Yet, excitement bubbled at the thought of exploring the mysterious Dusker kingdoms...and spending more time with Amara.

The conflict in my mind didn't last long. I was exhausted. A good night's sleep was exactly what I needed.

I don't care if you're tired. I also don't care that it's your birthday. You know the rules. Train with the Drifters during the day. Train with me at night.

I groaned and rolled over. *Shouldn't I sleep to regain my strength before we head into the kingdom tomorrow?*

Her laugh rumbled the inside of my head like a wheezy storm.

You're worse than Draven, I said.

I'll take that as a compliment. Now, close your eyes.

I closed my eyes, not knowing what to expect.

Ok, open them.

I gasped. I stood atop a mountain. *What did you do?* I scream thought to Amara, pulse racing.

Take a breath, use all your senses, Amara soothed.

I expanded my perception. The cold snapped at my nose. The air sparkled—crisp and electric. Yet I could still feel my real body, warm and heavy beneath the ship's blankets. Two realities stacked like glass panes.

How?

The Conglomerate trains its fighter pilots using advanced simulators. This allows them to train under pressure without the fear, and the cost, of actually crashing any ships.

I looked down. My hands were covered in unfamiliar gloves, warm and impossibly soft. My fingers wrapped around a strange pole planted in the all white surface. I tried to move. Nothing. Panic spiked.

Why can't I move?!

Because you're not in control. Yet. Aubrey's voice crackled, sharp and instructive. *I don't have Conglomerate sims. What I do have is memory— mine, yours, Robert's...even a few borrowed ones.*

I felt my hands clench around the rods in each hand. My limbs twitched, then began to move without my command. I slid forward, then back. That's when I noticed: my feet were bound to thin boards that curved upward like blades. Panic spiked again, I hated the lack of control.

I can superimpose those memories on to your conscious mind. Further-more, I can tap into your subconscious mind and your dream centers to allow you to play around in these memories, much like a simulation. A dream you can control.

I was only half paying attention as the person whose memory I was in had used the two rods to push himself to the edge of a very steep slope which yawned below us. My heart raced.

He's not actually going to go down this death trap on these stupid little sleds is he? The thought came out as a squeak in my mind.

They're called skis. And yes, Robert is an excellent skier. The memory froze for a blessed moment. *Was. Robert was an expert skier.*

Why are you doing this to me?

As you train against opponents like Amara and Draven, you will get faster. To fight at full speed, you need control over momentum, balance, and instinct. And nothing teaches that faster than barreling downhill with gravity trying to kill you.

But I don't know—

That's why you're only watching. For now. It will be your turn next.

And then—he jumped.

We dropped and my stomach hit the roof of my mouth. Skis hit the white powdery stuff with a soft *thud*. The world blurred into streaks of white and shadow as Robert yelled and leaned forward. Why would he lean forward down a steep slope? My instincts screamed to lean back, to brake, to fight it—but he welcomed the fall.

The white stuff is called snow.

He twisted our body, throwing weight to the right and forward, lifting his heels and snapping the skis around. Powder exploded around us like frozen smoke. Then he pivoted left. Another explosion of snow. He screamed again—but not in fear.

He was *laughing. Laughing.*

He's insane!

No. He's free. Aubrey's voice softened. *Relax. Watch.*

Maybe if I was controlling it. Right now I'm an unwilling passenger on an express trip to tumble town.

I can give you control right now if you really want it.

No! I shrieked inwardly. *I'll watch...for now.*

Good, then notice how his body is almost perpendicular from the slope. It requires a leap of faith to push yourself forward on such a steep pitch, but it is the only way to keep control.

I clung to the sensation of movement. Every turn felt like a gamble, like threading a needle on fire. But he did it—again and again—each time smoother, faster, more daring.

Soon, the cliff-like slope mellowed. Groomed trails emerged, cut with even ridges like the pattern of a freshly-drilled tunnel. Robert changed immediately—his stance shifted, skis widening apart, our body angling forward with predatory grace.

He attacked the snow now, carving deep arcs as we sliced through the trail. He twisted at the hips, not just the knees, lifting slightly before each turn, then carving in with precision and force. My heart surged with each sharp turn. I could feel the bite of the edges on snow, the grip, the flow, the *rush*.

Wind blasted my face. The mountain blurred. I couldn't breathe. I didn't want to.

It was *exhilarating*.

Finally, just as I felt we couldn't go any faster, we hit a flat. Robert rose, skis together, and snapped them sideways in one final, elegant stop. A wall of snow rose around us like a frozen curtain.

You ready to try? Aubrey asked, casually.

Can I start halfway down until I get the hang of it? I didn't love the tremble in my voice.

Fine. She sighed, a whisper of disappointment. *Recalibrated. Tell me when.*

Let's go.

And then, I was in full control—and already flying down the mountain at thirty miles per hour.

My breath caught. This was no dream anymore.

I tried desperately to lock every movement Robert made into my memory—every shift, every nuance—but all I really craved was to stop. Just pause for a second and catch my breath, to take stock of the storm raging inside me. But stopping? That was the hardest move of all, the one Robert made look effortless, like a whispered secret to the snow.

I ran it over in my mind like a broken record. Lift up a little. Turn. Shift your weight, push the knees back into the hill.

I got to the turn. I lifted, just like Robert. Then, the moment I shifted my weight, my uphill ski betrayed me, crossing over the downhill one with a cruel snap. Locked together. My body flipped wildly, tumbling end over end like a ragdoll in a nova-storm. The boots, mercifully, popped free, but my back slammed hard against the snow. I rolled four more times, a snow-covered wreck sprawled out beneath a sky that suddenly felt too close.

"Ow," I groaned, breath ragged and snow packed mercilessly into every crack and crevice of my gear.

A rumble vibrated deep inside my skull—a harsh chuffing that rattled my brainpan.

Are you laughing?

A pause and a faint sniff. *Not anymore.*

Could you have stopped the simulation before I jumped into that rock tumbler?

Hmm. Let me run the numbers. Yep.

Yep? That's all you got!?

Conglomerate simulators shock their users with a non-lethal jolt when they blow up a ship. Do you know why? Aubrey asked.

I didn't like where this was going. *No,* I whispered into my mind.

Because it's the best way to get a lesson to stick. Do better or there will be consequences. It adds real world pressure to the simulation. Nothing is happening to your real body, so suck it up, buttercup.

The pain felt real. I said.

It was real. The brain can generate pain just fine on its own. The difference is you will never have a lasting injury. Look at this as the perfect learning opportunity. All the real risks, without any lasting consequences.

I fell eight more times before I finally carved my first genuine turn on the groomed slope. Fell again on the next one. I learned I could turn right but turning left was a disaster zone. Twenty-six tries later, I stumbled to the bottom, breath ragged, muscles screaming.

Somewhere in the chaos, I discovered the wedge—turning the fronts of my skis inward, slowing down without that brutal full-stop Robert used.

But Aubrey wasn't impressed. No, she dragged me back to that stop again and again. Seventeen times. Each attempt ended in a chaotic mess of limbs and snow, a tangle of frustration.

On the eighteenth, just as I thought I had it, a sudden flash flickered at the edge of my vision—my right eye caught it this time. Before, it was just a glint off my goggles. *What was that?*

Focus, said Aubrey. *No distractions until you master this.*

Fine, how do I end this torture?

Simple—ski top to bottom without falling. Ready for the top?

No, but let's do it anyway.

My heart jumped into my throat as I leaned over the cornice. This was so much steeper than what I had already skied. If I fell, I was going to fall for a very long time.

I was right. Forty-three times. Was it possible to bruise your brain? I looked at my still prone body lying there in the bed and felt an unbearable jealousy.

On try one hundred and thirty-six I made it all the way to the bottom without falling. I saw the flash again because I was looking for it. This time I ignored it. Aubrey would let me know what it was if it were important.

I started having *fun* somewhere around my ninetieth try. I *might* have fallen intentionally several times in the last ten runs just to get another shot at jumping off the cornice. The screams I loosed going down the steep stuff shifted to joy.

I understood it now.

Overcoming fear. Learning a skill. Feeling alive in a way nothing else could touch.

I learned how to move at speed, how the slightest tweak in my joints could change everything when I was racing downhill.

I didn't know how any of this would help me in a fight, but I trusted Aubrey knew what she was doing.

At last, I stopped and shifted my gaze, hunting for that flash of light. It came from the peak next door.

I understand the lesson, what's going on over there? I asked.

You earned this. I'm giving Robert control over his body again. Observe.

We skated to the edge of the flat area where we had a good view of the next peak over. Robert stomped on the snow until he created a flat platform, then jammed his poles in the ground. He clicked out of his skis and took position behind a pine tree.

"There it is," Robert said. "Rhee, you seeing this?"

Robert adjusted the field magnification of our goggles and the small fire on the peak sprung into view. At the center of an impact crater an Ignavari moved slowly back and forth, looking for something.

"This is the closest I've been to one of these things. They're ugly. No sign of a ship," said Robert, "which confirms one theory—they don't need protection from entry burn."

"No other Ignavari scouts in the area," said Rhee in a tinny voice in our ear.

The Ignavari pulsed flame into the ground every minute or so. It then moved over the burned area and paused. Each pulse made it shrink and slow, dragging itself across the scorched snow.

"I'm surprised they sent a scout to an ice world," Rhee said.

"I'm not," said Robert. "They want it all to burn. I can feel its hate from here, but...there's pain there too. A lot of pain. Not sure what it's using the flame for now, I don't see anything living. Unless...," Robert adjusted his goggles to search specific light wavelengths. "What if it's using the flame like a mass spec for usable minerals?"

"I'm not sensing any signal back to a ship in orbit to share the information."

"They must communicate another way," said Robert.

The creature floated down the slope, growing more ghostlike, bursts of fire exposing patches of blackened ground beneath the ice. Its power was fading.

"I still can't identify a fuel source which powers their fire," said Rhee.

"I don't think it can either," Robert replied. "It's getting slower, weaker. It must have a way of burning something internally for power and it can't find something suitable."

It became even more transparent until, three minutes and fourteen seconds later, it disappeared.

"I don't like it," said Robert. "The Igni don't seem the type to sacrifice themselves."

"From the way they fight, I would agree," said Rhee, "but that's not what the data shows. The Igni willingly throw their lives away for their cause. Very similar to religious zealots across human history."

Robert paused. "Maybe. The last thing I felt from this one was... relief. Escape? Faith? There's still so much we don't know about these things."

Rhee paused, waiting for him to continue. When he didn't she said, "We have all the data we could gather. Ready for an evac?"

I wanted to ask a thousand questions, but exhaustion wrapped around me like a blanket.

Get some sleep, you earned it, said Aubrey as I sunk down into my body. Didn't need to tell me twice. I was out in seconds.

6

The Rose Gate

I finished packing early that morning, then raced down to Dain's workshop near the humming core of the ship. The air was thick with the scent of heated metal and ozone. Sparks danced as Dain leaned over the workbench, giving the final, delicate adjustments to the spider.

Don't call it a spider, Aubrey said, like I had offended it, or her.

I held it up with both hands. It had four legs on each side which poked out of a bulbous body where Dain had put the servos and logic gates. It was nowhere near autonomous, but it's actions could be loosely programmed through a series of switches on its underbelly. *Tell me this thing doesn't look like a spider,* I said.

She may look arachnid, Aubrey said coolly, *but we're not burdening her with that kind of baggage.*

Her?

Robert had a friend named Rachel once. Kind, a little round in shape, but strong when she needed to be. Her friends called her Rach. It fits. A nod to both arachnids and memories. Aubrey burned the word in my mind's eye so I had no choice but to pick up the reference.

"Rach," I echoed aloud, running a hand gently over her carapace. She wasn't sleek, and she definitely wasn't pretty, but she was something *new.*

Ask Dain if he has a control chip.

Dain laughed at the question. "Where do you think you are, kid, the engineering guild? They don't just pass those things out. Not as rare as a core, maybe, but they still cost a gemming fortune."

You think he knows what an integrated circuit is? Aubrey asked. *I'd kill for a transistor, or even an op-amp.*

I don't know what any of those things are and dad had a much bigger inventory than Dain. Why do you need them?

It would give me the power to control Rach remotely, she said. *It would give me some autonomy.*

I wasn't sure that was a good thing.

Suddenly, the Core Drifter lurched, subtle but unmistakable.

"We're close," Dain said, snapping shut the toolkit and thrusting a rugged duffel at me. It was just big enough to cradle Rach without letting her clatter around. I tucked her inside like she was something precious—and maybe she was.

I slung the bag over my shoulder and made for the bridge.

Kaley guided the Drifter into the dock like a musician hitting a perfect note. Outside, the kingdom's gates loomed—massive, ancient, and imposing. Two heavy crawlers crouched like beasts of war beside the entry platform, while smaller, sleeker vehicles clustered nearby like wolves waiting to pounce.

I climbed the ladder behind Amara, trying hard—*really* hard—not to stare at the way her leather pants hugged her legs. But when you're climbing behind royalty, gravity leaves you no modest angles. Of course, Sir Rouse came up right behind me. I could feel his judgment in the air like static.

The moment the princess's feet touched the dock, all the workers bowed low. When the dock master arrived, he took a knee. He spoke some rapid words in the Dusker language which I didn't follow.

We're so happy you're alive princess, Aubrey said. *You are the brightest light in our kingdom. We've been lost in darkness without our keeper of the crystal flame to light the way. Blah, title, blah, honorific, blah, blah, blah. Your princess has more titles than a bookshelf at a royal auction.*

My princess, what are you talking about? Wait...you speak their language?

Of course. I've been building a compendium since the captain allowed the Duskers to board the Drifter. Once I identified the core vocabulary and sentence structure, it practically unraveled itself. Honestly, it's not that far from modern Illeutian.

"Rise, Master Graven, and thank you," said Amara. "Please speak common around our tunneler friends."

The portly man bowed deeply. "Apologies, your majesty," he said in flawless common. I wondered if all of the Duskers spoke common so well. Then again, the dock master probably had to deal with a lot of foreigners. "Our two fastest riders were sent to the king the moment Sir Michael arrived."

"And did my protector ride with them?" Amara asked.

"No, your highness. He's...negotiating with the gate guards. Something about allowing special provision for your tunneler companions."

"Who has command of the gate?" asked Amara.

"Commander Thorne, your majesty."

Amara winced. The dockmaster saw the expression and she transformed it into a smile. "This ought to be good."

"The philosophical thought experiment of what happens when an unstoppable force meets an immovable barrier comes to mind, your majesty."

Amara gave the man a surprised laugh. "You think I should bail poor Sir Michael out?"

The man smiled. "It would seem a shame to ruin the experiment."

"I don't remember you being so entertaining, Master Graven."

A cloud passed over the dock master's face. "Dark times. I found keeping a sense of humor helps."

Amara replaced her light smile with the royal princess mask. "Indeed. Thank you for your service, Master Graven." She looked back to us and nodded.

Sir Rouse moved to her right side and, surprisingly, Draven took her left. Quiet, brooding Draven—who usually stayed in the shadows—now flanked the princess like he belonged there. The rest of us fell in behind as she made her way to the gate.

Only then, as we approached the towering doors, did I truly look at the companions I was marching beside.

To my right, Marek strode with the confidence of someone who *expected* people to move out of her way. Her crimson coat flared with every step, draped over a crisp white ruffled shirt. Her saber swung lightly at her side from finely pleated tan trousers—more a symbol of authority than a weapon. She looked magnificent. Commanding. Untouchable.

Draven, by contrast, looked like a shadow given form. His new armor—tight, black leather reinforced with dark blue rivets—clung to him like a second skin. I had never seen him wear anything so deliberate. He was clean-shaven now, his hardened features strangely youthful, like the weight of years had lifted.

Ravic moved on my left, silent and otherworldly. He wore a long golden tunic embroidered with ancient runes and delicate swirls that seemed to shift in the light. His blue metallic beard and hair were combed smooth and tied back, the hood of his tunic falling around his shoulders like a halo. He radiated a quiet power—the Watcher of the tunneler clans in full regalia.

Behind us, Dain and Rory brought up the rear, opting for quiet dignity over grandeur. Rory's crisp white shirt and black leather pants gave him an elegance you wouldn't expect from the ship's cook. His wide belt, adorned with a pewter buckle shaped like two gleaming chef's knives, gave the outfit a kind of whimsical deadliness.

Dain wore a black leather vest over his white shirt, top two buttons undone to let his bushy blue chest hair breathe and exaggerate his bearish masculinity. His black pants were much tighter than Rory's but looked freshly brushed. Even his usually grease-stained hands were spotless—like he'd scrubbed them with steel wool just to look respectable for once.

The Drifters looked *sharp.*

Except for...me.

I glanced down. Compared to everyone else, I looked like the understudy to a royal parade. My armored shirt gleamed, polished earlier that morning, but my boots were scuffed, the knees of my pants frayed and stained, but they were the best I had. I tugged at my vest self-consciously, feeling the weight of the parchment and royal ring in its pocket like a boulder pressing against my ribs.

I was here on a mission, not to represent my people.

Well, you are the only Grounder in the group, Aubrey said, *so by default, you are the representative of Dawnford.*

Thanks, I needed the extra pressure. My palms began to sweat.

You'll be fine. You are the only Grounder Watcher on the planet and you saved the princess's life. Own it. Head up, Finn. Now.

She was right. I forced my shoulders back and lifted my chin, locking my gaze on Amara's steady stride ahead.

"Eight external guards?" Draven muttered. "Last time I passed through the Rose Gate there were only two."

Ahead, the massive metal doors towered over us like the face of a mountain. Every inch of their surface was covered in breathtaking detail—etched roses in bloom, vines that wound together in a symmetrical dance, their thorns not just ornamental but *razor-sharp*. This wasn't just a gate. It was a warning. Beautiful. Deadly. Impossibly well-defended.

The guards stood motionless behind armored barricades, eyes locked forward, hands gripping halberds. The sheer presence of them made me wonder if the gates ever *actually* opened anymore.

Look at the ground for the answer to the gates, Aubrey said.

Deep, polished grooves on the stone flagstones were an indicator the doors functioned at some point, but with the guard barriers in front of them, it was likely they hadn't been opened in some time.

The guards. The barriers. The tension in the air. The sweat glistening on the dockmaster's brow.

Alyndor was on edge. Tightly coiled. A kingdom braced for war.

Thirty feet from the gate, the guards slammed the butts of their halberds in unison—*CRACK*—then struck their chests with armored fists. The sound echoed through the stone corridor like thunder in a canyon.

Their commander stepped forward, his plumed helmet tucked beneath one arm. He swept into a deep bow, a feat of agility in full plate armor. "Welcome home, Princess," he said, voice like a war drum.

"Commander Thorne," Amara said coolly. "Thank you."

The guards behind him split to either side, forming a narrow path toward a small door embedded in the massive right-hand gate. One of the guards strode to it and knocked—three raps, pause, then two more. A code. The sound of ancient locks sliding loose followed, metal grinding against metal.

"Round one to the unstoppable force," Amara whispered, more to herself than to us.

The door creaked open. One by one, we stepped through.

I had expected a sweeping view, perhaps the kingdom stretched out below in splendor. Instead, I found myself staring at a stone staircase that climbed *upward*, steep and unrelenting. A ramp paralleled it—wide enough for supplies, wagons, or maybe even siege engines.

It made perfect sense. From above, defenders could rain arrows and fire down with ease. Any enemy who breached the gate would be forced to crawl their way uphill into a kill zone.

We climbed. One hundred stone steps.

At the top, another gate. This one swung open with a groan of age and steel. A blast of trumpets rang out—clear, celebratory, almost defiant. A fanfare of return and revelation.

From high atop the wall, a herald's voice carried on the wind: "*Her Royal Highness, Princess Amara!*"

The soldiers stationed on the ramparts erupted in cheers.

"Accompanied by the heroes of the *Core Drifter!*" A smaller, more polite, stomping of feet and applause.

"And our Grounder ally from Dawnford compound, Finn Camlock." The applause turned to whispers.

The whispers turned to grumbles when Princess Amara grabbed my hand and pulled me forward. "Don't worry about them, they don't see a lot of Grounders in the kingdoms these days," she said, favoring me with a wide smile.

She pulled me through the gate and pointed down a gentle, green hill.

I gasped.

7

Alyndor

"What is that green stuff covering the ground?"

Amara let out a rich, unrestrained laugh—completely unprincesslike and utterly contagious. "You mean the grass?"

"Grass?" I echoed. "It's...a plant?"

She laughed harder, her joy echoing off the stones, but finally nodded her head.

"You mean the whole hill is...alive?" I thought about pulsing my perception outward, but I was afraid I'd be overwhelmed with data. I'd wait until I was in a place where I didn't risk making a fool of myself in front of so many people.

The grass wasn't the only living thing. There was life...*everywhere*. Goats roamed the rolling hills, munching on the grass, and stepping on the small yellow flowers which dotted the undulating meadow. Something about the goats seemed off, but I couldn't put my finger on it.

Small insects buzzed around the goats and the flowers, landing occasionally to investigate or do some other insect thing. Birds glided over the tops of the wall to swoop down the hills on their way to a gathering of tall sentinels, cylindrical at the base and bushy and green near the top.

Aubrey sighed. *I forget how little you've seen of the universe. Those tall 'sentinels' are called trees.*

I wanted to say something clever, but I couldn't look away. The trees were...majestic. Massive. Silent giants that stretched toward a sky that shouldn't exist.

Because this wasn't sky.

I glanced up—and was immediately blinded by a harsh glare. I flinched, reaching for goggles that weren't there. I'd left them in my pack. Squinting against the pain, I focused my slit pupils and saw it clearly now: not just *one* light source, but several. The brightest hovered in the east. It *was* still morning. Dimmer glows flickered to the north and south, casting weird, overlapping shadows on the terrain.

I turned my head upward and noticed a very faint light from directly above and behind us. The soft light allowed for my first glimpse of the cavern ceiling. It had to be at least a mile above us, but I struggled to make out any details. The cave roof was partly obscured by something nebulous. Wait, was that a cloud?

It is, Aubrey remarked in a tone bordering on wonder. *This enclosed environment seems to have created an atmosphere of its own. Fascinating.*

My breath caught in my throat. The air felt different—richer, cleaner. I looked back at the goats and finally saw what had been bothering me: their *shadows.* Not one, but three, cast from different angles, splayed across the grass in distorted silhouettes. Everything was lit, but none of it felt harsh. The light was diffused. Filtered and soft.

And still—utterly breathtaking.

Far to the north, the ground rippled and sparkled in tune with the light breeze coming from that direction.

"Is that a lake?" I asked Amara when I found my voice again. I hoped to impress her with the little bit of knowledge I gleaned from the Jackal when I set off on this journey.

She squeezed my hand. I had almost forgotten she was still holding it. "That's the Glassmere," she said. "On calm nights, the water is so still some say it shows glimpses of the future."

"It's so big. I've never seen that much water before."

"Oh, just wait," she grinned. "I'm going to teach you to swim."

We followed a cobblestone road that curved down into the valley. I shaded my eyes, tracking its path as it disappeared into a grove of trees. To the south, a haze loomed, like fog—but heavier, stranger. It looked...wrong. *Off.*

"What's that?" I asked Amara with a tilt of my head.

"The Murkmire Hollows. Old swampland, constantly shifting. The land continues to evolve more rapidly than the rest of Alyndor thanks to the experiments of our core crafters generations ago. Avoid them at night. In fact, avoid them all together. They're hard to navigate and magical creatures call them home. Those who live there tend to be....territorial."

The stillness broke.

A sharp, rapid *crack-crack-crack* echoed from the trees—loud, urgent.

Gasps rippled through our group as six goblins erupted from the forest ahead of us. Their twisted green forms scrambled down the slope, shrieking in panic.

Amara's hand slipped from mine as we both reached for our weapons. I heard the hiss and *shwick* of steel unsheathing behind me—Draven, Marek, Sir Rouse. Every instinct screamed *threat.*

Six riders exploded from the trees in pursuit, mounted on huge beasts that moved with terrifying speed and control. At their head rode a tall, bearded man, cloak streaming behind him. Sir Michael flanked him, and beside them galloped a man in full gleaming plate, as broad as a war golem.

The bearded man hurled his spear in one smooth motion. It pierced a fleeing goblin through the back. A heartbeat later, two more spears sang through the air, striking true. The goblins fell like broken dolls.

And then came the sword.

With brutal elegance, the lead rider drew his blade and surged forward, overtaking the last stragglers. One goblin's head flew from its shoulders. Another was cleaved in half by a whirling arc of steel.

The final goblin turned to run—but the man in plate armor raised a warhammer and crushed it mid-step. The crack of impact was sickening, final.

The bearded man scowled for a heartbeat, robbed of the last kill—but then grinned, satisfied. The panic among our group melted into relieved murmurs. Even the most hardened among us exhaled as the threat vanished.

We had all lost too much to goblins. No one mourned.

"What...are they *riding*?" I asked, still breathless.

Amara stared at the riders, mouth closed behind pursed lips.

"They're called horses," Draven answered, stepping beside me.

The riders crested the hill and spotted us. They waved and galloped toward us. The bearded man raised his sword in greeting.

"Well struck, General," he said to the armored man beside him, his voice strong and warm. "But I *almost* beat you to that last one."

"Can't let you have all the fun, your majesty," the General replied with a knowing smile.

My breath caught. "Wait...is that—?"

Amara didn't answer at first. When she did, her tone was colder. Sharper. Royal. All signs of the young woman joyful to be home vanished—replaced by the regal princess.

"Yes," she said. Her chin lifted.

"My father. The King."

The king gave a sharp nod to General Blacktide. "Burn the goblin corpses," he ordered, his voice iron. Then he swung down from his mount with the ease of a seasoned warrior.

He was taller than I expected—taller than me by at least two inches—and every inch of him radiated command. His purple surcoat fluttered over the shimmer of chainmail, the silver glinting in the artificial sunlight. His salt-and-pepper beard framed a sharp, noble face—the same aquiline nose Amara bore, only older, battle-worn. His eyes were steel— weathered, piercing...but not cold. There was warmth in them. A flicker of humanity beneath the authority.

The moment his boots hit the ground, our entire escort dropped to one knee as if tethered to the same invisible string.

I started to follow—until Ravic leaned close and murmured behind me, "Don't kneel. You're not his subject. You're a Watcher. Stand tall."

The words struck like a hammer forging a blade. I straightened. Despite my worn boots and travel-stained clothes, I met the king's gaze with my head high and my shoulders square.

He didn't even blink.

Instead, he stepped forward and seized Amara's face in both hands, his movements raw with emotion. "Oh, Mara," he whispered, voice cracking beneath his regal poise. "We thought we lost you."

Despite the vulnerability in his grip, Amara remained regal, poised. "I'm fine, Father," she said, steady. "Thanks to Captain Marek and the Core Drifters. And thanks to Finn Camlock."

Her words hit me like a wave—warm, but weighted. The king pulled her into a fierce embrace, arms wrapped around her like a man grasping his final water skin while marooned in the dunes.

Or a father clinging to the only child he had left.

I swallowed hard. That guilt—the thing I'd carried since we first found her—it surged from my chest like bile. I didn't want to tell him.

I *dreaded* it.

The king finally pulled back, holding Amara at arm's length, studying her face with desperate precision.

"I told you, I'm fine, father."

"You say you're fine," he said, voice softer now. "We suppose we'll have to believe you."

Then his gaze lifted—and locked on Marek.

"Captain Marek," he said, voice rising again with dignity. "A thousand thanks. You've brought my daughter home."

Marek gave a courtly bow. "It was my honor, your highness."

The king's eyes found me. "You must be the Grounder."

"Yes, sir. Your majesty," I replied, my voice a half-step behind my courage.

"And you carry a missive?"

I reached into my vest. "I do, your majesty. But...I regret to say the news it contains isn't good."

A sigh escaped the king—quiet, but heavy. The kind of sigh that carried too many funerals behind it.

"There's been too much of that," he said. "Hold it, for now. We'll speak in more...selective company."

I nodded, silently grateful for the reprieve, even as my heart clenched tighter. There would be no easy way to tell him what he needed to hear.

"Thank you, Master Camlock," the king said. "You helped bring my daughter home. For that, you've returned hope to a father who was nearly out of it."

Just wait until I tell him about his son. I felt so much guilt at his words. Anything I could say now felt awful and wrong, like they would come back to bite me.

Repeat after me: "It was my honor, your majesty," Aubrey whispered in my mind.

"It was my honor, your majesty," I echoed.

The king gave a small, approving nod, then turned toward the gathered crowd. "Forgive us! Please—stand. The wagons will be along soon. They were being fueled when we departed."

The word *fueled* snapped out of his mouth, and before I could stop myself, curiosity got the better of me.

"You use combustion engines?" I blurted.

A few nearby guards looked up in surprise, but the king only smiled, amused. "We do. We're fortunate that the Ignavari threat doesn't loom as close here as it does above. And, sadly, we lack those wonderful nova-fields you have on the surface."

"Apologies for speaking out of turn," I said, with only minimal coaching from Aubrey. I didn't intend to let her take over my responses completely.

"No apology necessary when speaking to concerns for our people's welfare." He signaled to several attendants who came out of the gate house on this side of the large stone wall which overlooked the stairs down to the Rose Gate.

If they used combustions engines, what about projectiles, explosives?

Nope, too big a chance for a cave-in, Rhee said. *The kingdoms signed off on a no explosive device treaty, based on the principal of mutually assured destruction.*

Mutually assured, what?

If one kingdom did it, all the other kingdoms would do it and everyone would die. They all have weapons and ways to bring down the other kingdoms.

What if the waxers or the Igni get a hold of those weapons?

It would be very bad indeed. Those weapons are likely their most tightly guarded secret and very protected.

I certainly hope so. I turned at a wonderful smell coming from those attendants.

53

The first attendant unfurled a long table, draping it in white linen. The others followed, unloading baskets of meats, cheeses, fruits, and loaves of bread. My eyes locked on a pile of small green egg-shaped things. Nearby were slices of something red and juicy—shimmering in the light like jewels.

"That's a tomato," Rory whispered, appearing beside me like a culinary ghost. I turned and saw him standing on his toes, eyes gleaming with reverence.

My stomach growled. Loudly.

The king chuckled at the sound. "There's plenty for everyone. But I would ask our honored guests to partake first."

He nodded toward Marek, who gave Rory a light tap on the arm. The man all but *leapt* toward the food, assembling a towering plate with the precision of an artist selecting colors for a masterpiece.

I followed suit a moment later, breathing deeply through my nose to take in all the scents of the food before us. The food was cold, so nothing wafted towards me, yet I barely caught a sharp scent from the little green eggs, and the deep earthy, sweet of the tomatoes. I grabbed several of each. I piled my plate high with the cured meats and a variety of cheeses before grabbing two pieces of barely warm bread with my hand as they wouldn't fit on my plate.

I sat next to Rory on the soft green grass. Who better to enjoy a meal with than the man who taught me how to love food? He reached for one of the green egg-shaped things first and I mimicked the motion. We popped them into our mouths at the same time.

"Ohhh," the cook rumbled. "I haven't had an olive in years. Notice the complexity of the taste. It's not really sweet, not really salty, but something else entirely. Almost meaty, yeah?"

I was thrown off by the initial taste. My teeth separated the pit from the meat, then rolled the flesh around my tongue. It was so new, I wasn't sure whether I liked it or not. I'd have to try again. And again.

54

The tomatoes went next.

Rory watched with anticipation, finding joy in each expression dancing across my face.

"It's all so good," I said. "I don't know how the people of Alyndor get anything done. If it were me, I'd do nothing but eat."

"Just wait until you try the cooked stuff," Rory said with a mouthful of bread.

I felt a hand touch my shoulder and looked up in surprise. All my attention had been on the food. My surprise tripled when I realized it was the king. His other hand rested on Rory's shoulder.

He smiled benevolently down at us. "The two of you truly know how to enjoy a plate of food."

Rory hastily swallowed the bread. "It's exquisitely prepared, your highness, your chef is an artist."

The king tilted his head, pondering. "Would you like to meet her?"

Rory held a hand to his chest and bumbled, "I...wha...I...," Rory bumbled.

"He would be honored, your majesty," I said for him.

"It appears that, for some, meeting the royal chef is a greater honor than meeting the king," the king said. He gave me a wink which Rory couldn't see.

Rory took a deep breath and his eyes widened. "No...not at all your majesty, it's just...meeting the royal chef, seeing the royal kitchens, it's always been a dream of mine."

The king relented. "We understand. It takes an artist to know an artist."

"Exactly!" Rory said with relief.

"Consider it done." The king stared down towards the forest.

I followed his gaze and saw a trio of four wheeled vehicles bouncing along the road, one pulling a large wagon.

"Finish up, friends," said the king. "Our transport has arrived."

8

The Castle

A mara chose to ride a horse for the final leg of the journey, her silhouette regal atop the saddle, hair streaming like a banner behind her. She and the king rode side by side behind their armored knights, their voices low as they conversed. From a distance, they looked like a perfect portrait of royal unity—but I could feel the tension radiating between them like heat from sun-baked stone.

Even without using my perception, I sensed the unspoken weight that passed between father and daughter. Maybe it was the secret she hadn't shared—the one about her brother. Or maybe something older and deeper ran beneath the surface of their smiles.

My own journey was...less dignified.

The vehicle I rode in lurched violently with every cobblestone, every bump in the road threatening to rattle my bones apart. My teeth clacked together hard enough I was afraid I'd chip one. The Duskers may have conquered cuisine, but when it came to vehicle suspension, they were firmly stuck in the past.

Dain groaned beside me, leaning out of the open-top transport to inspect the wheels. When he sat back up, he flung his hands skyward. "Springs!" he shouted over the roar of the engine. "Have they never heard of suspension springs?!"

"The transports may be bumpy but at least they're *really* loud," I yelled to Dain with a grin.

Birds flew from the treetops at our approach and small forest rodents ran for their lives at the sound.

"Makes it hard to enjoy the serenity of the forest, doesn't it?" Ravic asked, leaning close to my ear to be heard. "I'd recommend walking through these trees when there aren't vehicles around. It's as peaceful as the striations, maybe more so."

I looked around, and I could see what he meant. The canopy overhead filtered the simulated sunlight into a mosaic of dancing greens and golds. The trunks were massive, ancient things, and the air beneath them held a coolness and calm I'd never known underground. Even through the noise, I caught hints of the forest's natural rhythm. A whisper. A rustle. A promise of something sacred.

And then we emerged from the forest's edge, and the world opened.

Alyndor Castle stood before us, rising from the land like a crown carved from bone and gold.

Blue and gold pennants snapped in the breeze from towers that pierced the cavern air, their tips brushing the edge of the distant ceiling. The walls were pure white stone, flawlessly carved and fitted together like a puzzle solved by titans. Inside those walls, structures sprawled in graceful arcs and towering peaks.

On its western flank, the castle dipped into the shimmering waters of the Glassmere. Giant stone docks reached into the inlet like the outstretched toes of a giant testing the water's chill. Behind it, the white stone faded into the natural gray of the cavern wall, merging fortress with mountain.

A fortress with only two exposed flanks. *Smart*, I thought, recalling Jaxon's lesson. Fewer approach vectors. Easier to defend. Harder to conquer.

The architect had routed the inlet into a moat which encircled the castle in a ribbon of dark blue water which clashed with the light blue pennants streaming above the gatehouse. The drawbridge was down and the portcullis was up, leaving the entrance to the castle yawning open like a toothy maw.

To the north, nestled under the watchful eye of the castle, a town had sprung up—its roofs packed tight in neat rows, smoke curling from chimneys, life humming beneath the shadow of royalty.

As our convoy slowed, the wagon carrying the former prisoners came to a gentle stop. One by one, the survivors disembarked. They wept. Laughed. Clung to one another. Then, they turned to the king, the princess, the crew of the Core Drifter. Gratitude shone in their eyes, warm and deep.

I received four hugs—unexpected, fierce, and wordless. Each one a quiet thank-you that said more than any speech ever could.

We continued on foot toward the open gate. Another fanfare rang out, bright and triumphant. Horns blared. Flags snapped.

And there, standing just inside the great archway, was a woman wrapped in silks the color of the sky at dusk, her gown woven with flecks of sapphire and shimmering threads that caught the light like stardust. She was older than Amara, but radiant, ethereal—like someone molded from moonlight and royal blood.

Her presence stole a tear from Amara which sealed her identity—her Majesty, Queen Emilia, the Blue Lady of fairy tale. The queen opened her arms wide and the royal princess façade crumbled for good. Amara ran across the second half of the bridge and into the waiting arms of her mother.

They hugged and a cheer rose from the walls and echoed through the cavern.

Princess Amara was home.

Our quarters in the castle were ridiculously opulent. "They spared no expense, my boy," said Ravic with a grin at our shared room. "These must be the quarters they use for foreign dignitaries."

Two enormous beds dominated opposite corners of the cavernous chamber, each covered in layers of thick linens and silken throws. The ceilings soared like the top of a chapel, the walls inset with glowing crystal sconces that bathed the room in warm amber light.

Ravic made a beeline for the adjoining bath chamber. Moments later, the sound of rushing water echoed through the stone like a song I didn't recognize.

Concern prickled at my chest. I rushed in, half-expecting something wrong.

Instead, I found Ravic shirtless, casually pointing to a wide, inlaid basin that sprawled before him like a small pool. Water flowed from a sculpted faucet shaped like the neck of a delicate bird—similar to those gliding across the Glassmere.

I stared, mouth agape, as the basin began to fill.

"You've never seen a bath?" Ravic asked.

I froze in the doorway, jaw slack. "That's...that's a bath?"

He arched an eyebrow. "You've never seen one?"

"Not like that." We took showers on the ship. Back home, we used metal basins. Cold water. A cracked bar of soap if we were lucky. "Where's the water coming from?"

"Why don't you tell me?" he said, a playful challenge gleaming in his eyes.

I stepped closer, inspecting the faucet, listening to the smooth, gurgling stream. "They've got a network of pipes—must draw from the Glassmere. Probably filtered. Heated too...I bet they've got thermal reservoirs deep in the rock and pressure pumps to cycle it through the castle."

Ravic pointed at me. "That would be my guess, but maybe you can ask one of the water engineers at the castle."

My mind raced. We could do something like this back at the compound. Maybe not *hot* water, but just *running* water? That would be revolutionary. It wasn't a question of the engineering—no, it was the sand. Always the sand...

The thought evaporated as Ravic waved me out of the room. "My turn for luxury," he said with a grin.

I laughed, retreated, and collapsed onto the nearest bed. It cradled me like a cloud. For a moment, I let myself sink into the impossible softness.

Then I sat up again, guilt prickling like static across my skin. I didn't want to dirty the covers.

Ravic's singing echoed from the bath, cheery and off-key. I smiled faintly and pulled my boots back on. A hot soak could wait. My restless legs—and my thoughts—needed a walk.

The heroes of the Drifter have free reign of the castle, the king had said, with a wink toward Marek. *Save for the royal chambers...and the vault.*

He'd said it like a joke, but it still surprised me—this level of hospitality from a reclusive ruler. Then again, we had brought his daughter home.

Brought her home, I thought, and just like that, the weight came back. The ring in my vest pressed against my ribs like a stone, and the words I still hadn't spoken twisted in my gut.

Honesty goes a long way when delivering bad news, Aubrey said.

I harrumphed. *Didn't seem to work too well with Amara.*

Different situation, Aubrey said. *You didn't know. You pulled the bandage quickly, and I thought she took it amazingly well. Remember— royalty, or anyone in leadership, has to give or take this news too often. Doesn't mean it hurts any less. But they're trained to hear it. Robert used to agonize over having to tell the family of dead crew members. But he did it. He was always honest and he was always kind, regardless of what he thought about the person who died.*

Even if that person was a brakking idiot?

Especially if that person was a brakking idiot. It's not the idiot that needs comfort, but those who loved the idiot.

Not that the commander was an idiot, but this is hard enough when I respect the person.

It's harder when you respect them. Because it requires you to share your own grief.

I kept walking, boots thudding dully against the rich rugs and polished stone, barely seeing the fine tapestries or gleaming armor on display.

Until I collided with someone...again.

Princess Amara stood in the hallway, arms folded, head low. We both kept our feet this time.

"Hi," I said, caught off guard and reduced instantly to a monosyllabic fool.

She gave me a tired smile. "Hi, Finn."

I saw them—the faint, glistening tear tracks down her cheeks. Something about them hurt more than any bruise gained in the circle.

"I thought you'd be with your family," I said gently.

She shook her head. Her breath trembled. "I can't. Not when they don't know about Calder."

Her brother. His name hit like a punch. I'd never thought to ask it. To me, he had always just been *the commander*.

We stopped near a tapestry that stretched from floor to ceiling. It showed a brutal battle—blue and gold knights clashing with red and black foes in a titanic tunnel.

"This one was his favorite," she murmured, voice small.

"Who are the knights in red and black?" I asked.

She scowled. "Not knights. Thal'Naris. Traitors. They broke their oath and stabbed us in the back."

Her venom surprised me. Not even goblins had drawn such fire from her.

"They're another Dusker kingdom?" I asked.

She nodded and pointed to a rail track running along the base of the tapestry. "That's the Veilspoke Transit. Over a century ago, the kingdoms and the tunneler tribes built it together. Spoke and wheel design, with Saenar's Veil—home to the great Library and the famed healer's monastery—at its hub. It was meant for peace. Each of the Seven Kingdoms signed an alliance that the rail would only be used for trade between the kingdoms or for bringing students or the injured to the Veil, never for war."

"After seventy years, Thal'Naris broke the pact. They used the rail to attack Alyndor. This is the Battle for Alyndor Station. My grandfather died here."

I nodded solemnly. "Why did Calder love the tapestry?"

Her eyes grew distant. "Because little boys dream of glory."

She reached out and gently touched a blue-and-gold figure. "I've spent five days trying to figure out how to tell my parents."

"Let me do it," I said quietly. "It's my burden too. I have the parchment. The ring. I made the promise."

She turned sharply, voice cracking. "But he was *my brother!*"

"I know," I said softly, stepping closer until our shoulders touched. "I've been replaying that moment—telling you—ever since it happened. I'd do it differently if I could."

She leaned against me, her head tilting ever so slightly, letting herself feel the weight for just a breath.

"Maybe we do it together," she whispered.

Then she straightened. The warmth against my shoulder vanished.

She turned to me, eyes blazing again with the fire I'd missed. "Yes. Together. Right now."

I blinked. "But I—"

I'm not ready, I wanted to say.

But I would never be ready.

And neither would she.

So I swallowed the words and nodded.

"Okay," I said, steadying my voice. "Lead the way."

9

A Royal Audience

When we reached the royal family's private wing, the air felt different—*heavier*, like a nova-storm pressing in, threatening to break. Voices echoed down the marble corridor, sharp and raw. The door to the solar stood slightly ajar, and the conversation beyond spilled through.

"That is *not* under your authority to grant, brother," hissed a low, sibilant voice, each word laced with cold disdain. "That falls within the dominion of the Church. If you press forward with this decision, I *promise* the Oracle will be outraged. Don't be surprised if she abandons Alyndor altogether."

Amara mouth tightened. "That's my uncle Drennic, Duke of the Deep."

Another voice chimed in—a stark contrast, jovial and half-slurred, yet not lacking in bite. "Would that be so bad?" he said. "If she *did* leave? Or at least stopped preaching that isolationist drivel?"

Amara leaned close and whispered, "That's Uncle Althar. Duke of the March."

"You *dare*," Drennic snapped, his words brittle as glass ready to shatter.

"Oh, I *dare* plenty," Althar replied, his voice rising now, a mocking lilt giving way to vehemence. "I remember another war sparked by religious rhetoric and sacred mandates. Hard to forget—it's *immortalized in tapestry* right outside our entry hallway!"

"You forget yourself," Drennic growled, tone turning glacial. "Without the Oracle, without the Church, the core wards that keep the dark at bay would fail. We sleep peacefully because of her."

"Funny," Althar spat, "I don't remember the core wards doing a thing about the goblin incursion! Tell me, brother—how exactly do you and the church plan to spin that disaster?"

"Brothers, please," the king interjected, calm but firm. "I value your counsel. But my decision is made. I will accept the consequences."

"You *will*," Drennic hissed, and the venom in his voice made the hairs on my neck rise. "Mark my words, brother—the consequences will be grave."

The solar door flew open with a bang. Duke Drennic stormed out, tall and rail-thin, his long black jacket sweeping behind him like oily tendrils. His eyes locked on Amara—then flicked to me. A sneer curled his lips, but he said nothing. He simply turned and stalked away, the air seeming colder in his wake.

Duke Althar followed a moment later. Barrel-chested, broad-shouldered, with the sturdy gait of a man who trained with knights but preferred a feast to a fight. He caught sight of Amara and his entire face lit up. "Mar!" he boomed, striding toward her. "You're safe. Thank the stars."

He wrapped her in a bear hug, lifting her slightly off the floor. Amara's stoic mask cracked as she buried her face in his chest.

"I'm sorry I wasn't there to greet you," he said, voice muffled against her hair. "But I've been busy sweeping the tunnels clean of those blasted goblins. The farther out we go, the longer it takes."

"Nice to see you too, Uncle," Amara murmured into his chest.

Althar turned to me and grinned. "And *you* must be the Grounder everyone's talking about." He clapped a hand on my shoulder. "Well done, lad. You brought her home. That makes you family in my book."

"I'm honored, sir," I said, giving him a small bow.

With a warm laugh and a farewell pat on my back that nearly knocked the wind out of me, he waddled off down the hall, humming to himself.

Amara and I stood in silence, watching him go. Then she drew in a slow, steadying breath and turned toward the open door.

"Let's do this now," she whispered, her voice quiet but firm. "Before I lose my nerve."

Inside the solar, the air was heavy with silence. The Queen sat beside the King on an elegant divan, their hands clasped, their expressions carved from grief and dignity.

"We know, my beautiful, brave daughter," said the Queen, voice soft as black silk at a funeral. She looked at Mara with pride, knowing how hard it must have been to tell them. "The news reached us last week. A border patrol found the remains of your brother's command. After the Dawnford checkpoint went silent."

The king's hand tightened over hers. His other hand wiped hastily at the corner of his eye. "We didn't know how to tell *you*, Mara. Not after everything you'd been through. You've already carried so much."

Amara stood still, her chin trembling as she fought to hold herself together.

I stepped forward and told them what I could. No embellishment. No dramatics. Just the truth: Calder had fought with courage, led with honor, and died saving lives. I spoke of his bravery. His sacrifice. Then I reached into my vest, pulled out the sealed parchment and the ring, and placed them gently into the King's waiting hands.

I stepped back, suddenly unsure where to look, my eyes fixed on the carpet while Amara fell into her mother's arms.

Queen Emilia held her daughter like she was fragile glass. The king wrapped them both in a protective embrace, his eyes closed, lips pressed together in silent anguish.

"We'll grieve tonight," the queen said, stroking Amara's hair. "Just the three of us. After the ceremonies."

I felt invisible, and maybe that was how it should be. This was their moment. Their loss.

The king eventually sat up and broke the seal on the parchment. His eyes scanned the contents quickly, his expression tightening with each line. When he finished, he passed it to the Queen and looked down at the ring in his hand, spinning it between thumb and finger.

"Tell me, Finn," he said, locking eyes with me. "What do you think he meant by 'Beware the Melt'?"

I blinked. I'd nearly forgotten the scorched words Calder had found beneath the drawer in the checkpoint bunker. They'd seemed cryptic then, meaningless. Now, they felt like a warning whisper from beyond the grave.

"I believe it has something to do with the waxers, your majesty," I said carefully.

The king frowned, biting the inside of his lip. "Perhaps," he murmured. "But it's vague. Too vague. Melt could mean so many things..."

He trailed off and looked to his wife, who was still scanning the letter, her brows knitting.

His gaze returned to me. "And it was you who uncovered the diverted lectric? The energy your people trade with us?"

I nodded. "Yes, sir. But we didn't have time to investigate who was stealing it."

The queen folded the parchment with delicate care and placed it on the small, ornate table beside her. Her voice, though soft, rang with conviction. "We have to tell her."

"*Not yet,*" the king snapped, his voice suddenly sharp, cutting through the room like a blade. "Not here."

The queen's jaw tightened. "She's your heir now, Aeron—even if not officially. She deserves to know."

The king stood abruptly, pointing a warning finger in her direction. "This is a *family* matter."

I dropped my gaze to the floor, heat rising to my cheeks. I hadn't meant to overhear. I felt like I was trespassing in sacred space.

But the queen wasn't backing down. Her voice was steel wrapped in velvet. "We kept the circle too small last time. That mistake cost us our son."

Then, to my shock, she turned to me. "Mara could do far worse than an ally like this one. Calder himself vouched for the boy's integrity."

The king's hands were still. He stared off into some invisible distance, spinning his son's ring between his fingers like it was the only thing anchoring him to the present.

Amara stood silent, watching, listening, until her patience wore thin. "Tell me *what?*" she demanded, her tone low but unwavering.

The queen took a long breath. "Your brother was investigating—"

"*Emilia...*" the king growled, a final warning.

But the queen rounded on him. "*Aeron.* If she doesn't know, she won't be able to protect herself. She's already in danger. Knowledge is her only shield."

Amara planted her hands on her hips, every inch the royal she was born to be. Her voice was clear and commanding: "Tell. Me. What."

A heavy silence fell. Then, at last, the king nodded.

The queen faced her daughter. "Calder uncovered a plot. One aimed at toppling Alyndor from within."

Amara's face paled. "From *within?*"

"We don't know who's involved yet," the king admitted, "or even how deep it goes. But we know it has to be someone close."

"Someone on the inner council," the queen added grimly. "Because only they would have knowledge of our vulnerabilities—where to strike, how to bypass our core ward defenses."

My heart hammered. I hadn't planned to speak, but the silence begged to be filled.

"I don't know much about core crafting," I said cautiously, "but if your mesh lines are anything like our pylon grid...then your theory's probably correct."

The king turned to me sharply. "Explain."

"The waxer we fought in the caverns," I said, "he was my neighbor in Dawnford. He tried to disable our grid to let the Ignavari into the compound. I don't know what the Igni wanted—but I doubt we would've survived it."

The queen's eyes narrowed. "Was he in power?"

I shook my head. "No. But he was...manipulative. He could turn people. Made the entire compound believe I was the threat. That's how I ended up banished."

I told them everything. The lies. The accusations. The exile. And the betrayal that sent me away.

When I finished, the king and queen exchanged a long, heavy look.

"This distrust has been the source of tension between us for months," the queen said, voice low. "How do you question those closest to you without tearing your kingdom apart?"

"Once you start," the king murmured, "you can never be sure who to trust again."

"If it's *not* someone on the council..." The queen didn't finish the thought.

"Then the rot runs deeper than we feared," the king finished for her. "It widens the search, but I'd rather trust and verify than see enemies where there may be none. I'll eat my crown if Thal'Naris isn't somehow involved."

A chill settled in the air.

Amara stepped forward and dropped to one knee. "What would you have us do, my liege?"

The king looked down at his daughter—his *only* child now—and something in his expression softened, then hardened again into grim resolve.

"Continue your brother's work," he said. "Root out the traitor. I know it's a heavy burden for one so young—but the truth is, we *cannot* trust anyone else. Only you."

Amara bowed her head. The queen reached out and gently took her hand.

"Sending you into danger would never be our choice," she said, her voice barely holding steady. "But danger has already found you. This... gives you a way to fight back."

The king's eyes met mine. They were no longer heavy with grief. They were searching. Measuring.

"Finn," he said. "My son believed in your ability, in your insight. If you aid my daughter in this investigation and help safeguard this kingdom, I will grant you honorary citizenship. You will be empowered to renegotiate trade agreements with Dawnford as Alyndor's envoy."

My breath caught. An emissary with full authority to determine the terms that governed the future of my people—and possibly, my return.

I could go back...not as an exile, but as a hero.

Accept it, said Aubrey. *Robert may have asked for more, but these people need help. If you successfully help the kingdom, you help yourself and your compound. It's a fair offer.*

It is, I replied. *But I want to go home. I honored my pledge to the commander, delivered his message. My month is more than up. I want to see my parents, see Shea. Find out what the compound decided.*

Go back now and you'll be judged by the same fools who banished you, said Aubrey. *Finish the mission, and you'll return not just with leverage, but with power.*

I knew she was right. But I was sixteen. I was tired. And homesick. And completely in over my head.

I glanced at Amara. Her expression was impassive, but her eyes weren't. They were full of uncertainty. Of fear. She didn't want to do this alone.

And I couldn't let her.

Even if she could be stubborn. Even if she drove me nuts sometimes. *Stars help me,* I thought. *I'm really falling for the princess-in-peril bit.* I let out a long breath. "I'll do it," I said, steady and clear.

The king nodded solemnly, but I didn't miss Amara's reaction—her shoulders slumped in relief, and something bright shimmered in her eyes.

"You'll have to be sworn in, of course," the king said. "Oaths of secrecy. Loyalty. Trust."

I opened my mouth to agree—but Aubrey shouted in my mind.

Stop! Not one word until you see it in writing.

"Gladly, your majesty," I said, reframing the suggestion. "Once I have the offer in writing. If the information is too sensitive, I suggest encoding it and placing the record in the castle vault. Or my safe."

The king arched a brow. "Perceptive indeed."

The queen smiled. "We appreciate caution, Master Camlock. We'll draft it ourselves."

"Good," the king said. Then he turned to Amara. "Princess, you'll bring him up to speed on the court. I expect him to know every major power broker before tonight's awards ceremony."

Amara's eyes widened at the request, but she didn't complain or make excuses. "Yes, father, but I have one request before we start."

He raised that imperious eyebrow once again.

"Please order Finn to take a bath."

I raised my hands in protest. "I tried! Ravic beat me to it."

The king waved us off with a tired smile. "Get out of here, both of you."

10

Pomp & Fancy Pants

The bath was amazing.

Steam curled in lazy spirals around the marble-tiled room, the hot water biting into my skin in the best possible way—like it was scouring off weeks of grime, guilt, and goblin blood all at once. The moment I lowered myself in, I nearly melted. Every tense muscle sighed in relief. I could've stayed there for hours.

The soap, dispensed from a tiny bronze pump shaped like a water lily, filled the basin with thick bubbles that carried the scent of wildflowers and something sweet and strange I couldn't name. Overpowering, maybe, but it beat the scent of stale sweat and fear.

I'd just finished scrubbing myself raw and had leaned back with a blissful groan when it happened.

Three booming knocks.

They echoed through the chamber like war drums, breaking the fragile spell of peace.

Another round followed. Then Ravic's voice, half startled, half amused. "Princess, a pleasure to see you."

"Is he ready yet?" Amara's voice shot through the door like a crossbow bolt. Sharp and impatient. Regal.

"You're the one who *ordered* me to take a bath!" I shouted, scrubbing at my face one last time.

"And now I'm ordering you to finish! We have work to do!"

"Will there be snacks?" I called back, hopeful.

"Is he always this annoying?" she asked flatly.

"Only when he's awake," Ravic answered with a traitorous chuckle.

I flipped the drain and dragged myself from the warm hug of a bath. I toweled and dressed in the same threadbare clothing I wore this morning and opened the door to face my tormentor.

Amara stood with arms crossed, eyes scanning me from head to toe. Her judgment was instant.

"You can't go to the honoring ceremony dressed like *that*," she said, voice laced with horror.

"Sorry, princess, but these are my best clothes."

"Not anymore." She pointed to the bed where a black tunic with golden thread and blue toggles sat next to a pair of dark azure pants. "How are you going to style your hair?"

I frowned at her. "What do you mean?"

"Is he kidding?" Amara asked Ravic who, I was happy to see, also looked confused. She took a deep breath and looked up at the ceiling. "I don't think he's kidding."

I shrugged. "I'll change before the ceremony. You're the one who's in a hurry, are we doing this here or..."

She glanced meaningfully at Ravic then shook her head. "No, the royal library is far more conducive to study. Besides, my mother still requires a chaperon for me, and the librarian will do in a pinch."

We made our way through the east wing, her explanation floating beside me as I tried, and failed, to keep my thoughts focused. The "small" royal library looked larger than the entire compound archives back home. Shelves rose like stone towers around us, crammed with knowledge carved into bindings.

We found a quiet study nook: a circular wooden table carved with dancing four legged creatures with spindly horns, surrounded by four high-backed chairs. Sunlight filtered through a stained-glass window, draping colors across the floor like spilled jewels.

Amara launched into a primer on Alyndor's power structure, listing names, alliances, rivalries, and courtly vendettas like a battlefield strategist mapping enemy positions. I nodded along, but my eyelids drooped. The simulated daylight, the warmth of the room, and my recently boiled limbs conspired against my focus.

Back home, this was the time I'd normally sleep. Midday was sacred rest for Grounders. But here, the Duskers ran on sun and ceremony. My head nodded once, then twice.

Salvation arrived in the form of a serving woman with a tray.

Snacks!

I perked up instantly.

Later, I stood in the center of the room while a tailor circled me like a hawk. No one had measured me—not formally, anyway—but the new clothes fit *perfectly*, like they'd been stitched onto me by magic.

The woman had a permanent scowl as she eyed my armored shirt. "Unacceptable," she muttered.

"I'm not removing it," I said.

She grumbled but showed me how to loosen the toggles on the tunic so it would still fit. Then she got to work with a blade as sharp as her tongue, trimming the wild hairs from my face and reshaping the uneven haircut I'd been wearing since the Drifter. She mixed a greenish goo, warm and fragrant, and massaged it into my hair, brushing and tugging until strands obeyed her like troops answering roll call.

When she finally spun me toward the mirror, I didn't recognize the person staring back.

Gone was the scruffy exile. In his place stood a young man with squared shoulders and armor-bulked arms. The facial hair was gone, revealing sharp cheekbones and a jawline I didn't know I had. My skin was pale now, like the Duskers, but clean, smooth.

It was the hair which made all the difference. She separated strands and batches which propped my bangs up before letting them fall down in a manner which looked haphazard, but was anything but. She had sculpted the hair exactly where she wanted it. It framed my forehead and made those dark, sandy locks look...masculine.

I'd never looked in a mirror and *liked* what I saw...until right now.

When we arrived at the great hall, I walked beside the Core Drifters with a new kind of confidence. We moved like a unit—polished, hardened, undeniably changed. Their outfits hadn't changed. They didn't need to. They'd always looked like heroes.

But me? I no longer looked like a pauper begging for chits. I looked like I belonged.

A herald stood in the arched doorway, cloaked in deep violet and gold. His sculpted jaw and perfectly trimmed goatee looked carved from stone. He held a tall staff topped with a silver hawk, and every time he announced a name, he slammed it against the stone floor with a thunderous crack that echoed across the hall like judgment being passed.

He raised a hand, stopping us with a flick of his wrist.

"You'll be announced last," he murmured. His eyes scanned the group before settling, and lingering, on Marek. "The stars of the show should never enter before the crowd is ready to adore them."

I braced myself for Marek to gut him with her glare, but...no. Was she actually *blushing*?

No time to think about that. I turned, scanning our group—only to realize one of us was missing.

"Where's Rory?" I asked, a little too loud.

Dain shrugged. Draven answered.

"He was invited to the royal kitchens," Draven said. "The chef asked for his help preparing the feast."

Dain looked personally offended. "He chose *cooking* over a royal ceremony? Over applause? Over *drinks?*"

"A passionate fool, indeed," said Ravic. "The royal kitchen is his summit—a holy place. Don't tell me you'd make a different choice if they let you roam the royal workshops."

Dain shook his head. "Nope, work is work. I may love what I do, but tonight, we drink and be merry."

Then, the herald began his incantation of introductions.

"Sir Draven of Alyndor," he called, voice like thunder. Draven blinked at the unexpected title but walked with quiet dignity.

"Dain Underforge, master engineer of the Core Drifter." Dain flexed as he passed, making sure everyone saw him.

"Watcher Ravic Tunnelseer." Ravic gave a slight bow and glided in like he belonged in every throne room that ever existed.

Then came my name. "Finn Camlock of Dawnford Compound."

The world slowed. My pulse thudded like war drums in my ears. I straightened my spine and walked beneath the archway, stepping into a hall carved from grandeur itself.

Heel to toe, heel to toe, Rhee counseled in my mind as I made my way down the aisle.

Polished floors reflected the light of hundreds of mounted crystal lanterns. Banners of blue and gold swayed gently from the rafters. The air smelled faintly of scented smoke and lilacs.

At the far end, elevated on a three-step dais, sat the king and queen, cloaked in majesty. Between them, a step below, was Amara.

She looked radiant in ceremonial blue, but it was her smile—the private, genuine one she saved just for me—that ignited something deep in my chest and burned away every trace of doubt.

I stopped worrying about tripping.

I let myself *see* the room.

Long benches lined either side of the aisle, filled with nobles draped in silk and velvet. Some ladies watched me with curiosity, even admiration. The men...less so. Their eyes sized me up like I was a pawn that had moved too far across the board.

Amara had warned me: the court was a viper pit, coiled in brocade.

At the top of the dais stood Sevrin Vexenholt, the Iron Quill—royal chancellor who rewrites history as often as he advises the king. I expected an old man with parchment dust on his robes. Instead, he was lean, sharp-eyed, and barely older than my father. He whispered something into the king's ear, and the king smiled faintly as I passed.

I held my gaze forward. Let them talk.

To the right, I recognized the dukes—Althar and Drennic. The king's brothers.

Althar was a broad-shouldered beast of a man, red-nosed and jovial-looking, one hand resting affectionately on the thigh of his younger wife. Drennic, by contrast, was a gaunt specter, all cheekbones and shadow, with a gaze like a dagger and the warmth of an open grave. His wife's eyes flicked to me with quiet interest. He noticed.

I kept moving.

Beside them sat General Garrick Blacktide, the Shield of Alyndor, the same man who stole the last goblin kill from the king. His square jaw and storm-grey eyes radiated discipline. He was a man of war, respected and feared, a rare general who saw *before* he struck. He was beloved by his men, loathed by the church and the core crafters. He nodded at me, just once.

Opposite him sat Oracle Seraphine Veilheart, her golden veil glinting in the crystal light. The Voice of the Veiled God, seer of disasters. No one knew her age. No one knew if she was the same Seraphine from decades past. No one had ever seen the face behind her golden veil. Her priestesses flanked her like moonlight shadows.

Healer Elyndra Moonsong sat beside them in green, vines in her hair, serene as spring. She was sometimes referred to as the Bloommother—current head of Saenar's Veil

Then, last—an unwelcome guest. The Thal'Nari ambassador, cloaked in blood-red silk. His presence was an act of political theater. I learned in the library earlier that Amara didn't even know his name. He smiled at me like he was imagining how I'd taste over a fire.

Behind him were the guildmasters, each one watching us like a banker eyeing a risky investment. I'd meet them all soon enough.

I reached the dais at last and took my seat beside Ravic, directly across from the court and just below the throne.

The herald boomed once more. "Captain Marek of the Core Drifter."

The crowd murmured with interest. Marek strode down the aisle like gravity itself bent to her will. The herald trailed three paces behind her, eyes fixed politely on the throne.

She took her seat next to mine, closest to the king.

Then, the herald took center stage and slammed his staff down a final time.

"Lords and ladies! Allies of the throne!" His voice rang through the hall like a bell forged from steel. He turned to us, smile bright. "And new friends..."

He bowed low.

"The king has words to share."

The hall fell silent. All eyes turned to the throne.

11

Heroes of Drumsorrow

The king stood. The low murmur of the court dissolved into silence. Even the banners seemed to still, the room hushed by the weight of what was coming.

"Thank you," King Aeron began, his voice deep but lined with fatigue, "for joining us in celebration of our daughter's return to Alyndor."

He looked directly at Amara, his composure momentarily cracking with unspoken emotion, then turned his gaze to the gathered crowd. "Tonight, we honor the heroes of the Core Drifter—those who did not just defy death, but wrested hope from its jaws."

A ripple of reverent murmurs passed through the crowd. In the back, the former prisoners we had saved bowed deeply, dressed in their best—though many still wore the weariness of their ordeal like another layer of clothing.

The king's gaze softened. "And our loyal knights, Sir Michael and Sir Rouse," he continued, "who stood their ground in hopeless odds. They would have fought to their last breath—many of their brothers and sisters *did*—had my daughter not surrendered to spare their lives."

Gasps. Nods. Whispers of admiration and horror stirred the chamber like wind over grass. But not everyone was moved.

General Blacktide's jaw was a clenched iron trap, his scowl like thunderclouds on the horizon. I didn't need Amara's insights to guess those knights were already paying a quiet price behind closed doors for allowing the princess to get captured.

Then, the king's tone changed. Softer. Raw.

He looked to the queen, and in that flicker of vulnerability, his royal mask cracked. "We wish..." he hesitated, the silence deafening, "we wish that joy was all we brought you this evening."

A shiver passed through the room.

"The rumors that have haunted our halls are true," he said, voice trembling. "Our son, Prince Calder, has fallen. Slain by goblins...and darker forces still."

A collective gasp surged through the crowd. Some reactions were real—hands to mouths, sobs stifled. Others, especially among the nobles, were theatrical, forced—like performers playing a tragedy they'd already rehearsed.

The king pressed on, steadying himself like a man leaning into the wind. "The news was confirmed by one who stood with him at the end: Master Finn Camlock."

His eyes met mine. Not stern. Not distant. Apologetic. As if, somehow, *he* owed *me* something. I didn't understand it. Not yet.

He took a shaky breath, voice catching. "We grieve the loss of a future never lived...a king who might have been. A brother. A son."

And then—tears.

Tears rolled unashamedly down his cheeks.

The court froze. This was not the mask of a monarch. This was a father, stripped bare.

Even the ever-cheerful Duke Althar lowered his head, and General Blacktide's stony façade cracked as he wiped a tear away with one thick, calloused hand.

The queen sat unmoving, her expression frozen in grief, her hand clenching the arm of her throne with white-knuckled fury. Amara sat beside her, proud but pale, every breath drawn like it cost her something.

I couldn't imagine being the target of the queen's stony gaze. But someone would be. Someone who betrayed this family, this kingdom. And I'd be there to see justice fall.

After a long, aching pause, the king lifted his head. His eyes were red. His voice was steady.

"We will hold a memorial for my son..."

He faltered.

Aubrey's voice whispered into my mind: *He said 'my.' Not 'our.' Not 'we.' That wasn't a royal decree. That was a father speaking. This is deeply personal for him or...he slipped up intentionally.*

Of course it's personal! He's talking about the death of his son.

Aubrey made a hmmm noise that tickled my ears from the inside.

"...seven days from now."

Sevrin Vexenholt, the Iron Quill, stepped forward and leaned in to whisper something. The king shook his head sharply. Whatever the chancellor suggested, Aeron would have none of it.

Then, with an audible clap of his hands, the king rallied a smile— fragile, but real. "But *tonight*," he said, "tonight we *celebrate*. The return of our beloved daughter. And the courage of those who brought her home."

The room slowly lifted from the tension. The court shifted, breaths exhaled, spines straightened.

"I name these brave souls the *Heroes of Drumsorrow Cavern*," the king declared, "a title that grants you free passage through Alyndor's gates, now and always."

The applause began slowly—then swelled like a wave.

The king's eyes found Dain first. "To Dain Underforge, master engineer, we offer full access to our royal workshops for one week.

Create anything your heart desires, up to one hundred gold in value on the crown's credit."

Dain blinked, mouth agape. I wished I could sketch the expression— it was a perfect mirror of every time he'd surprised *me*.

"Rory Eggsberry," the king said with a chuckle, "though not in attendance, has found refuge in the only place holier than this hall— our kitchens. We grant him access to the royal larder for five years and, in recognition of his culinary valor..."

He opened a small wooden box and handed it to Dain. "Rare spices, gathered from the Seven Kingdoms. See that he receives them."

Dain rose and bowed. "Aye, Your Majesty. I'll make sure he cooks something worthy of it."

"Sir Draven," the king said, turning. "I name you *Lord Draven Stonepath*, and grant you two hectares of land at the foot of Whisper Ridge. Thank you for seeing our daughter home, Lord Stonepath."

Draven stood and executed a courtly bow, leg out front, making it look like a martial form. "Thank you, my liege. I'll do my best to be worthy of the title."

"To Ravic Tunnelseer, Watcher of the Clans," the king said next, "we grant unrestricted access to our royal libraries and sages, including those who study the Last Song."

Ravic bowed low, his voice reverent. "A kingly gift indeed."

Then, the king turned his full gaze on me.

"Master Finn Camlock of Dawnford Compound," he said, and every heartbeat in the hall paused, "you risked your life to save my daughter and, in doing so, you may have saved the future of this realm. For your courage, we offer one year of training with the Royal Guard and the right to study with every guild in Alyndor. A new start of sharing information between our peoples. What better way to defeat our shared enemies."

The air grew thick with reaction. The nobles murmured, but the guildmasters scowled—uneasy, offended. Amara hadn't lied. They guarded their secrets like dragons hoarding gold.

I did my best to mimic Draven's bow and said, "Thank you, your highness."

Oh, he's good, Aubrey spoke into my head. *He just gave you full access to root out the traitor. Don't know how much of a gift it is to you though.*

Are you kidding me? I said. *I get to learn combat from the Duskers and learn ALL their trades — engineering, lens creation, cooking, everything.*

"And lastly..." the king turned to Marek. "Captain Marek Shadowdelver. For valor, for skill, and for returning my daughter whole, the crown will fund full repairs of your drillship and offer you a ten-year exclusive contract to manage all royal tunnel expansions."

Marek stood, stunned. Even she—calm, impenetrable Marek—was speechless. An exclusive contract for a drillship captain was the brass ring. She bowed. "An honor, my liege. One I will not take lightly."

The king raised his goblet high.

"Let Alyndor never forget the names of those who dared the dark and brought back the light. Heroes of Drumsorrow Cavern—tonight, we feast in your honor!"

The entire court rose in a thunderclap of applause. Music flared. The chandeliers blazed. The tide of celebration crashed forward.

And I knew, beneath the light and wine and laughter, a shadow still moved.

* * *

The banquet passed in a golden haze of wine, laughter, and dishes so exquisite they belonged in a dream. I tasted a bit of all of them—Rory made sure of that.

84

He'd arrived with the head chef herself, beaming like he'd been crowned, and served the opening course with a proud flourish. The applause he received for both saving the princess and seasoning the soup nearly outshone ours. And somehow, impossibly, he kept showing up at our table just when a courtier leaned in to whisper something slippery.

"What herbs do you think they used in the glaze?" Rory would ask, eyes wide and innocent, effectively cutting off the noble mid-ploy. "There's definitely saffron—no, wait, starroot. Has to be. Don't you think so, Finn?"

His timing was so perfect, so precise, that after the third interruption I caught Draven's smirk and knew.

"You planned this," I accused quietly.

Draven raised his glass in a toast to Princess Amara and took a slow sip. "Not I," he said. "But *she* did."

I blinked.

"She's not just quick with a blade, Finn," he continued, his tone quiet but firm. "You're not just watching a fighter. You're watching a tactician. She's using Rory like a shield."

I glanced across the table at Amara, who was chatting serenely with a guildmaster's wife, her laughter soft and practiced. But then—just for a heartbeat—her eyes flicked to me and held.

She knew exactly what she was doing.

It wasn't the last time she shielded me.

Over the next two weeks, she made sure I was never alone. Every tour of the city, every audience or gathering, one of the Drifters was always nearby. She played the court like a seasoned musician, keeping me safe with the right harmony of allies, distractions, and subtle threats.

But there was one thing even Amara couldn't stop.

The rumors.

They bloomed like mold in dark corners—quiet at first, then spreading, persistent and vile. Whispers turned into certainty: that I was the only one with Prince Calder at the end. That I'd helped the goblins. That I'd manipulated Amara into trusting me.

Having Carl Stinz as my brakking neighbor only stoked the fire.

Within a week, the warm smiles shifted. My name was still on noble lips, but now it came with frowns, narrowed eyes, and veiled accusations. The other Drifters were celebrated. I was studied like a crack in the foundation.

"I'm so sorry, Finn," Amara said one afternoon as we lay on the warm dock of the Glassmear, breathless from a long swim. The suns reflected off the water, throwing ribbons of light across her face.

"It's my fault. I should've crushed the rumors the moment they started."

"No," Draven said as he dried his hair beside us. "You couldn't have."

Amara sat up, water dripping from her hair, anger in her eyes. "You doubt my influence with the court?"

Draven pulled on his tunic. "Not for a moment. I'm saying your father's outweighs yours."

The memory clicked—the way the king looked at me after naming me as Calder's witness. That strange flicker of guilt.

"He *knew* this would happen," Amara whispered. "He let the rumors grow."

Draven nodded solemnly. "He needed to shift the spotlight. You were too exposed. Now they watch Finn instead."

I stared between them. "That's insane. I'm supposed to be Amara's ally in—" I stopped myself just in time.

"...strengthening our kingdoms," Amara filled in, eyes flicking toward the attendants nearby.

Draven snorted, not buying it. "It doesn't take a genius to smell something rotten in the highest echelons of the court, your highness."

"Do you think the traitor will come after Finn?" she asked, voice tight.

"Maybe. Or maybe they'll think he's one of them."

Amara's eyes widened. "Of course. If they think he helped Calder die, they might try to *recruit* him."

Draven shrugged. "Doubtful, but it was a smart play by your father. As you know, princess, rumors have a short shelf life in the kingdom. They fade as quick as the next scandal pops up."

"Is that why you fled the kingdom for seven years, because of how short their shelf life is, *milord*?" she asked.

Draven stared out over the Glassmere for a long moment. "I hadn't learned that lesson yet, your highness." He looked to the attendants. "You're in good hands. I'll take my leave."

As he walked away, I turned to her. "Why poke him like that?"

She sighed. "It's something my mother taught me. The best way to know someone's truth is to press on their wounds and see what bleeds."

"Sounds cruel," I said.

"It's better than dying because you trusted the wrong person."

All too soon, the Drifters began packing up. The drillship gleamed in the royal yard, fully repaired, squawk boxes humming with life. They had their first contract—tunnel work near the southern border—and with it, a steady route back to the capital.

The goodbyes weren't dramatic. We'd see each other again. That didn't make them easier.

Dain pulled me aside before he boarded. He handed me Aubrey's spider.

"Didn't change a thing. Rojer says it's a perfect apprentice test. Show this to the right engineer and they'll skip you past the basics."

"What did you build with the credit from the crown?"

Dain smiled mysteriously. "You're just going to have to wait and find out. It'll be a fun surprise the next time you board the Drifter."

I scowled at him, but it didn't have any bite. "There's nothing fun about your surprises."

Ravic interrupted our hug. "Move on, engineer, I have something I need to tell Finn." He glared at Dain. "Privately."

"Fine, *Watcher*. I need to get the Drifter prepped anyway."

"Find anything new about the Last Song at the library?" I asked Ravic.

"A little," Ravic said. "But most of what I found is more of the same myths running through our culture."

"What myths?"

"That the songs can be harnessed, used to protect." He shrugged. "No practical information on *how*, of course."

Ravic waited until everyone was out of earshot then leaned in close. "I didn't just research the Last Song the past two weeks." He paused dramatically. "I chased some trog holes on what transformed the Stone Serpents."

"What did you find?"

"There are ways to *change* people, Finn. Dark ways. The core crafters once used them to create the magical beasts of the forest and swamp. But there were *rules*. Laws. What we saw? That was no accident. Someone broke those laws."

"The goblins?"

"Doubt they're smart enough. Could be rogue crafters, maybe the waxers, maybe even the Igni."

My chest tightened. "You think Carl—"

"I think you've underestimated him once. Don't make that mistake again."

Ravic gripped my forearm.

"Be careful, Finn. The court watches you. Our enemies watch you. And if the rumors do their work..."

He let the warning hang in the air.

I nodded. "I'll watch them back."

12

Igni Prime

3 Years Before Finn's Pilgrimage To Iron Mountain

"Carl?" Denis said again. "Are you okay?"

Carl looked up slowly, fingers still curled around the handlebars of Finn's new speeder. What did a little kid need with a new speeder anyway? The weight of Denis' voice grated against his skin like sandpaper. *Okay?* The word nearly made him laugh. *Was he okay?*

He forced a stiff smile. "My bad," he muttered, gesturing vaguely at the busted lock. He couldn't bring himself to apologize to Denis. "I'll replace it."

Denis didn't even look angry. That was what twisted the knife.

He looked *pitying.*

Of course he did. That was the Grounders' currency when it came to Carl—pity handed out like ration chits. But not anymore.

Carl swallowed the bile rising in his throat and let the moment stretch, feeling the bitter taste of humiliation twist into something colder. Sharper.

Let them pity me.

He'd *use* it. Let their guilt and misplaced kindness grease the wheels of his rise. Let them underestimate him all the way to the edge of ruin.

"I'm just glad you're okay," Denis said, voice warm with sincerity. Carl's stomach turned. *So sincere. So brakking noble.* The worst thing about Denis Camlock was that he actually meant it.

Carl gave a crooked smile that nearly cracked his face. He stuffed down the manic chuckle bubbling in his chest.

"I'm fine," he said, trying to sound weary but hopeful. "Just got a little lost in the sands."

Denis glommed on to the smile, grasping it like a lifeline. "Good, I'm glad you're back," he said with a relieved sigh. "What were you trying to do out there?"

The way he asked the question implied he thought Carl was trying to kill himself. He wasn't exactly wrong, but...that story wasn't going to get him what he needed.

Carl shook his head. "No, nothing like that. I was just...trying to say goodbye...is all. I think I'm finally ready to move on."

Denis' eyes sparked with interest and relief. Carl knew right then he could ask this man for anything—the guilt Camlock carried, for his role in killing Amber, would make sure he got it. No matter the pirate attack which took her life happened over thirteen years ago—wounds that big never healed.

"That's good, Carl. Really good. You look...better. Let me know if you need anything."

Carl stifled the smile which threatened to ruin the facade. "Since... you're offering, can I borrow the speeder one more time?"

Denis gave him a quizzical look. It wasn't distrust, but he burned to know why. The man would lend him the speeder regardless, but his story needed to be strengthened, for those who weren't quite so trusting.

Carl pulled Amber's wedding ring from his pocket. He stared out at the sands as he spun the ring in his fingers. "It's time to let her go.

Once and for all. To do that, I need to see where she fell, where they found her body." He held up the ring. "I'm going to bury it with her."

He'd never give up his token of the woman he loved, but Denis needed a reason.

Denis took a breath and winced. "That's really...unsafe. You'd have to be out on the sands for at least three days."

Carl patted the handlebars of the speeder. "I know. I *need* it to be unsafe. It's not a trial if it's easy."

Denis walked around the speeder, checking it for damage. "Want me to come with you?"

Carl couldn't think of anything worse. "I'm afraid this is a solo mission." Could he summon the will to be gracious? He'd have to. "But thank you for the offer," he forced out.

Camlock caught his eye and held it. Carl stared back. Surprisingly, Denis was the first to break the gaze.

That was new, but Carl had purpose now.

"The speeder's yours for as long as you need. I'm not giving it to Finn for another couple of months. Chlo won't let him have his own vehicle until he's fourteen."

Carl could care less about Denis and his perfect family. Be gracious, gotta be gracious. "Afraid he's going to race the rim?" he asked.

"Oh, I know he's going to race the rim. I just don't want him to be stupid about it."

Carl forced another smile, then a nod. "Thanks again."

The heat blasted him from all sides as he streaked across the sands, the sun a white hammer overhead. The speeder hummed beneath him, steady and reliable, while the little device Malik had given him pulsed softly in his pocket.

The green dot—*his* location—drifted ever closer to the black one on the screen.

92

He'd brought two extra nova batteries, just like Malik instructed. Sixteen hours straight in the saddle, and his body ached in places he forgot had nerves. But he didn't stop. Couldn't.

Ahead, the jagged spines of the Droughtspire Range rose like the bones of some dead titan, tall and sharp enough to pierce the sky. Their red sandstone shimmered with green streaks—veins of metal or ore, maybe. Or something worse.

He veered slightly south as a yellow-green flame floated silently across the dead hardpack. Another Ignavari. His third sighting of the day.

His heart thudded once, then steadied. The fear wasn't gone, but it had dulled. The Igni ignored him. Just like Malik promised.

Soon, the shadows of the spires stretched around him, cool and welcome. He eased off the throttle, scanning the base of the mountains.

And there—narrow and dark as a slit in the world—was the entrance.

Smaller than he expected. He could ride the speeder through it but he wouldn't have much room on either side.

Carl swallowed the dryness in his throat and revved forward. Malik stood in the mouth of the passage, holding the twin of the device in Carl's pocket. His silhouette was framed by jagged stone and shadow, waiting.

"You made it," said the thin man in the black duster, his voice little more than a whisper carried on the furnace wind that sighed from the tunnel's depths. Malik's red hair stirred like blood smoke, his eyes fixed, unblinking, aglow with a hunger which had nothing human left in it.

Carl parked the speeder and swung his leg over the side, stretching his spine with a grimace. His muscles screamed after the sixteen-hour ride, but his mind—his mind was locked on the goal.

"Now what?" he asked.

Malik's gaze pinned him. "Have you been nursing it? That pain?

That hollow where your wife used to be?" His voice coiled, low and venomous. "Feeding the hate for the filth who took her from you?"

Carl didn't blink. "The pain and hate never left. I don't know how much bigger it can get."

"Good," said Malik. "Fall back on it when you meet the Igni. It's the only way you'll keep your sanity."

He handed Carl a mask—industrial, ugly, with a thick tube that clicked into a humming box clipped to his belt.

"Put it on," Malik said. "Otherwise, the air inside the cave will peel your lungs like fruit."

Carl fitted the mask over his head and inhaled. The air was stale, metallic, hot—like breathing through an oven's exhaust.

Carl glanced at Malik. "Where's yours?"

Malik smiled, slow and skeletal. "Don't need it anymore."

Then he turned and strode into the dark.

He followed Malik down the tunnel which narrowed until they could no longer walk side by side. When the tunnel widened again, a greenish-yellow mist took over the space. Or maybe it was just green—hard to tell through the mask. The temperature had increased, and Carl worried his skin would burn if he spent too much time here. He could feel the heat of the ground through his boots.

Malik walked into the dense mist and changed. His head ignited, eyes boiling with a wet pop that echoed. Flames coiled around his skull like a crown of agony, and still, he walked.

The tunnel opened into a giant cavern dominated by a lake of molten fire. Dozens of Igni floated through the fire, sinking or rising to avoid bumping into each other as they staked out spots in the lake.

Carl couldn't prevent the terror which burbled his gut at this nightmare come true. The heat was so intense, he felt he could burst into flame any moment.

What had he been thinking?

Revenge, he reminded himself. *For Amber. For everything.*

He passed the reins to his hate—of Dawnford, of the Dead Crows. It countered the fear, the heat. Barely, but enough to move forward. He followed Malik past the pool of fire and up a ramp which had been melted through the rock.

At the top, the tunnel curved into something different. A perfect tube, smooth and seamless, as if poured from a mold. Malik ran a flaming hand along the wall. Carl dared not touch it—every instinct screamed that it would sear his flesh.

At last, the tunnel opened into a perfectly spherical chamber, lit not by fire, but by something purer. Something worse.

At its heart floated a single Igni, utterly unlike the others.

A star in miniature. Blinding white, rimmed in flickering fire so intense it felt clean. Controlled. *Alive.* While other Igni looked slightly insubstantial in their flaming coherence, this Igni had presence, like gravity manifested.

Carl squinted through his mask, trying to absorb the impossible. Around the chamber's spherical walls, thousands of tiny alcoves had been carved into the rock, each holding a single object—metal shards, bits of bone, tools, seeds, teeth. Junk, or trophies. Some hung upside down from the ceiling, perfectly still.

Only the ramp to the center remained bare.

Malik descended it first. Carl followed, boots slipping slightly. The heat pressed into him like a second skin. When he reached the platform, the white Igni floated at eye level—radiant, pulsing.

Carl couldn't look directly at it. It seared through the mask, burning into his skull. His questions died in his throat.

Malik leaned his flaming head towards the spherical Igni. Flames jumped between them for several seconds before Malik stepped away.

He looked to Carl. "Your turn with the Prime. Be honest with your intent, with your need for revenge. Feel it, let it own you."

Carl took the burning man's advice as he stepped close to the stark white flame of the Igni. He let his feelings for Dawnford and the Dark Crows suffuse him. The hate burned so strong, he already felt close to bursting into flame.

The Prime floated his way and tendrils of flame reached towards his head, his eyes. Carl almost forgot he wore a mask.

He tried not to flinch but the heat was intense and he drew back.

"Don't move!" Malik hissed from his side. "You flinch, you die."

Carl closed his eyes, forcing himself to stillness. The flames kissed his throat.

It felt like his core caught fire.

But he didn't scream. He leaned in.

The flames surged into him, *through* him, burning along his memories. It *saw* him—every weakness, every humiliation, every failure.

And it *fed*.

It lapped up his hate like wine, recoiled from his love, sneered at his grief. It watched eagerly as Carl received news of her death, then cheered him as drunkenness and sorrow turned into hate. It *feasted* on his pain and demanded more.

And then—Carl saw *its* mind.

A world in collapse. A sun bleeding light like a wound. A column of white flame that split the sky, worshipped or feared or both. A glimpse of Ignavari piling into huge mountains morphed with slag metal— those mountains levitating off the ground.

And underneath it all, the Prime's own hunger. Its own hatred.

Its *loathing* of change. Of weakness. Of hope.

Then—silence.

The Prime floated away.

The white Igni floated towards Malik again and the waxer accepted the flaming tendrils without flinching. After a moment it was over. Malik gestured for Carl to follow him.

They walked back, past the flaming lake of floating Igni, back through the misty haze of the tunnel and out to the exit where the hover bike waited for Carl.

"The Prime sees potential in you, but it is not ready to trust you with powers."

Carl frowned.

"Yet," Malik continued. "You have to prove yourself first."

"What does that mean?" Carl asked.

"You have to not only face your past, but conquer it. You need to visit the Dead Crow camp, face the pirates who took her from you."

13

Indexing & Shields

When I finally sank into bed that night, I wanted only one thing: oblivion.

Sleep. Blessed, silent, dreamless sleep.

It had been another exhausting day, one in a long line of them. The king's edict might've been carved into stone, but the guilds treated it like a suggestion. Three weeks of petty obstacles, paperwork, and procedural delay—all designed to make me quit.

The engineer's guild had been the worst. They'd granted me access to one of their vaunted workshops...but only to the tools. Tools without materials. It was like being handed a bow with no string, a promise with no path. Torture.

They weren't outright defying the king. That would've been suicidal. Instead, they wielded their autonomy like a scalpel, cutting me out of everything that mattered, hiding behind rules and "reviewal processes" as transparent as glass. I was the fulcrum of a tug-of-war between royal decree and guild independence, and it left me feeling like little more than a pawn.

Thank the stars for Sevrin Vexenholt—the Iron Quill. The royal chancellor wielded guild law like a broadsword, slicing through red tape with surgical precision. But his help came at a price: constant runs from one end of the capital to the other, ferrying arguments and counterarguments like a glorified messenger. It was a battle of parchment and patience, and most days, I was outmatched.

When it got to be too much, I escaped to Whisper Ridge. Draven was turning his crumbling estate into something worthy of the name *Lord Stonepath*, and I helped where I could. Rebuilding walls, planning defenses, carving out spaces that felt safe—even that was a reprieve.

But I couldn't hide forever. I *needed* the guilds. I was dying to get my hands dirty, to learn from the masters, to build something that mattered. Amara and I had a mission, but I also had a hunger—to understand, to become *more*. And the guilds were the gatekeepers to both.

Sevrin said the resistance was wearing thin. The guilds were running out of legal excuses to stall me. But that didn't make the rejection sting any less. They weren't just blocking access to training. They were blocking *me*. Dismissing me not as a threat, but as irrelevant. Forgettable.

That kind of rejection was harder to swallow than any insult. At least insults meant you were seen.

With nothing else to do, I threw myself into training with the royal guard. Halberd, spear, falchion, greatsword—every weapon became a language I fought to learn. Draven's brutal drills aboard the Drifter had taught me *how* to learn, and I devoured everything the Guard offered. I still lost every sparring match...but I had a secret weapon.

A *very* annoying one.

We both know you need the training, said Aubrey.

Do we? I sighed back, dragging a pillow over my head. It didn't matter. She was *in* my head.

You continue to improve at a ridiculous rate, she said, stroking my ego to gain compliance. *Why do you think that is?*

Because we train every night, I said.

Because we train every night. Now stop whining. You're weight distribution is good, but you're too hesitant. And you still haven't learned the secret to up close fighting. Lucky for you, I've got just the drill.

Fine. Closing my eyes made the transition easier.

When I opened them, I stood in a room built of gleaming metal and simple machines. Circular weights rested on bars. Strange pulley devices stretched cables taut across polished rigs. The walls bore mirrors and windows—beyond them, the endless black of space.

A gym, Aubrey said. *Robert trained here when he was still just a second lieutenant.*

I saw him—Robert—sitting up from a set of crunches, our uniform a sleek, one-piece suit that hugged our frame. He stared into the mirror, and for a second, I felt like he was looking *at me.* A shiver ran down my spine.

Then the door hissed open and a dozen fighter pilots strode in, swagger dripping off them like heat from an engine. They wore the same gear, same confidence. One of them—huge—nodded at us.

"Crossfire," he said. "Early as always."

Crossfire? I asked.

New callsign after his first mission. He saved two pilots with a gutsy move.

What was his first callsign?

Bobblehead. Robert...Bob. Aubrey chuckled. *Fighter pilots are savage to rookies.*

We stepped onto a glowing blue mat with the biggest pilot, "Rabbit," across from us. Robert pulsed his awareness, scanning the man's joints, posture, microexpressions. He was looking for any tell, any twitch that gave away intent.

Ride the first couple of matches then it's your turn, Aubrey said. *Tonight, I want you to focus on two things. Robert was a master of the counter attack.*

Whenever he was the aggressor, he did it with purpose, see if you can figure it out.

And the other?

Their shields. They are similar to a nova-shield, but they don't pull from a nova-field. See if you can identify their source.

I didn't see an edge and neither did Robert as they lined up, bare-handed, across from each other.

Rabbit moved—fast, way faster than a man his size should move. A feint kick to the ribs. Robert blocked and kept contact, sliding his hand along the plane of his opponent's leg. That's when the *real* kick came—a whip-fast strike to the head.

Robert ducked under it and *slammed* his fist into Rabbit's hamstring. Shields buzzed as they clashed.

The man yelped. "Easy, Cross! Way too close to the family jewels."

Robert smirked. "Hate to break it to you, Rabbit, but polishing 'em every night doesn't make 'em worth more."

Rabbit snickered. "Pretty sure your mom would say otherwise."

Robert smiled and lined up again. How did he move so quickly into that counter strike? I was missing something.

This time Robert attacked first. His first kick a feint which got us close to Rabbit. Rabbit responded with a punch which Robert blocked. He held on to Rabbit's arm, shields buzzing against each other. Robert's free hand shot out, faster than thought, and knuckled in to Rabbit's ear.

Rabbit grimaced and the two fighters lined up again.

Contact. That's what was different. When Robert attacked, he did so to make contact with his sparring partner.

Robert called it indexing, Aubrey said.

Cross made contact to *read* his opponent. With Rabbit's arm in hand, he knew where his head was. He didn't have to guess.

I could have punched Rabbit blindfolded, I realized.

Exactly. Never forget the power of touch in a fight.

The next round, Rabbit tried to stay elusive—a flurry of kicks and spins, forcing distance. I had no idea what to do, but Robert timed it, stepped inside the whirlwind, and drove his knee into Rabbit's kidney.

Rabbit hit the mat hard. "How do you always know where to be? It's *so* annoying."

I had the same question. Muscle memory, sure, but it was more than that. Robert had a full library of moves burned into his memory of how to counterattack when one of a thousand attacks came his way.

Robert just laughed and helped him up. I marveled—not at the strength, but the precision. His body didn't react. It *anticipated*. Each counter felt inevitable.

It must have taken hundreds of hours of practice to make each move instinctive.

Hundreds of hours? Try thousands, said Aubrey.

I ran the math in my head. That wasn't possible. Unless...

You were helping him, doing the same night training I'm doing.

She didn't answer, but I could feel her satisfaction ooze over me.

She briefly handed control to me. I rubbed my arm and felt only the soft exercise fabric. Of course. Just like a nova-shield. Subtle. She gave control back to Robert so I could ponder.

So...how did it work?

While Robert fought our next two opponents, something caught my eye.

A small bump—barely noticeable—tucked behind the second woman's ear. I saw it as we locked her in a hold.

Your turn, Aubrey said.

Intrigued, I reached back and ran my fingers over the skin behind our own ear.

There it was. The same bump.

Conglomerate tech, embedded into the skull of every conglomerate soldier.

I rubbed it, trying to get a sense of the shape beneath the skin. Small. Precise. Part of me wanted to claw it out, to feel it between my fingers and *know*. How could they all agree to this? Let someone slip a leash straight into their heads?

In the rest of the 'verse autonomous enhancements are commonplace.

I rubbed at the chip again. *And these chips are like you?*

I felt Aubrey's snort like a clearing of my sinuses. *Please. These are standard military issue. I am worlds apart from crude, standard issue tech.*

I had offended her. Good. *And how would I know that?* I asked.

She ignored the question. *Save for several specific medical conditions, everyone in the 'verse has the ability to Meld to tech to some degree—the great promise of the Synth Core. In this training sequence, I'm controlling the Meld for us, but you need to feel it on your own, without me.*

With a pop, she vanished—only a vacuum in my mind's eye where she normally perched.

The gym around me dulled. My perception dimmed like a light losing power. I tried to pulse, to bring back the awareness...but what returned was messy, like trying to read data through broken glass. I hadn't realized how much I relied on Aubrey filtering the data. I couldn't track body movement. I couldn't anticipate. My edge was gone.

No. I can do this. I functioned before Aubrey went for a ride on my brain stem. I could do it now. I closed my eyes and slowed my breathing. Focus inward.

Three breaths. Four.

There—faint but familiar. A signal near my right ear, like a quiet heartbeat. I reached for it, mentally and physically. Latched on.

Suddenly, the world snapped back into brutal clarity. Not quite what I had before, but a hollow similarity.

Sound returned in layered waves. I could hear footsteps on the far side of the gym. Voices bounced off the metal walls. I could feel my heart rate—72 beats per minute. Blood chemistry. Hormone levels. Oxygen saturation. Data streamed in fast and heavy.

I blinked—and as I wondered what the numbers meant, a full rundown of red blood cell function, normal thresholds, and my own stats appeared in perfect clarity.

A sharp *snap* in front of my face jolted me back to the room.

"You good, Cross?" Rabbit said, raising an eyebrow.

"He's doing that thing again," said the woman I sparred. "Zoning out, then coming back with a new way to wipe the floor with me."

"What'd you figure out this time?" Rabbit asked.

"Still working on it," I muttered, already distracted again. "Can you toggle your shield on and off?"

Rabbit gave me a weird look. "Yeah, sure. Spec on the body core allows a 200-millisecond delay before the auditory shield comes back up."

I nodded slowly. "Auditory shield off," I said, and the soft hum vanished from my awareness. "On." It returned.

I pulsed my perception. The shield wasn't just sound. It was *dense*, tightly woven sound waves vibrating at dangerously high frequencies. It was like a skin of thunder wrapped tight against the world.

"You're trying to use the shield as a weapon somehow, aren't you?" the woman asked.

I ignored her. The implications were enormous.

Could I *pulse* an Igni with one of these shields? Would it disrupt their flame? Would the frequency matter?

"Before you zone out again," Rabbit said, "real question: Say you had to fight an Igni hand-to-hand. No backup. No weapons. What do you do?"

"Run," I said, not even pausing to think about it.

"I know *that*," the fighter jock said. "But, let's say your back's against the wall, nowhere to run. What do you do?"

I wanted to call for Aubrey, reach into her endless memory bank of military history—but she was still gone. Or hiding. My mind rifled through what I *did* know. Had any of the jocks ever fought one?

"Why? Planning on entering the sparring circle with one of em?"

"No, smartass," Rabbit snapped. "If I get shot down in atmo, I want more than just prayers. I don't want to end up like Juicebox."

I gulped. So one of the jocks *had* fought an Igni. And lost.

"I'd rupture the coolant system in my suit. Blast it at the thing. *Then* run."

"Why not just hose it down?" Rabbit asked. "Use the water stores in the suit."

We'd tried water against the Igni in Dawnford. Of course we had. Water didn't run cold enough. Even when we used a lot of it, water we didn't *have* much of, the Igni merely turned it to steam.

"Doesn't run cold enough," I said. "Extreme cold seems to be the only thing that slows 'em down. But to kill one?" I winced and left the question open.

Maybe if we dunked one in the Glassmere? Could I use the auditory shield to pulse at one of the Igni? Could sound be used to lower temperature? I *needed* to learn more about this shield! About what Conglomerate tech could do. At the very least it could serve as inspiration.

"There he goes again," said Rabbit. "Let's get some chow, by the time he comes back, he's gonna need test subjects."

The others filed out. I barely noticed. My mind was lost in the Meld.

What else could this conglomerate tech behind Robert's ear do? The minute I asked the question, the answer appeared. Vitals, comms, weapons readouts, personal shield, interface to Mark IV fighters.

This must be what a Meld felt like for those without an Aubrey.

See! Aubrey's voice rattled into the void she had left so loudly, I jumped. *Now, you see how limited the standard license tech is?*

At least it can create a personal shield, I said.

You think I can't create a shield?

Well, can you? I asked.

With the right materials, of course I can, Aubrey said. *All it takes is a simple transmitter. We can build one the minute we get access to the guilds—your next assignment after you finish Rach.*

Now, practice what you learned on indexing, she said. *After a hundred bouts you can tap out and sleep.*

After the sixty-third bout of hand-to-hand combat I was finally getting the hang of using touch to understand exactly what my opponent would do next.

I was about to start the next round of sparring when Aubrey interrupted. *Finn, someone just slipped something under the door.*

The simulation ended and I opened my real eyes. I got out of bed and padded over to the door. An envelope embossed with my name on the front was sealed with red wax using the impressive stamp of the Glass and Light guild.

I hurriedly opened the envelope and read.

Finn Camlock,

After further review and in agreement with the edict of the crown, we offer you admission to the Glass and Light Guild training program. Your orientation begins at six bells tomorrow morning. Failure to appear on time will result in the guild rescinding the offer.

—Sheldon Farsmith III, Guildmaster

Aubrey, what time is it?

A little after second bell in the morning. They're playing dirty.

Yes, they are. Please wake me at fifth bell. I'd like to get some sleep.

14

Glass & Light Guild

A sharp knock startled me as I stepped out of the bath.

Another knock—faster, sharper, urgent.

I grabbed a towel and wrapped it around my waist, water still dripping from my hair. I already knew who it was. Only one person knocked like that.

Amara.

I cracked the door open, smoothing my wet hair back with one hand.

Her amethyst eyes widened. She stared, *openly*, at my bare chest, her gaze lingering far too long before snapping to mine.

I cleared my throat.

She blinked, flustered for half a heartbeat, then lifted her chin, the princess mask sliding into place. "Why answer the door if you're not decent?"

"This *is* decent. You've seen me wear less. We swim together all the time."

A flicker of color bloomed in her cheeks before she recovered. "I wanted to make sure you were awake and that you got the G&L guild's summons. Sevrin said they'd pull something like this."

Her gaze shifted past me, locking onto the open envelope on the desk.

The room was a far cry from the original suite I shared with Ravic—modest, functional, servant-class—but it had a bath and running water. That was all I cared about.

I looked at the princess. She was wearing her sparring clothing, but her hair was only slightly mussed and her amethyst eyes were sharp as ever. I shook my head. "What time do you get up?"

She frowned. "Why?"

"Because you look...good. I thought women had to do a thousand things in the morning to look that good."

Her mouth opened, then shut again. "Thanks," she said, and a flush crept up her neck. "Actually, I just got up ten minutes ago, the moment I got the note from Sevrin. I wanted to make sure you were awake."

I smiled. "You said that already."

She tucked a loose strand of hair behind her ear and straightened. "I know," she said, the princess mask sliding into place. "Get dressed. I'll walk you down there."

She stepped backwards. I held up a finger as I slowly shut the door.

Aww, you two are adorable, said Aubrey.

No. I towel-dried my hair aggressively. *You do not get to comment on my personal life.*

I dressed quickly in Dusker trousers—infinitely more comfortable than Grounder gear—and my armored shirt beneath a plain tunic. I hesitated at the door, suddenly missing home. Missing *them.* Patrice, Shea, my parents... Were they even still alive? It wasn't easy convincing myself that the vision I received from my grandfather's pocket watch was just a vision.

I'd asked Ravic and Captain Marek to watch for news from the surface. But the last caravan from Dawnford had come a week ago. Another wouldn't arrive for three more.

Her knock came again. "Let's go, Finn. You can't be late!"

Amara stood with arms crossed and foot tapping. I'd learned that was a *very bad* sign. "Being late shows you have no respect for the other party," she said when I was two minutes late to our last swimming adventure. Draven was the same way. I didn't know if timeliness was a Dusker thing or just a Draven and Amara thing.

"I dressed as fast as I could."

She turned, already moving. "Guildmaster Farsmith is a pretentious ass who takes himself way too seriously. Now, pick up the pace."

We sprinted through the narrow halls of the servant quarters, dodging trays of food and bundled laundry. One servant shouted, but choked it back the moment he recognized the princess.

Down the main stairwell. Through the torchlit gate. Over the drawbridge and into Alyntown's waking streets, where flickering lamps lit our way through the misty dark.

The Glass and Light Guild loomed like a cathedral of refracted fire—a kaleidoscope of colored panes glittering in the light of the gas lamps, even this early. It was a building meant to awe, and it succeeded.

A golden seal shone above the grand stairway—a prism splitting light into fractured color. The message was clear: We control the power of light.

I paused. She didn't.

Amara took my hand. Her fingers were warm, confident. The contact sparked through me, sharp as a nova-shield buzz but soft. I followed her up the stairs, heartbeat quickening, but not from the run.

We reached the door before the sixth bell. Right on time.

Naturally, it was locked.

Amara seized the knocker and slammed it, three times, on the heavy bronze door.

A smaller side door creaked open. A spectacled guildsman blinked, bleary-eyed and half-dressed. "Wards, girl, it's barely dawn—"

He froze mid-sentence. His jaw dropped as recognition dawned.

"Princess Amara," he stammered, sweeping into a lopsided bow.

"Apologies. I wasn't expecting—"

"You should have Finn Camlock on your list," she said, crisp and cool.

The man shuffled through a clipboard and frowned. "Ah...no visitor listed under that name"

I handed him the letter.

His eyes widened. "Ah! *Not* a visitor. Master Camlock, you're listed as a potential entrant for the spring quarter. That's why you weren't— yes, yes, of course. Please, follow me."

Amara breezed past him without waiting. I trailed her into the towering entry hall.

The doorman blinked again. "Ah, princess—I, uh...wasn't instructed to let you in—"

"Oh, don't worry," she said sweetly. "I just couldn't resist seeing my dear Uncle Sheldon."

"U-Uncle Sheldon?" he squeaked. "You mean...the Guildmaster?"

She patted his shoulder like a doting aunt. "Who else would I mean, silly?"

The man swallowed audibly. "I...suppose that's alright, then."

The princess gave him a theatrical eye roll and we entered the great hall. Every wall was a display of mastery and legacy. Glass cases housed inventions spanning centuries. Lenses, tools, and tech so intricate they bordered on magical. Some Ancient, some homegrown.

On the left: a strange, spindly device.

Compound microscope, Aubrey helpfully chimed in, *about the best you can get from lens technology.*

On the right: a sleek, ancient telescope.

Refraction telescope. Long range precision. Before quantum optics, this was cutting-edge.

After the Ancient technology, the homegrown displays were remarkably crude. Early lenses, eye glasses, progressing to better and better devices at the foot of the wide golden stairs leading deeper into the guild.

At the top of the stairs stood a small man in a black-and-gold suit so perfectly tailored it looked like it had been forged, not stitched. The seal of the Glass and Light Guild gleamed on his chest. He adjusted his gold-rimmed glasses, peering down his nose at us like a man examining a smudge on crystal.

His face was all blade—sharp lines, cold disapproval, no warmth. If he smiled, the world might crack.

"Uncle Sheldon!" Amara squealed with unrestrained delight, and before I could process what was happening, she launched herself up the steps and into the guildmaster's arms.

The look on his face was priceless. Pure, frozen horror. Like he'd just been hugged by a feral animal. For a full breath he stood there, stiff as stone—then awkwardly, tentatively, *barely* returned the embrace.

"Princess," he said, voice clipped and tight, "we weren't expecting you this morning."

"I know!" she chirped. "But it's been far too long, Uncy."

I stared. *Uncy?*

I'd seen Amara spar like a war goddess. I'd seen her navigate court politics like a seasoned predator. I'd never seen this.

From the wide-eyed expression on Guildmaster Farsmith's face, and the slack-jawed doorman, I wasn't the only one.

She broke the embrace, stepping back with an affectionate smile. "I was helping Finn prepare for his first day. Father thought it was a fine excuse for me to drop by and say hello."

Then, casually, like tossing a stone into a calm lake, she added, "Oh, and he sent a message. He said the guild's quarterly funding from the crown will be a tad delayed."

Farsmith's brow darkened. "How delayed?"

"Four weeks and three days," she replied, bright-eyed and innocent as a kitten.

The guildmaster's nostrils flared. "A coincidence, I'm sure—that's precisely how long our review process delayed Mr. Camlock's entry. We have these processes in place for a reason, princess. I hope your father knows that delays in the funding will likely delay the deliveries of new G&L tech to the crown."

Amara's smile never wavered. "Papa thought you might bring that up. He said something about...prudence. Then he said...autonomy is fine, but it's important to remember which side your bread is buttered on." She nodded helpfully, like a child reciting her lines. "Or something like that."

Farsmith's expression iced over. He leaned back on his heels, studying her like a chess piece that had just grown fangs. "You may tell your father the message was received."

She clapped once and gave a delighted little hop. "Wonderful! Oh—and feel free to share that message with your other guildmaster friends."

Farsmith's jaw tightened. "Of course."

Amara turned to me, all warmth again. "Have fun on your first day, Finn," she said with a wink—then skipped lightly down the stairs, like she hadn't just threatened an entire economic pipeline with a smile.

She walked to the side door and let herself out. The door clicked shut behind her.

Silence.

"Harold, return to your post," the guildmaster said through gritted teeth.

The doorman fled like he'd just been released from a gallows sentence.

"I trust you received our invitation?" Farsmith asked, smoothing his cuffs.

"I did. I was...lucky to be up late studying."

I looked around for a moment. "Won't there be other students joining us for the orientation?"

The guildmaster gave me a hard look, before deciding the question was an honest one. "This is the spring quarter. You are the only new student." He paused again. "Provided, of course, you meet the same standards our other students do by passing an entry exam."

I didn't know there was going to be an exam, but I wasn't surprised by it. Nor was I overly concerned by it. I had the foremost encyclopedia of knowledge in the world rattling around in my thought cage.

If I deign to help you, you mean.

Who are you kidding? I said to Aubrey. *You need me to get in as badly as I do.*

"And that's why I was requested to come early?"

The guildmaster began to walk and I fell in beside him. "Classes begin at eight. The test shouldn't take more than an hour or so. Consider this a tour."

He motioned for me to follow, and I fell in beside him as we entered a curving corridor. The outer edge was lined with office doors and lecture halls, but it was the interior windows that caught my eye— some frosted, others clear. Through them, I glimpsed labs that looked more like the guts of a spaceship than a school.

Devices I didn't recognize. Lenses arranged in labyrinthine patterns. Light sources mounted on adjustable rigs, some focused so tightly they burned pinholes through metal sheets.

Are they advanced enough to make lasers? Aubrey whispered in my mind.

I was about to ask her what she meant, but just then Farsmith made a subtle gesture with his fingers and one of the frosted windows cleared instantly, revealing the room beyond.

The lab was massive. On one side, bins of powders in every imaginable hue and texture—from coarse grit to fine, glittering dust. The largest bin overflowed with something all too familiar.

Sand. Coarse, sun-bleached, reminded me of home.

I stepped closer, transfixed. There were furnaces and kilns, molds and hollow rods, delicate tools I didn't yet have names for. The room was still and silent, but it buzzed with potential.

"This is one of three student labs," Farsmith said. "The glass creation lab. Care to guess what the others might be?"

I thought for a beat. "Lens refinement...and something related to manipulating light?"

A pause.

"Not bad," he said, lips barely twitching. "Yes. We teach advanced lens crafting and focused light applications. What's your background in this field?"

I hesitated. Aubrey was quiet, but I could feel her temptation to intervene.

"Very little," I admitted. "I know the basics—glass from sand—but surface crafters guard their techniques like treasure."

Farsmith grunted, and I couldn't tell if it was approval or disappointment. "Then let's see what you *do* know."

He stopped in front of an unremarkable door, hand resting on the latch.

"This is your entrance exam. Beyond this door is a test of your knowledge, intuition, and perceptiveness. Use what you know about light, lenses, focus, and refraction to reach the other side."

He opened the door.

Pitch black.

I turned to him. "What am I supposed to—?"

He shoved me forward.

The door slammed shut behind me with a solid thud, plunging me into absolute darkness.

15

Entrance Exam

I pulsed my perception and began to hum. The small corridor "lit" up with sound wave energy. The hallway was not quite four feet three inches wide, slightly taller than me, and it appeared to end twenty-two feet in front of me.

With my perception trained by the likes of Ravic, picking up the fake wall at the right end of the corridor was trivial. I couldn't sense any danger directly in front of me so I took a cautious step forward—and instantly felt the floor shift under me with a subtle *click*.

Light exploded across the floor. Panels beneath my feet flared to life, a kaleidoscope of dizzying color that pulsed and shimmered. A visual assault, a distraction.

I slowed, resisting the urge to shield my eyes. The corridor *appeared* to stretch on straight ahead.

When I reached the end of the hallway, my perception confirmed what I'd already suspected—the "continued corridor" was a mirage, conjured with a precise arrangement of mirrors. The real path turned sharply to the right. Anyone relying on eyes alone would slam into the wall.

I wondered how many poor initiates had done just that. I smirked and made the turn.

As soon as I crossed the threshold into the next hallway, the hidden door behind me slid shut with a hiss.

This hall felt...*wrong*. The floor glowed with a soft yellow light—almost inviting—but the moment I stepped forward, my senses screamed. I froze.

Walls moved.

No, *closed in*.

Two massive panels lined with wicked metal spikes began grinding toward me from either side, like some monstrous beast meant to crush me to paste.

Panic surged.

I inhaled sharply. Hold. Think.

My humming picked up again, sharper now, more focused. The sound bounced, scattered—and told a different story.

The spikes were real, yes, but they weren't here with me.

They were on the other side of transparent, expertly treated glass.

The lenses embedded in the glass warped distance and scale. A precise optical illusion designed to trigger panic. Someone had engineered this space to trick the eye and rattle the mind.

I didn't take the bait.

Instead, I pulsed ahead.

Near the far end, on the second-to-last floor panel, my perception snagged on something hidden. A sliding door to the left—concealed and silent. Just ahead, on the final panel, a mechanical void yawned below.

A trapdoor—a trap for the overconfident. Or the panicked.

I moved forward, calm but swift. The spikes *appeared* to close in, shadows dancing along my periphery, but I didn't flinch. I stopped on the second to last tile. I paused a moment. I still had plenty of time.

I expanded my awareness through the paper-thin ceiling above me.

I opened my perception wide, searching for lifeforms.

Sure enough, I was being watched. Seven heat signatures. Human. Watching thirty-one feet above me. I couldn't see any of their faces, but the energy pulsing from them felt...angry.

Not the heat of a goblin or the rage and hate of an Igni, but I got the sense they didn't want me here. Then again, maybe I was projecting based on how long they delayed my acceptance.

I turned to the far wall and examined that wall panel too, to build their curiosity as to how I was figuring out their test. I didn't want them to know how easy this was for me. I spun back and opened the hidden door to the left.

The corridor beyond was a stark contrast. Gone was the soft yellow glow. This space *blazed* with white light—ceiling and floor aglow, banishing all shadow. Sterile.

The hallway was three times wider and taller than the last.

And waiting at the far end—three identical green ladders, each with six rungs, each leading to a shadowed recess above.

But my perception painted a clearer picture.

Only one opening, one exit, was real. The others? Elaborate illusions, crafted by an array of mirrors and focused lenses spanning the upper third of the walls.

A clever trick, but not clever enough.

I walked forward, turning slowly in place as I studied the angles and reflections. Aubrey's voice whispered helpfully in my mind, overlaying lines and vectors in my perception, mapping the false entries with surgical precision.

Elegant physics, Aubrey said. *Almost weaponized deceit.*

I let the silence stretch a little longer—thirty-three seconds, precisely—before I moved.

I crossed the hall and reached for the left ladder, the only real exit.

The moment my fingers curled around the cool green metal, all three ladders began to retract.

No second chances.

I leapt upward, boots slamming onto the first rung, and scrambled fast. The ladder groaned beneath me as it pulled back into the wall, but I was already at the top. I hauled myself through the opening as the last inch of the ladder vanished behind me.

There were five more puzzle rooms. Each one a clever showcase of mirrors, lenses, and light, designed to trick the senses and rattle the nerves. By the third room, I felt almost guilty for how easily my sound-based perception cut through their illusions.

Almost.

But guilt didn't mean complacency. I slowed down, studying each setup with Aubrey's help—angles, lens magnification, light refraction. Credit where credit was due: the guild may have been full of insufferable elitists, but they knew their craft.

They'd built artificial suns beneath the ground, reflecting and amplifying light from the surface through a series of tunnels to create a livable, underground paradise. That wasn't just impressive—it was awe-inspiring.

I walked into a long straight hallway twice the width as the hallway in the beginning. It seemed straightforward. No trapdoors, no mirrors or lenses in sight. I pulsed my perception and could feel the same seven lifeforms waiting for me on the other side of the final door.

This must be the last hallway. A victory lap, or a final trap?

I took another step and something changed.

A new signature flared to life. Human and fast. Slipping into place ahead and to my right, like a spider slinking through cracks. The seven on the other end didn't react, but maybe they weren't supposed to.

Then came the opening—a subtle shift in the wall. Just a crack.

Aubrey's voice exploded in my head. *Careful!*

I caught the glint of metal, the whisper of a breath drawn—and *moved.*

I twisted sideways just as a poisoned dart shot past my ear, embedding itself into the far wall with a sickening thunk.

I didn't hesitate. Rage and instinct surged together. I sprinted toward the wall and kicked with everything I had. The panel buckled inward with a crunch. I felt the attacker scramble back, fall, then retreat, the thump of fleeing footsteps echoing away.

I crouched and peered through the damaged wall. Whoever it was had already vanished into shadow. All I caught was the tail end of a long black duster vanishing around a corner.

Footsteps behind me. The final door at the hallway's end cracked open.

A tall, gray-haired woman in a modest brown dress peeked through, eyes wide. "Master Camlock, are you hurt?"

I didn't answer. I stalked toward the dart still quivering in the wall. My fingers wrapped carefully around the shaft. A drop of green ooze clung to the tip.

Recognition hit like a knee to the gut. I'd seen this poison before—back on the sands, during the Leadsled ambush. The same slow-killing toxin that dropped Margot.

This wasn't just a test. Not anymore.

The other observers gathered at the damaged wall, murmuring amongst themselves. Guildmaster Farsmith stood with his arms crossed and lips pursed as if *I* had done something wrong.

He motioned toward the shattered panel. "Would you care to explain this, Master Camlock?"

I stared at him.

I stepped forward, slow and measured, the dart held delicately between my thumb and forefinger. "Yes," I said, voice ice-cold. "I would love to explain."

I stopped inches from him, raising the dart until it hovered before his face. "Someone tried to murder me in the final hallway of your test. Note the poison."

Gasps. Audible shock from a few of the observers.

I didn't let up. "I kicked down the wall to stop the attack. I don't know if it was an intruder or one of your own, but they fled, wearing black, moving like they knew this place."

The room fell into stunned silence.

I watched his face very closely. The guildmaster went pale, as did the others around him. It confirmed my theory—the attack was not part of the test. What I didn't know was if he or one of the others orchestrated the attack or if it was another party entirely.

I doubted it was them. The blame for the attack would fall heavily on the guild if it were successful. But it was impossible to know.

I gave a soft smile and signaled at Farsmith's hand with my chin. He held it open in front of me. I stifled the urge to drop the dart and gently placed it in his hand instead. "I'm guessing you don't test all your applicants with poison darts?"

The man gulped and shook his head. He reached into a pocket at his breast and pulled out a silk handkerchief. He dumped the dart into the handkerchief and carefully wrapped it several times. He placed the wrapped dart into a side pocket. "Of course, there will be a full investigation," said Farsmith.

"Of course," I said airily, "the king would expect nothing less."

The guildmaster pursed his lips together in a pained expression. "I don't *suppose...*," he drew out the word, "you could delay telling him for a day or two until we have more information to share with the crown?"

I stroked my chin for a second. "I don't know. I guess that depends on whether or not I passed your test."

The large woman gave a small chuckle. "I like him. Knows what he wants and how to go get it." She turned her wide eyes in my direction and gave me a big smile. "You didn't just pass. You broke the course record by five minutes."

"Huh," I said. "Who held the record before me?"

She pointed at Guildmaster Farsmith.

"Yes, you passed," spat the guildmaster. "Thirty-six hours is all I ask before you share the news with the royal family."

I clapped my hands and stilled the urge to act like a small child, following Amara's lead from earlier. There was something about the pretentious nature of the guildmaster which made it so obvious he hated children. I suppressed it.

"Great, where's my first class?"

16

Optics

As I stepped into the classroom, the buzz of whispered conversations hit me like a wall. Most of the students were already seated, their eyes flicking over to me as I entered. The room was laid out in a way that felt almost like an arena—three descending platforms with a wide staircase between each, creating a subtle divide between the tables and the podium at the base. Two towering chalkboards loomed behind it, a silent testament to the professor's command of the space.

Each platform held four large pegboard tables, each accompanied by two chairs. The students lounged lazily, clearly expecting the professor's entrance—but when their eyes met mine, the mood shifted. Most of them glared, as if I had interrupted something sacred.

I felt the familiar surge of tension in my chest, the instinct to shrink away, to hide from the piercing stares. But today was different. I didn't flinch. I didn't cower. I met their glares head-on, unwavering, until they dropped their gazes one by one.

Good.

I was done backing down from challenges.

Besides, any one of these students could have been the person holding that blowgun earlier this morning.

Unfortunately, Draven's prediction that the rumors swirling around me would have a short shelf life was wrong. Very few of the rumors were flattering. My hero status had been tainted by the association with Carl and my proximity to the prince's death. Training with the Royal Guard competed with my access to training with the guilds to create a heaping dose of jealousy from the young nobles and wealthy scions of the major power brokers in the city.

Those looking for a scapegoat didn't need to look far.

Of the four open chairs, I received death glares from two of the young men and one of the young women who occupied the other chair at the table. I almost sat to spite them.

I doubted that whoever sent the person who tried to poison me with a blow dart would be a student at the G&L guild, but I wasn't about to show potential enemies weakness. I had to say they all looked a little soft for that kind of work but I assumed nothing—desperation made tools of anyone or anything.

Look at me, an agent of the king.

I turned my eyes to the fourth table where a massive young man with silver hair sat.

"Mind if I sit?" I asked, pointing at one of the table's open chairs.

He smiled at me and I couldn't help but notice the stubby fangs jutting from his lower jaw like shaved tusks. They fit his wide face, small enough to be concealed by a closed mouth, yet they added a wild fierceness to his smile.

"I'd love the company," the young man said, deep voice matching his large frame. "This lot treats me like a scabie-ridden leper."

I smiled back. "I know the feeling."

He chuckled, showing off his fangs again. "Name's Valdrath Marsten, but you can call me Val." He extended a hand, and I almost flinched when I saw the thick, silver arm-hair covering his forearm, resembling fur. The grip was firm but not unkind.

"Finn Camlock," I replied, shaking his hand. "I don't meet many people who greet me with a handshake down here."

Val gave a low grunt and squeezed my hand just enough to leave an impression without being a jerk about it. "I'm Nyxian," he said as if that explained everything. "And I know who you are. The whole kingdom's buzzing about the young Grounder who saved the princess and is plotting to take down the kingdom from the inside."

I gave him a chuckle. "Don't tell me you believe the rumors."

He flashed those teeth again. "You should have heard the rumors about me when I first showed up. According to them, I'm either a silver orc from the land of Trasmatan or my father mated with a dire-sow and I'm the result of that unholy union."

I frowned and said, "So which one is it?" with as much innocence as I could manage.

"Oh, you're hilarious," Val said.

"I've never met a Nyxian before. Is that a Dusker kingdom?"

He frowned at me, as if wondering if I was still joking. "You've never heard of Nyxhaven?"

I shook my head.

"Well, you're a Grounder, I guess," Val said. "We're a small kingdom, far from here. Some call us the last stop on the Veilspoke Transit. As far as us being Duskers? We're more like a hybrid kingdom. Most of our people live underground, but we're close to the surface. Some Nyxians still live under the stars."

Which explained the Grounder handshake. "Any compounds nearby?"

"Salthook is only a couple miles away from our cave system, but it's dying," Val said. "The Igni ignored the compound for almost two hundred fifty years, maybe because they live in a dried up seabed, but everything changed three years ago. Loads of Salties try to join

Nyxhaven every day. We're bursting at the seams."

I wondered if this was because of the waxers and the Igni's new scanning technology or something else.

Impossible to know, Aubrey said, *though salt can impact a scan, especially with older tech.*

My next question died on my lips when the tall woman from my earlier exam walked through the main door and made her way down to the podium. I took a seat. She wasted little time, dropping her bag at the foot of the podium before stepping behind it. She stooped to remove the small stool another professor must have used in a previous class.

"Class, I'd like you to welcome our new student, Finn Camlock. Finn, tell us something about yourself."

Thanks for putting me on the spot professor! I cleared my throat and stood. "Thanks, Professor...?"

"Cloud," she said with a nod.

I turned from her and addressed the nearby tables. "About me...well, I'm a Grounder from Dawnford compound. I was banished for a crime I didn't commit. I've encountered the Ignavari at least four times in my life. I ran every time. I'm the only Grounder in Dawnford without access to the nova-field...and I'm excited to learn everything I can while I'm here."

That ought to feed the rumor mill for awhile.

I glanced over at Val. He had a big grin on his face. "Smart," he whispered. "Can't beat them, might as well join them."

The professor nodded to me and I took my seat. "Very humble," she said. "What Finn neglected to mention is he broke the course record for the entrance exam earlier this morning."

That caused several students to look back at me, reassessing.

Professor Cloud pulled out a black pen and a transparent page which she set on a glowing device sitting on a small table next to the podium.

She pulled down a screen behind her then flipped off all of the lights but the ones in the back of the classroom. She drew a diagram on the transparent page and I blinked as the drawing appeared on the screen behind her, four or five times the size.

More fun with light and lenses, and a lot more effective than writing on the board.

I got lost quickly as we dove into reflection, refraction and a whole lot of other terms I'd never heard.

Aubrey provided a running commentary of the physics involved, but I was quickly lost in all the jargon.

Val took furious notes next to me, but I set my pencil down after about five minutes. Hopefully, I could catch up by reading some basic manuals on the subject. Then again, the G&L guild were so protective of that knowledge maybe they never wrote anything down.

After a tortuous two hours the class finally ended. If anything, I felt like I knew less about the subject than before I started. Or maybe I started to understand just how much there was to know about the topic.

As the final whispers of the lesson faded, Professor Cloud's voice cut through the air like a blade. "Mister Camlock, a moment."

I gathered my things, brain still numb from the intensity of the lecture. Val slung his bag over one broad shoulder. "I'll wait for you outside," he said, flashing a grin. "We can walk to Materials Lab together."

I gave him a nod and stepped up to the podium. Professor Cloud handed me what felt like a brick of paper—dense, thick, and heavy with expectation.

"These are the lectures from the first semester," she said, her tone sharp but not unkind. "If you want a chance in this class, you need to be caught up by next week."

I flipped through the packet, stunned by the sheer volume. Hundreds of pages, covered front and back in tight, spidery script. My fingers traced the paper, still amazed at how freely the Duskers used it. So much smoother, easier than the wax tablets we'd scraped on in Dawnford. At least the packet was written in common. If it had been in High Cellarian, I'd have been doomed before I even started.

I glanced up at Professor Cloud, eyebrows raised. She met my stare without flinching.

"Do the work, Mister Camlock," she said, her voice dropping low with intent. "The first secret you'll learn about G&L is we were all offered entry because we're talented with math and optics, but we stay because we grind. Every day."

Out of the corner of my eye, I spotted Renaux—the smug noble who'd practically snarled at me when I first entered the room—strutting past like he owned the place. I tilted my head toward him. "Even that one?"

Cloud let out a sigh. "Even Renaux. He wouldn't have made it past week one without discipline. The arrogance is earned—unfortunately."

I frowned and gave her a solemn nod. "I believe you. I'll get it done."

For the first time, she smiled, crooked and faint, but genuine. "I believe you will. Office hours are third to fifth bell. If you hit a wall, come get help."

Aubrey chuckled in the back of my mind as I bounded up the stairs toward the hallway. *If she teaches you optics better than I do, I'll officially consider myself obsolete.*

Val was waiting, just as he promised, and together we headed off down the long corridor toward the Materials Lab.

"This is the good stuff," Val said as we stepped into the wide, high-ceilinged space. The room buzzed with energy—students already hard at work at benches covered in tools, materials, and half-finished projects. "We started with raw glass. Now it's all lenses and mirrors. Honestly, polishing's kind of addictive."

I scanned the room, the scent of scorched sand and hot metal thick in the air. "You started making any control chips yet?"

Val laughed, loud and genuine, then stopped. "Oh, I thought you were kidding. No, the control chips and anything that smells like a Synth Core is tightly controlled information by the guild. Only full-time members have access to it, though there's a rumor going around that they're going to start teaching it at the graduate level."

"And I'm guessing most people don't get to the graduate level in a year."

Another laugh. "Try four or five. Minimum."

Brak! That's why I was here, to learn how to make a control chip or even a Core. Well, that and figure out who's trying to take down the crown.

He saw the disappointment on my face. "Don't stress about it, making lenses is fun. And you really do need to understand this stuff before you can even think about a control chip. Come on, I'll help you get started."

Our assignment was straightforward but intimidating: craft one of each mirror and lens the guild used. These would be our foundation for future builds, and any mistakes now could haunt us later.

Val, already deep into shaping a concave lens, nodded toward the empty station beside him. "Start there. I'll walk you through it."

I glanced around. "No professors?"

"Not here," Val said. "Just lab assistants and the occasional check-in from Guildmaster Farsmith. This lab's for self-discovery."

That made me smile. "That's how I learn best."

Val was right. It *was* fun. Hot, dirty, hands-blackened, sweat-dripping fun. Instead of blowing glass like back home, we melted down a cocktail of sand, quartz, soda, and cokes into shimmering pools and poured them into molds.

I was mid-pour when something strange caught my eye.

At the far side of the lab, Renaux sat at his bench, polishing a lens with the kind of smug precision I'd expect from someone raised on gold and praise. But floating next to him—barely visible—was something... unnatural.

A vaporous creature danced across the surface of one of his lenses. Bluish-green, about six inches tall, mostly transparent and disturbingly fluid. It was teardrop-shaped, its arms morphing in and out of its central body like tendrils of mist. Wherever it touched the glass, it smoothed and polished it to an impossible sheen.

"What is that?" I whispered, tension creeping up my spine.

Val's voice rose, sharp and hard. "That is *cheating*."

The entire table around Renaux froze. The vapor vanished with a snap, leaving no trace. Renaux turned slowly, face twisting into a scowl as he met Val's gaze. "Dirty Nyxians," he muttered to one of his hangers-on.

Then he looked at me and sneered.

My blood burned, but I kept my voice low. "Was that core crafting?"

Val's face darkened. "A weak trick. Aeromancy. Renaux knows better than to summon an essentia vapor in a shared lab—especially in front of a non-crafter."

"Why?" I asked, genuinely confused.

Val didn't answer.

"Val," I pressed. "Why?"

"Focus on your lenses, Grounder," he snapped brusquely.

I clenched my jaw. Another locked door. Another circle I wasn't allowed into. Just like Dawnford.

I straightened, rolled my shoulders, and poured the next mold.

By the end of the session, my first three lens molds were cooling on the rack. Val had helped the whole way, and his earlier tension had faded like smoke. We cleaned our bench in companionable silence.

"Nice working with you today," he said, grabbing his satchel. "I study most nights at the Crooked Oak in Cheapside. It's not fancy, but it's clean and quiet. If you want help catching up, I'm there."

I paused, surprised at the offer. Truth was, I hadn't had many friends since arriving in the kingdom. The Drifters were off working their contracts. Draven had his estate. Amara was drowning in court politics. I hadn't realized just how lonely I'd gotten until that moment.

"I'll meet you there tonight," I said. Val was still a mystery, still a possible threat—but he was also the first person here who didn't seem to want something from me or hold my past against me.

And if I was going to survive—really survive—and uncover whatever dark threads were knotting together beneath the surface of this kingdom, I'd need all the allies I could get.

17

Crooked Oak

When I returned to the small room I'd been calling home for the past four weeks—tucked away in the servant's quarters like a secret someone didn't want discovered—I immediately spotted something new: another letter, slipped under the door like a whisper in the dark.

I picked it up.

An invitation from the engineering guild.

I let out a slow breath. *Amara's threats worked.* She must have pushed harder than she let on.

As if summoned by the thought, her voice floated through the doorway behind me.

"There you are."

I jumped, the letter crinkling in my grip. I turned to see her standing in the frame like a living painting—her formal regalia catching the last of the hallway light, all layered lace and gold-threaded silk, gemstones clustered at her throat like a noose.

"That looks...wildly uncomfortable," I said.

She sighed, plucking the golden laurel from her hair and tossing it onto my bed like it offended her. "You have no idea. Sitting in court all day, trying to look engaged while traders and farmers complain about our security measures destroying their way of life? I'd rather wrestle a bear."

I smirked. "Have you tried explaining what a goblin war band would do to their way of life instead?"

She snorted. "Right? I'd *love* to say that. But most people still think of goblins as scary bedtime stories. Same with the Ignavari. Doesn't matter that we're still cleaning their rot from the forests." She waved her hand, dismissing it all. "Ugh. Enough court talk. I'm done for the day."

She peeled off her stiff jacket with a groan, flung it onto the bed beside the laurel, then turned to me with sharp eyes and a tired smile. "Your turn. Tell me everything."

So I did—everything *except* the attempt on my life. I talked about the class, the endless packet Cloud gave me, and the new guild invitation. I mentioned how terrifyingly effective her innocent act was on Farsmith. "Honestly, that little-girl routine? It was equal parts hilarious and nightmare fuel. I'd hate to be your enemy."

The air in the room changed.

Her smile dropped, and her eyes turned to ice. "Then why," she said, each word clipped, "are you leaving out the assassination attempt during your entrance exam?"

My stomach sank.

Of course she knew. The royal family had ears in every wall, even the ones in G&L.

I sat slowly on the corner of the bed, careful not to touch her discarded jacket. "If you already know, then you know I promised Farsmith thirty-six hours before I reported anything. He wanted a chance to catch whoever did it—or learn something first."

Amara crossed her arms, her voice trembling with fury. "Full disclosure, Finn. That was our deal. No secrets from each other. You can keep stuff from my parents, your professors, the entire warding city if you want—but not from me."

I blew out a breath and looked down at the floor. Then I lifted my eyes and met hers. "You're right. I'm sorry." I ran a hand down my face, feeling the guilt settle like dust. "I've just...never been...a part of something like this before. When I tell someone I'll do something, it's important to me to do it. Even now, telling you about Farsmith's request feels...wrong. Breaking it—even for you—felt wrong. Does that make any sense?"

She didn't answer at first. Instead, she gently swept her jacket to the top of the bed and sat beside me, eyes unreadable. "No. It doesn't. Because this isn't about feelings, or trust, or pride. It's about the kingdom. The stakes are too high. You *know* what's out there. You saw what just *one* waxer did to you. To your compound. You lived through it."

Her voice hardened, sharp as a drawn blade. "If we slip, if we hold back, people die."

I stood, tension running like static through my body. "I should've told you. But I won't abandon everything I believe in just to win a war. I need to *have* a line. You don't win a fight by turning into your enemy. Will you lie? Cheat? Break oaths? Kill?"

Her eyes dropped to the rug, her voice quiet now. "Maybe," she whispered. Then, looking back at me with something ancient and raw in her gaze, "Probably."

"And if those you hurt are innocent?"

She didn't hesitate this time. "Then I'll mourn them when it's over. But this is war. And it's one we *can't* lose. Not against the waxers. Not against the Igni."

I shook my head slowly, resolutely. "Then we're fighting two different battles. I'll only harm another to protect myself or others. If we don't have a code...if we win at the cost of who we are—it's not worth winning."

Silence stretched between us, heavy and tense.

Finally, she nodded once. "I can live with that. But you have to promise—*no more secrets.* Not from me."

"I swear," I said without hesitation, the words steady and true. "And...thank you. For holding me to it."

She didn't echo my promise—not about killing only to protect, not about morality. And I didn't ask her to. We were shaped by different fires.

"I'm going to clean up," I said, grabbing a towel and motioning to the stack of papers Professor Cloud had buried me under. "Then I'm heading into town to study. That packet's a beast."

"You know you're welcome in the palace library," Amara offered, her voice softer now.

"I know," I said with a small smile. "But it was good to be out of the palace for a while. I think we need to widen our search anyway. We have too many blind spots in Alyntown."

She nodded, a sharp gleam in her eye. "Agreed. That's why I'm coming with you."

I raised an eyebrow. "You *know* I have to study in town, right?"

She smirked. "You study. I'll start poking around."

* * *

Cheapside was refreshingly seedy. It was gritty, unpolished, and gloriously alive with the pulse of the forgotten. Amara walked beside me wearing a gray duster with a hood to conceal her features. She explained that most of the neighborhood sat in perpetual shadow— morning gloom cast by the cavern wall, afternoon swallowed by the looming shadow of the castle above. Simulated sunlight didn't reach here often, which made it a haven for those who preferred the dark...or couldn't afford the light.

We passed our first beggars—ragged, hollow-eyed souls huddled against the stone walls, their cups outstretched without hope. A gang of street toughs lounged at the corner like vultures waiting for something to die, their eyes following us as we walked. They clocked the sword on my hip, then looked away.

Smart.

Even with its edge, Cheapside was cleaner than the warehouse district back in Dawnford. The scent of stale beer and piss lingered in both places, but urine evaporated quicker on the surface.

Then I saw it—the painted sign of a crooked oak tree, sagging on a background of faded pink like it hadn't been cleaned since the last dynasty.

"That's the place you picked to study with your new best friend?" Amara asked, eyeing the sign like it might peel itself off the wall and attack us. "Charming."

"Only the best for Cheapside nobility," I muttered and pushed open the door.

The interior of *The Crooked Oak* matched the outside: dimly lit, dusty, and utterly indifferent to appearances. A man and woman spoke in hushed tones at the bar. Empty tables stretched across the room like a boneyard, except for one—occupied by a silver-haired Nyxian with a grin that split his wide face like a sunrise.

"Finn!" Valdrath called, raising a hand. "Didn't think you'd show."

I frowned. "I said I would."

He shrugged. "People say a lot of things."

"Val, I want you to meet—"

"Hiya, Val," Amara said brightly, already grinning.

Val's tusks showed in a wide, fond smile. "Hiya, Mar. Fancy seeing you in Cheapside."

"Us stuck-up royals don't get out much," she replied.

My brow furrowed. "You *know* each other?"

They laughed. *At me.*

"What happened to full disclosure?" I asked, glaring at Amara.

"I thought it'd be a fun surprise," she said, her hand resting gently on my arm. Soothing.

Val laughed. "You've already got the poor lad wrapped around your finger." Then he turned to me, voice lower, more sincere. "The princess and I go way back. Summers at the royal retreats at Saenar's Veil. While our parents debated treaties and borders, we swam, sparred, and did our best to avoid the parade of entitled brats."

My mouth opened. "So you're a...?"

"Duke," Amara said with a smirk.

Val winced. "Technically an *earl*. My father's the duke of Nyxhaven."

I stared. "Why didn't you say anything?"

Val grinned. "Because announcing your title in the first ten minutes of conversation is exactly what an entitled brat *would* do." He slapped the table. "Sit. Mead's on the way—real Cheapside mead. Almost tastes like it's not poison."

"I'll just take water," I said.

"Not in Cheapside," Val replied, deadpan. "Trust me. The mead's fermented, which means it's...mostly safe."

I looked at Amara for backup.

She shrugged. "It's safer than the water."

"Like she'd know," Val added. "When's the last time you deigned to set foot in a Cheapside tavern, Your Highness?"

"I don't know," Amara shot back. "When's the last time *you* came to the palace for a proper dinner?"

Val pointed at her. "Fair. But your family's chancellor? Severin? That man has it out for me. Every time I visit the palace, a new rumor grows like mold on a moonfruit."

"I wonder why that is," Amara said innocently.

"Seriously, he can't *still* be sore about the egg thing," Val said.

Now I was curious. "What egg thing?"

The bartender walked over with a pitcher of mead and three mugs. He plopped them on the table hard enough to spill mead over the rim of the pitcher then walked away.

"That's what I love about this place," said Valdrath, "no bowing and scraping. They do their job without twisting my ear, asking for favors, or starting rumors."

He poured mead into each of the mugs and passed them out.

I took a sip of mine. It was slightly sweet but also tasted slightly... dirty? I swallowed and tried not to think about the source of the dirt. "What happened with Severin?"

Amara shrugged. "I love Severin, but if there's a man who knows how to nurse a grudge better than our chancellor, I haven't met him."

Val leaned in conspiratorially. "Years ago. Saenar's Veil. I was thirteen. Severin called me an insolent brat—unjustly, I might add—so I did what any reasonable boy would do: snuck a chicken egg into the foot of his bed. Nothing says revenge like yolk-covered toes."

Amara nearly choked on her mead. "He *still* claims it was just an egg. But what Val conveniently forgets to tell is that Renaux's pet snake had a bizarre craving for eggs."

"A creepy little beast," Val said, chuckling. "Could smell one from a hundred feet away, but I never thought about the snake, I swear."

"That night," Amara continued, "we're all jarred awake by a blood-curdling *scream*. Everyone thinks the dowager queen is having night terrors again, until we track the sound to Severin's room."

Val burst out laughing. "He was standing on his table, shrieking, pointing at this *tiny snake* with an egg halfway down its throat, with the chancellor's quill pinning it to his bed as it writhed about."

Amara grinned. "Renaux storms in, shouts 'Slither!' like it's a battle cry, and yanks the quill out of his pet. The poor thing makes a straight line for Severin, who shrieks again and nearly faints."

"The best part," Val added, tears forming in the corners of his eyes, "was your father holding up the bloody quill that had pinned the snake to the bed and declaring, '*I suppose the quill is mightier than the dagger.*'"

Amara wiped her eyes. "Severin turned so red he matched the drapes."

I shook my head. "How'd they know it was you?"

"Only one person wasn't there to witness the chaos," Amara said.

Val lifted his mug. "I'm a deep sleeper."

Her expression shifted, her smile fading. "Why did you really ask Finn to study with you?"

Val's grin slipped and he met her eyes. "Because I like him. He's got the right attitude. Doesn't suck up, doesn't pretend. And us misfits need to stick together."

I raised my mug. "To misfits."

Val clinked it. "To surviving the stuck-up prats."

But Amara wasn't buying it. "Val..."

He sighed and looked down into his drink. "Alright. Truth? I needed to see you. Something's wrong."

My buzz faded instantly.

He leaned in. "I went on one of my late-night walks near the Murkmire. Found two unicorns—a mare and her foal. Dead."

Amara gasped, hand flying to her mouth. "How?"

Val's voice was flat with horror. "Their horns were hacked off. There was silver blood and shredded hair everywhere—like someone *tortured* them before they were killed."

"And you didn't report it?" I asked.

"I wanted to talk to you first," Val said. "But that's not even the worst part."

He swallowed. "Their hearts had been cut out. Split open. And then—somehow—ignited from the inside. Their organs were *burned from within.*"

A heavy silence settled over the table, darker than the room around us. The warmth of the mead turned to ash in my throat.

"That's not some twisted poacher," I said quietly. "That's a message."

Val's jaw tightened. "Yeah. And I don't like what it's saying."

18

An Old Flame

2.83 Years Before Finn's Pilgrimage To Iron Mountain

Carl adjusted the field magnification on the goggles for the third time, his fingers twitching with restless energy. It had been only three weeks since his meeting with the Ignavari Prime, but there was no reason to delay.

He refocused. Something about the two sentries pacing between the ancient rib bones of the long-dead behemoth didn't sit right with him. Their movements were off—too casual, too relaxed. They kept bumping into each other like drunkards. Or... was that laughing?

Were they flirting?

Carl grimaced. Whatever it was, he'd take it. A distraction was a distraction. He'd been watching them for two straight days, counting their steps, memorizing every loop. He knew their shift didn't end until deep into the night, and their patrols were a joke.

He pulled the goggles off, stowing them in the saddlebag of his recently acquired hover bike—new to him, though the cracked leather seat and whining repulsors told another story.

Ever since that terrifying, almost surreal journey through the Ignavari base, Carl had returned to Dawnford like a ghost walking in his own life. He applied for a janitor's job with Wright & Co. Samson Wright had hired him on the spot, full of that greasy smile and whispered praises for Carl "getting back on his feet."

Pity. That's what they gave him. Sweet, simmering, backhanded pity. Carl knew the truth—Dawnford loved a failure. It gave everyone else someone to look down on, someone to throw scraps to so they could feel righteous. Nothing made people feel more generous than watching someone crawl.

But he wasn't crawling anymore. After his first payday, he used his chits to buy a used hover bike. Denis Camlock told him he could use Finn's hover bike for as long as he wanted, but he refused to be beholden to that brakking spitbag a moment longer than he needed.

Now, here he was, crouched three dunes away from the Dead Crow camp under a moonless sky. The last breath of twilight had vanished behind the dunes. The Igni were all but nonexistent after dark, and nobody traveled during the baking daylight—so the guards were always relaxed in the early hours of night. Lazy. Overconfident.

Perfect.

He buried the hover bike beneath a thermal blanket and hoofed it the rest of the way. The titanic ribs of the ancient beast loomed like jagged white cliffs, curving skyward from the sand. The camp had spots—sloppy, swinging arcs of bright floodlights—but they left pockets of shadow wide enough to drive a crawler through. Pirates didn't understand perimeter discipline. They relied on cruelty, not strategy.

Carl dropped to his belly as a floodlight swept his dune. He lay motionless, counting out ten heartbeats...then twenty...before the beam finally moved on.

He exhaled and shifted his weight, easing the shotgun from the makeshift holster on his back. The barrel had been digging into him all night, and now he wanted the cold comfort of it in his hands.

With a flick of his thumb, he activated the battered nova vest strapped beneath his duster. It hummed to life, the shield forming a soft pressure against his skin. He *could* summon one himself—he had enough flux—but he didn't want to maintain it or risk someone sniffing out the energy signature.

He peeked over the dune.

The sentries were giggling. *Definitely flirting.* One of them reached out to touch the other's hair, and Carl took his chance. He sprinted low and fast across the sand, a silent shadow beneath the stars.

Getting past them was child's play. These weren't hardened guards. They were young and cocky. Sentries expected attacks from bands of pirates or Igni, not a single ex-drunk looking for retribution.

Carl ducked behind a rusted-out speeder and pulled his duster tight to hide the shotgun. He ran a hand backwards over his shaggy, unkempt hair to conceal his face. He walked straight into the camp with the posture of someone who belonged—fast, confident, but not hurried. No one questioned him.

The Dead Crows weren't in their nightmarish battle armor. In the firelight, they looked like anyone else—dirty boots, worn jackets, slouched shoulders. Not so different from the people in Dawnford.

Not that it mattered.

They had taken everything from him.

The well stood at the base of the ancient skull—the behemoth's hollow eye sockets towering above it like the gaze of a god long dead. He approached casually. No one challenged him. He was just another body in the crowd.

He hesitated for half a second—there was no pump, just a rope and bucket. Crude. But no one noticed as he grabbed the crank with one hand and palmed the small tablets Malik had given him with the other.

He lowered the bucket, cranked it back up, and scooped a ladleful of water, sipping it slowly to sell the ruse. The water was tepid but clean enough. He slipped the tablets into the scoop and dunked it again. They dissolved without a trace.

Malik had sworn they weren't poison—"just something to make them more... suggestible," he'd said with that sly, firelit grin. When Carl pressed him, the Igni sympathizer's demeanor had shifted—wild, burning, unstable. Carl had dropped it.

He released the crank, letting the bucket descend back into the black below.

Mission complete.

He turned—and slammed straight into someone.

He started to mumble an apology when their eyes met.

And the world fell out from under him.

Carl stumbled back, breath stolen, knees buckling. He caught himself on the rim of the well, chest heaving.

No. No no no no.

He'd seen those eyes in dreams—nightmares—for fourteen years.

"Carl?" she whispered, her voice impossibly familiar.

His lips moved without sound. Then, hoarse, "Amber? How are you—how are you *alive?*"

She grabbed his arm with a strength that shocked him and pulled him close, threading her arm through his like they were lovers again. "You shouldn't be here," she hissed, dragging him away from the well. "If they see you—if they *recognize* you—they'll kill you."

"I *shouldn't* be here?" he hissed back. "You're supposed to be *dead!* What—"

"Quiet!" she whispered as a few heads turned their way. Her grip on his arm tightened, almost bruising.

She hustled him around the edge of a tent, then into a sandstone building nestled against one of the massive ribs. Two Crows inside glanced up but didn't question her. They dipped their heads in quiet respect.

Carl's mind reeled. *Respect?*

She pulled him through a narrow door into a clean, well-appointed room that looked like a personal study. Metal desk, padded chairs, curtains instead of flaps. It smelled of lavender and iron.

She locked the door behind them.

Carl stood in a fog, spinning, disoriented. But he knew this place. He *knew* this style. Amber's style. Every piece, every placement, was her.

She pushed him into a chair and took the one across from him, crossing her legs. "Talk," she said. "Now. Why are you here?"

The pain and rage that had stewed in Carl for fourteen years—slow, corrosive, and all-consuming—flickered beneath a new flame. *Betrayal.*

It didn't burn like anger. It hollowed him out. Left him gutted.

He took a ragged breath and met her eyes—the eyes of the woman he once dreamed of building a future with. "How could you let me believe you were dead?" His voice cracked under the weight of it. "I chased everything. Every rumor. Every trace. I buried you in my heart, Amber. Your death *destroyed* me."

He stepped forward, chest heaving. "My world ended the day they said you were gone. How could you do that to me? How could you disappear without a word?"

He hadn't thought he was capable of this kind of hurt anymore. He thought hate had burned it all away. But here it was—raw, jagged, and so alive it nearly knocked him off his feet.

Amber didn't flinch. Her face was stone. Cold. Silent.

"*Why?*" he demanded. "Just tell me why."

"Because it was better this way," she said, finally. Her voice was quiet, but it cut like a blade.

"*Better for who?!*" The shout ripped out of him before he could stop it.

Amber lifted a finger to her lips. "Keep your voice down, Carl. You'll get us *both* killed."

He shook his head, fists trembling. "I *don't care.* You owe me the truth. So talk. *Now.*"

He clenched his hands into claws, fury flooding every vein. It wasn't just betrayal—it was confirmation. *Iron Mike had been right. The Camlocks had been right.* He *had* been played. He'd loved her like a fool, worshipped a ghost, wasted half his life chasing a lie.

She must have seen it in his face—what was boiling there. "Did you know my real parents were pirates?" she said, her tone suddenly brittle. "No. Of course you didn't. I never told you. They were Mesa Lords. Executed by the Igni."

Her eyes darkened, voice thick with old bitterness. "We didn't have the luxuries of the compounds. No walls. No grids. No guards. Only fire and pain."

"Don't talk to me of pain like I don't understand it," Carl growled.

She leaned forward, searching his face. "Maybe you do," she admitted. "When I was little, the Igni used to come once a month. Not to kill. To *maim.* They'd burn a limb, scar a face, cripple someone's mind. It was like they wanted the pain to last. Like they were...*farming* it."

Carl said nothing, though his stomach turned.

"The Igni murdered my parents. My father tried to stand against them. My mother died with him. I was eight. I walked to Glass Compound alone and begged them to take me in."

"They did," Carl muttered. "They made you one of their own."

"They gave me a roof," she said. "But they never really understood me. *You* never understood me either."

Carl's jaw clenched. "Hard to understand someone when their life is built on a *lie.*"

Amber shrugged. "Maybe so. I learned to channel flux better than most. They praised me. Said I'd be one of Glass's next leaders. But I was never there for them. I was there to learn what they knew. How they defended themselves. I needed to bring that knowledge back to people who didn't have walls."

She toyed with a lock of her hair—an old gesture that used to make his heart flutter. Now it only made his blood boil.

"On one trip back to the Mesa Lords," she said, "I met someone. A man from the Dead Crows. His name was Jalil. He was charming. Clever. And he believed in building something stronger than a fortress. He believed in uniting the scattered clans."

Carl's fists dug into his legs until his nails broke the skin.

"I don't want to hear about your romances," he snapped.

She raised a brow. "I thought you wanted to know *why*."

He clenched his jaw and nodded. He did want to know. He *needed* to know why.

"I fell deeply in love with Jalil," Amber said softly. "He's the one who told me about Dawnford. About the *grid*."

Carl's vision tunneled. The urge to find this Jalil and introduce him to the business end of his shotgun became a craving.

She continued. "Glass had walls, but they still suffered. Dawnford didn't. They had something *better*. So when traders from Dawnford came to Glass, and one of them happened to be an awkward but sweet young man...I saw opportunity."

He knew what was coming. But still—when she said it, it shattered him.

"You were the perfect mark."

Carl couldn't move. Couldn't breathe. Her words hit harder than any fist. "I cared for you," she said, voice dipping. "Truly. But I never *loved* you. My heart always belonged to someone else."

The last pieces of his heart crumbled into ash.

"You stayed," he choked, "just long enough to learn how the grid

146

worked."

She nodded.

He blinked hard and looked around the room like it might offer escape. "So where is it? The grid? The one you're building for the Dead Crows."

Amber's eyes flickered.

"You don't have one, do you?" Carl said, voice quiet now, deadly cold. "You know how to build it—but you don't have the power. Not yet."

His mind clicked through the pieces. "You're going to steal it. From Dawnford's solar farm."

Amber winced.

"I don't remember you being this smart," she said softly. "I'm sorry you figured it out so fast."

Sorry? He frowned. Then he understood.

She was going to raise the alarm.

"Me too," he said.

In one motion, he yanked the shotgun from his back and leveled it at her.

Amber rose from her chair, hands half-raised. Her eyes widened, not with fear—but with sadness. "You're not a killer, Carl. That's never who you were."

He tilted his head. "You don't know me anymore. Death, pain, betrayal—they change a man." He cocked the gun with a sharp *clack.*

"Please," she whispered. "For what we once had. Don't—"

"What we had was a lie," he said.

Then, without another word, he whipped the butt of the shotgun across the table and slammed it into her temple. Her eyes went wide for a heartbeat, then she crumpled to the floor like a broken promise.

He stood over her, heart thundering. Her chest moved—still alive. Maybe she was right, maybe he didn't have the spine to kill her. But he would visit pain on her and these Dead Crows.

He would have retribution.

He spat on the ground beside her limp form, shoved the shotgun into its holster, and strode to the door.

His hand trembled as he turned the latch, but when he stepped into the night, a strange calm settled over him. Cold. Untouchable.

Malik was right. The Ignavari were right.

He needed this. He needed to face the ghosts. To see her for what she really was.

No more illusions.

Nothing could hurt him now.

He disappeared into the night, and all that followed was the wind.

19

Cap of Cheapside

"We have to report this. Now. At the very least, the game warden needs to know," Amara said, her voice clipped with urgency.

"I would," Valdrath replied grimly, "but it gets worse, Mar." The usual playfulness in his tone had vanished, replaced by something harder, colder. "I went back this morning. The bodies were gone."

Amara and I exchanged a look—tight, unreadable, but full of quiet alarm.

Val leaned in, his sharp eyes flicking between us. "What do you know?"

Amara's head moved barely an inch—just a slight shake, subtle enough to miss. But I saw it. And judging by the way Val's gaze darkened, so did he.

His jaw tightened. "It made me think of what happened to *you*. Of the waxer. Of the battle in Drumsorrow Cavern. That thing you fought— was it real?"

Amara set her mug down slowly, her voice quiet but unwavering. "It was real."

Val's brows knit together. "You think one of those *things* got past the wards?"

Amara let out a long, measured sigh. "Three months ago, I would've sworn it couldn't. But..."

"The goblins got in," Val finished grimly.

I stood up too fast. The mead in my blood caught up all at once, sending a dizzy wave through me. All the warmth the drink had stirred—fake and fleeting—evaporated.

"I'm annoyed with you," I said, pointing at Amara. "For not telling me you knew him." Then I turned to Val. "And I'm annoyed with *you* for using me to get to her."

Val took a slow sip of mead, unbothered. "Don't take it personally, mate. I'd have invited you either way. Can't stand the rest of the class. This was just a bonus."

I groaned, pulling Professor Cloud's behemoth packet from my satchel. "And we didn't study at all! I've got a week to get through this. A *week.*"

Val shrugged. "I've seen how your mind works. Basic optics will be child's play."

I slung my bag over my shoulder. "Doesn't matter. I've got the engineering guild first thing in the morning. And I mean first thing. The guilds are making it their mission to make sure I get no sleep."

I wasn't sure what pleased me more—Amara rising with me in solidarity, or the comfort of not leaving her to walk back to the castle alone. Not that she needed protecting. Amara was twice the warrior I was. Still, Val could've walked her back.

I still wasn't sure how I felt about their friendship. Neither was making googly eyes at the other, so I took it at face value. It was none of my business anyway.

So why are you thinking about it at all? Aubrey whispered in my mind.

"Because I'm tired and a little drunk," I said before realizing I said the words out loud.

Amara raised an eyebrow. "Because...?"

Oh, stars.

I was just answering a question the autonomous device in my head asked me, I didn't say. "Because I'm a little drunk," I recovered quickly. "I meant to say *besides*."

Valdrath squinted at me, unconvinced, but let it slide. "You two be careful. Cheapside has teeth after dark."

I gave a lazy wave over my shoulder as the door to *The Crooked Oak* creaked open and spilled us into the cold, grimy night. The sour tang of old urine and smoke clung to the cobblestones like a second skin.

We'd barely gone two blocks when the sound of echoing footsteps matched our own.

I stopped. Spun.

No one behind us.

I opened my perception wide—something I didn't love to do in the city with the noise of all the people around. Hundreds of life forms burst into my mind's eye, though the closest was much closer than I expected.

I turned forward again—and nearly walked into a man standing *directly* in front of us.

He was tall, dressed to kill—literally, maybe. A charcoal pinstripe suit hugged a frame that was all muscle and menace. A bowler hat perched atop his head, and in the flickering torchlight, he looked like something peeled from one of those crime stories Amara liked to read.

He struck a match. The flare lit his face in brief, ghostly orange as he brought the flame to a long pipe that had appeared between his teeth. The first puff of smoke curled around his face like mist.

"Princess," he said, his voice a smooth, dark purr—like velvet soaked in whiskey. "Didn't expect to see you prowling the alleys of Cheapside."

My hand instinctively reached for my sword.

Amara's hand was faster, pressing firmly over mine.

"Drake," she said, his name spat like a bitter fruit. "I wasn't expecting to be *seen*."

"Oh, princess," Drake said with a grin. "You know better than anyone—nothing happens in Cheapside without me knowing."

As he spoke, the buildings around us seemed to come alive. Second and third-story windows creaked open. A woman leaned over a balcony rail, wearing little more than a smile and a threadbare sling barely covering her breasts.

"You alright down there, Cap?" she called.

"Never better, Melinda," Drake answered smoothly. "Appreciate your concern."

"You come up and visit anytime," she cooed. "Friends and family discount." She winked, then vanished into the shadows.

Valdrath's voice cut across the street like a sword through mist. "What're you doing harassing my friends, Drake?"

He stepped from the shadows like a summoned beast, sleeves rolled up, silver-furred arms catching the lamplight. I hadn't even sensed him until he spoke. That was...alarming.

I need a better way to hone my senses in the city, Aubrey! I near shouted in my head.

Body temp drops a little while sleeping. Try this.

My perception shifted—half of the blips around me dimmed. Dozens of lives, most of them asleep. But five—no, six—were close, too close.

From two alley mouths, thugs stepped out. Clubs, chains, daggers. Drake's backup.

But I wasn't surprised. Aubrey's technique worked like a charm.

Val laughed and the sound carried real joy. "And here I was thinking I wouldn't get any exercise tonight." The large Nyxian rolled up his sleeves even farther.

Drake raised a hand. "No need for theatrics, Val."

The thugs stopped mid-step. After a curt nod from Drake, they melted back into the alleys.

"Then why *are* you here?" Amara asked, her voice flint and fire.

Drake took another long pull from his pipe, but this time, something shifted in his expression. Not satisfaction—disgust.

He exhaled slowly, curling wisps lit by the flickering lamplight. His lip curled as if the words themselves tasted bitter. "Because I owe you, Princess. And your Grounder friend here. And I don't like having unpaid debts." His eyes narrowed. "They always come back to bite at the least opportune time."

I looked to the princess, confused. She locked in her regal princess mask. "I'm listening."

Drake gave a half-smile. "You met my sister, Scarlet, after the battle at Drumsorrow, didn't you?"

"I remember her," Amara said. "Charming. Gorgeous. Not sure how you two shared a parent."

That earned a rare laugh from the kingpin of Cheapside. "Two parents, if you'd believe it. Scarlet got the charm, the looks, the grace. Me?" He spread his arms. "All I got was an enterprising spirit and a knack for creative solutions."

"I'd hardly call extortion creative," Amara replied, tone sharpened. "Protection rackets are as old as dirt."

Drake raised a finger. "Ah, but I *actually* provide protection. That's the difference. And that's why helping you settle this little debt also helps the people of Cheapside." His grin widened. "Efficient, isn't it?"

Amara's voice softened slightly. "Go on. How do you plan on paying this 'debt'?"

Drake's eyes gleamed. "Information."

That one word hung in the air like a blade.

"You and your family," he said slowly, "are being *played*."

Amara's posture didn't shift, but I saw the tightness in her fingers. "How and by whom?"

Drake shook his head. "Not here. Not in the open."

Valdrath's voice cut through the air like a blade through silk. "I thought these were your streets, Cap."

I blinked. Val was suddenly standing just behind Drake, silent as a ghost. I hadn't even noticed him move. My gut twisted. I must have had more to drink than I thought. It surprised me so much I immediately opened my perception as wide as it would go.

Drake didn't even glance back at Val. "They're my streets, yes. But no one owns *every* eye and ear. Anyone who tells you otherwise is selling something."

He pulled a crisp envelope from his vest pocket and handed it to Amara. "Inside, you'll find a location for a private meeting. And a little taste of what I've got to offer."

"You can bring the Grounder and the orc," he added with a wink.

From behind him, Val chuckled, voice full of dark amusement. "One day, you and I are going to settle it. Snake or orc—who's faster?"

Amara ignored the posturing. "I'll need at least two guards for this meeting."

"One," Drake countered. "And they don't speak."

"Done," she said without hesitation. She tucked the envelope into her coat without even glancing at it. "If what's inside is as juicy as you claim...we'll see you tomorrow."

Drake's grin was all teeth. "Oh, we'll *definitely* be seeing each other."

He turned, giving Val a once-over before patting him on the shoulder. "The snake, of course. Come prepared tomorrow. With any luck, we'll be undisturbed, but my luck hasn't been that great as of late."

Then he disappeared into the night like smoke blown into the wind— silent, almost weightless. Even with perception wide open, I couldn't hear his footsteps. *Core crafting?* Possibly. But if it was, it was like nothing I'd seen before.

I had seen almost no core crafting performed since coming to

Alyndor, as if the Duskers were given an order not to craft in front of me. Or maybe they did it in a way I couldn't perceive. If anything, what I saw in class earlier in the day made core crafting even more of a mystery to me.

Even Amara refused to craft in front of me. It made me think it was some royal edict.

I was going to ask—but not here. Not while Cheapside was watching.

Sensing the tension, Val spoke quietly. "I know you two can handle yourselves. But I'm going to shadow you until you're somewhere with fewer rats."

I nodded. "Thanks."

Amara gave a curt nod of her own.

We kept our pace brisk, weaving through the crooked alleys until we reached the brighter, cleaner edge of the city. At the edge of the glow, Val gave us a wink and a casual wave before fading back into the shadows.

We walked up the road to the castle. All I wanted was a bed, a blanket, and a way to skip time until morning. I couldn't wait to hop in bed, but still had a fair amount of studying to do. I also had to train with Aubrey. Maybe she'd give me a night off.

Not a chance.

Ugh.

The road ahead was mostly empty, so I finally voiced the question that had been clawing at the back of my mind.

"The Grounders use novamancy all the time. But I've been in Alyndor a month and a half and I've barely seen *any* core crafting. Once, maybe twice. What gives? Why hide it? Is that some kind of royal restriction?"

Amara shook her head. "No. It's not us. But...I'm not allowed to talk about it."

We stepped onto the bridge leading into the castle, moonlight dancing off the water below.

155

"You're royalty. Who can stop *you* from talking?"

Her gaze turned to steel. "The crown has no power over the crafters."

"Then who?" I asked. "The guilds?"

She shook her head again. "They run logistics. Training. Discipline. But the real power? That comes from the church. From the Oracle herself."

I stopped mid-step. "The Oracle? You mean the lady in the veil at the awards ceremony?"

Amara didn't slow. "She sees the future—or so they say. No one crosses her. Not openly. And no one questions why she does what she does. If the Oracle commands that core crafting remain hidden, then it remains hidden."

"And everybody just falls in line with her edicts?"

Amara gave a tired laugh. "Not even close. You'll see evidence of that tomorrow. The engineers are notoriously pragmatic. Try telling an engineer not to use a tool they have at their disposal and see what happens."

I chuckled at that. If there was one thing the Dawnford mechanics and engineers valued most, it was their tools. "And that doesn't ruffle the church?"

"Of course it does," said Amara. "But have you ever known an engineer who cares about ruffling the feathers of those in power?"

20

Engineering Guild

I was ready when the knock came.

Already bathed, dressed, and pacing my room like a caged coyote, I ran through everything Dain and my father had drilled into me—mental checklists of traps, expectations, protocol. If today was anything like my "interview" at the G&L Guild, I had to be ready for anything.

I flung the door open.

Amara stood there—not in her sparring gear, but in full formal regalia. A high-collared, embroidered jacket sat over a crisp white blouse. Her slim-fitting trousers were deep purple, trimmed with gold weave that shimmered like starlight. Her hair was pinned, her face flawless, her posture imperial. She looked every bit the princess.

"Come to escort me to my first day at the engineering guild?" I asked, managing a half-smile.

She snorted, a flicker of warmth behind her cool expression. "No. I'll be stuck in court all day again. But the engineers are going to love you." She nodded toward my sword. "You've got something they worship—real experience with engineering on the surface. Drillships. You'll end up teaching them as much as they teach you."

I frowned. "Okay, then. As much as I love seeing you, princess, why are you here?"

She didn't react to my words but for a small flush above the high collar of her white blouse. "You were tired last night."

"And a little drunk," I added with a rakish smile. "I don't have a low tolerance. I have zero tolerance."

"Not a bad thing, though it might get you in trouble around the nobles in this place." She gave me a distracted smile and looked inside my room.

I opened the door wider. "Please, come in."

She swept into the room like a gust of wind. I hadn't made the bed yet, but she sat on the edge all the same. "I read Drake's note last night. I almost came banging on your door at two bells."

In truth, I'd been up reviewing Professor Cloud's leviathan of a packet before diving into training with Aubrey. Shields, mostly. Shields were a big thing to Robert and therefore Aubrey. Fast-deploy, counterflow, projection locking. Grueling work—but I was getting better. *Sharper.*

I didn't say any of that. I just met her eyes and said, "We're in this together. You can wake me anytime."

She brushed invisible lint from her pants and hesitated before pulling a sealed envelope from her coat. "I didn't want to start rumors. The castle staff runs on loose lips."

She flipped the envelope between her fingers. "I couldn't sleep after reading it."

My smile faded. "That bad?" I searched her face for fatigue but nothing cracked the regal princess mask.

I had only gotten four hours of sleep myself, but last week I finally accepted Aubrey's offer to "optimize my serotonin receptors" to immediately drop me into a much deeper sleep cycle. I hated having her mucking around in my head, but her tweaks were effective. I woke up each day fresh and ready to go.

She nodded. "Drake claims he has proof... that we're about to be betrayed. *Again.* By the Church."

My stomach tightened. "Again?"

"He claims the goblin attacks...weren't just a failure of the wards. He says they were orchestrated. That someone in the Church—maybe even the Oracle herself—was behind them."

My thoughts stalled for a heartbeat. "That...honestly doesn't seem that far-fetched."

She tucked the envelope away with a hard breath. "I want to say it's ridiculous. The Oracle has always been a trusted ally of the crown. But...this isn't the first crack in that trust."

"Could be someone in her inner circle," I said quietly.

Amara stood, folding her arms across her chest. "Or it could be smoke and misdirection. Either way, we need to know what Drake knows."

"Where's the meeting?"

"Ribald's Junction. Tonight, at dusk. Near where Val found the dead unicorns."

I winced. "Sounds charming. Should I pack a picnic basket?"

She stepped closer. "That's why I came. Not just to warn you, but to ask you something important."

"Shoot."

"I love Sir Michael. He's loyal, brave, and unshakable. But he's also...*devout.* If he hears what Drake has to say about the Church—"

"He might take it as heresy," I finished for her.

She nodded. "Would you mind if we brought Draven instead of Michael?"

My face broke into a grin. "I've missed the arms master. If I'm going to be marching into cursed woods with possible traitors and known criminals, I'd rather have a swordsman than a sermon."

She smiled faintly. "Five bells. Front gate."

"Looking forward to it," I said. Then I glanced at the little clock on my table and swore. "I've got to move."

The Engineering Guild sat across from the G&L guild like a rival titan, its wide stone facade bustling with motion even at this early hour. Sunlight glittered off the fountain in the center of the plaza, where four mythic beasts spat water in arching streams—one of them a unicorn.

Exactly how close was this Ribald's Junction to where Val found the dead unicorns?

I tore my eyes away from the fountain and focused on the Guild itself. Unlike the austere grandeur of G&L, the Engineering Guild was chaos perfected. Carts rattled. Golems hauled lumber and steel. A line of civilians stood outside the main doors, waiting for service. The real flow, though, was through a side door—engineers in dusty coats and tool-belts streaming in, barked greetings tossed between them.

I headed for the side door.

A guard stepped into my path. "Customer line's over there. This door's for engineers only."

I straightened my jacket. "I'm not a customer. Name's Finn Camlock. I'm here as a guild candidate."

Recognition sparked in the man's eyes. "Ah, the Grounder. Hang on." He whistled into the guild, sharp and precise.

A moment later, a stout man jogged over and motioned me inside. "You're with me. You'll be meeting Rojer Varn. He'll get you sorted."

Rojer? Could it be the same Rojer Dain used to mention? If so, this was going to be interesting.

The interior lacked the decorative ego of G&L's entrance. No marble columns, no soaring ceiling. Just a front service desk that looked like it had seen a hundred years of oil stains and burn marks. On either side, massive hangar doors framed the workspace beyond. Through a dirty window, I glimpsed the mechanical guts of the guild: massive siege engines, bridge struts, and the skeletal frame of what looked like a flying machine—or a very ambitious deathtrap.

My guide raised a hand, signaling me to wait by a glass window overlooking one of the hangars. "He'll be with you shortly."

I nodded, but my eyes were already glued to the strange siege weapon on the floor beyond the glass. It wasn't like anything I'd seen. The payload basket was mounted on a sled, not a simple pivot. A cord linked it to a heavy lever and counterweight. Whatever it was, this thing didn't throw like a normal catapult.

It launched.

And judging by the sheer mass of that counterweight, it launched *hard*.

What I didn't see was a winch system to reload it. Which meant either it was unfinished...or it required something very powerful to reset.

"It's called a trebuchet," said a voice like gravel poured over steel.

I nearly jumped out of my skin and spun on my heel.

The man behind me wore a crooked grin that instantly reminded me of Dain—that same amused smirk Dain got whenever he knew he'd startled me on purpose. Yeah. Definitely one of *his* people.

He was squat, broad across the chest and shoulders, built like a boulder someone taught to speak. His eyes burned with a fierce, inquisitive intelligence—the kind of stare that dissected everything it landed on. Midnight-black hair shot out from under his brow in every direction like he'd tried to comb lightning. His clothes were grease-streaked khakis and a short-sleeved button-up beneath a leather apron that looked older than I was. But it was the brace on his left leg that caught my eye—an elaborate exoskeletal frame of copper and chrome, all struts and gears that whirred softly when he shifted his weight. The boot on that leg was massive, easily twice the size of the one on his right.

He saw where my eyes had landed and gave a dry grunt. "Massive explosion. I was the only survivor," he said grimly. "Never mix incendiary powders with a magmatite construct if you're fond of your limbs...or your drinking buddies."

My eyes went so wide they nearly shot out of my head.

Then he barked a laugh. "Dain said you were gullible. I like you already." He tapped the brace with a wrench. "Nah. Clubfoot. Born with it. It's what got me into engineering in the first place. Had to outthink my body just to keep up. Now? I can outrun most of my colleagues. Save for the young'uns."

I nodded awkwardly, still reeling from the sudden energy this guy carried like a storm cloud. Before I could recover, he jerked his thumb toward the hangar window and the siege machine beyond it.

"You've been eyeballing my baby for a while now. Tell me—what's missing?"

I turned back to the trebuchet, squinting at its mechanical guts. "No winch," I said after a beat. "There's no mechanism to lift the counterweight again. Not one I can see, anyway."

His lips curled into a full-blown grin. "Dain said you were a fast thinker. The winch is housed in the reinforced casing on either side— tucked in tight. Dual access. If one side gets slagged, the other can handle the reload."

I nodded slowly, piecing it together. "And the housing's thin enough to avoid interfering with the sling track. So, you've miniaturized the lateral profile?"

"Close." He jabbed a thick finger at the glass. "Vertical miniaturization. Compressing function *downward*, not *outward*. Keeps the center of gravity low and the range long. Not bad for a Grounder."

He thrust a hand toward me. "Rojer Varn. Welcome to the guild."

I blinked at the offered handshake, caught off guard again.

Rojer frowned. "What, am I doing it wrong? Dain said you surface folk still like to clasp hands, yeah?"

I quickly shook his hand. "You're doing it right. Just surprised me is all. Most people down here look at my customs with a sneer."

His grip was firm but not crushing. I was touched Rojer took the time to learn one of my customs, though I didn't say it.

Rojer pulled back and spread his arms. "Now then, you've got questions. I can smell 'em. Fire away."

I tripped over my words, three questions crashing into each other on my tongue. I swallowed, regrouped. "Uh...Will there be some kind of entrance exam? Like at the G&L guild?"

Rojer snorted so hard I thought I saw oil mist puff from his nose. "That *was* your exam, lad. You passed. G&L made you take a test?" He shook his head and barked a laugh. "Farsmith's got a brass rod up his backside and a nameplate on it to prove it."

"Professor," said a new voice—sharp and electric.

A young woman strode toward us, wiping grease from her fingers with a rag that looked like it had lost a fight with a golem. Her spiky white hair had streaks of fire-red running through it. A long smear of oil streaked her cheekbone, and she wore it like war paint. Her apron matched Rojer's—functional and filthy.

She tossed the rag over her shoulder and pointed a wrench at him. "Quit talking deep rot about Farsmith and open the damn lab, would you?"

Rojer gave her a glare that could have melted steel. "Pushy brat. Fine. I'm coming. Spindle, this is Finn Camlock, the Grounder."

She gave me a quick up-and-down. "Ah, the Grounder. I'm Korra Jex, but everyone around her calls me Spindle." She grinned. "Word is, you're skipping straight to the graduate level."

I turned back to Rojer in disbelief. "Seriously?"

"Dead serious. I saw the crawler you built," he said. "You're using techniques most of my third-year candidates haven't even heard of."

"I had help," I admitted. "From Dain."

"That's what he said," said Rojer. "He also said you did most of the work on the Drifter and you were a sharp hand in your father's machine shop up on the surface. Any truth to that?"

I nodded.

Rojer slapped me on the back hard enough to jolt a lung loose. "Then you're wasting your time with the basics. That muck up with the guild bosses upstairs flexing against the king was annoying for all of us. Real engineers don't let politics get in the way of talent. You should have joined us a month ago! Anyway, I imagine you're dying to get your hands dirty."

"To be honest?" I smiled. "It's been *way* too long since I held a spanner, sir."

"No sirs here," he said. "Call me Rojer—or Professor, if you're mad at me like this one."

Spindle rolled her eyes. "Let's go, old man. I've got an AD to finish and I'm *not* getting younger."

As we walked, the whir of Rojer's brace ticked out a rhythm against the stone floor.

"AD?" I asked.

"Autonomous Device," said Spindle. "Automaton, golem, robo-buddy. Call it what you want."

My eyes lit up. "What are you using? Core or control chip?"

"Control chip, obvi," said Spindle. "Grublickers over at G&L won't share any of their toys with us unless ordered by imperial decree."

"How'd you get the control chip then?"

She gave me a sideways look. "I built it, of course."

My jaw dropped. "I didn't know the guild could do that."

"Technically?" She smirked. "We're not supposed to. But I built a functioning chip using copper wire and solder on a board. It's not etched like the fancy ones, but it works."

Rojer gave me a look like he was reassessing my abilities. "You never worked with 'lectric and bread boards up on the surface? I thought you Grounders were the experts with fields."

I snorted. "Of course I have, my dad's been pushing circuits at me since I was five. I just thought a control chip was more..." I searched for the word, "core crafted I guess."

"They can be, but they don't have to. Nothing magical about a chip, lad. They're just machines," he said. "But a real Core? Not those knockoffs G&L tries to peddle. The Ancients' Cores?" He shook his head. "Those things...I don't know what they are."

"The guild's never cracked a Synth Core open?"

He gave me a tight smile. "Never dared."

Then he fixed me with a long stare. "Has your father?"

Both he and Spindle leaned in, eyes like laser drills.

I shook my head. "No way. Our Melders would blow a gasket just hearing the question."

"Exactly," Rojer murmured.

We stopped in front of a large door. Rojer grabbed the key chain attached to his belt and fumbled through a couple dozen keys until he found the right one.

He opened the door and Spindle pushed past him to get into the lab. She issued a command and lights flickered on.

My eyes widened again. "By the stars," I whispered.

21

Magmatites

I took a slow breath. Then let it out in a rush, like if I didn't, I might actually explode. I pinched my arm, just to be sure.

Nope. Not dead. Not dreaming. Still very much alive and staring into the most beautiful place I'd ever seen.

The hangar sprawled before me, massive and humming with potential. It wasn't just a workspace—it was a kingdom of creation. Towering tool closets lined the walls like armored guardians, silent and proud. Between them, neatly coiled wires hung in a rainbow of colors, each spool tagged and sorted like sacred relics.

Metal sheets gleamed in stacks along the far wall, wood planks and pipes neatly arranged in vertical bins, separated by size like some grand offering to the gods of invention. The back half of the room was dominated by machines that loomed like slumbering beasts—saws, presses, cutters—each one humming with the quiet threat of power.

Sixteen workbenches formed rigid lines in the front half, bolted to the floor like anchor points to something greater. Each bench was surrounded by drawers, tools, and the promise of brilliance.

I stepped forward, and a strange, powerful sensation washed over me.

Home.

Not the one I'd left behind. Not my bunk in the castle. Not even my father's shop.

This. This was the home of my future.

Off to the side, Spindle was already in motion. She moved like a tornado with a mission—tools flying out of chests, gears clinking into place, materials pulled like cards from a magician's sleeve. At her table, a half-assembled AD rested on its side like a beast mid-transformation. It looked incomplete...but somehow dangerous.

She caught me staring. "Come on over," she called.

Rojer and I crossed the room to her station—third one down on the left. She patted it like it was an old friend.

"This here is my bench," she said, reverently.

I blinked. "That's what you call it? A bench?"

She smirked. "Of course. Sounds better than 'work table.' Gotta treat it with respect. This is where the magic happens."

I chuckled. "Bench it is. What kind of AD are you building?"

Her smile turned sly. "A seeker."

I tilted my head. "What's that?"

"A finder golem," she said casually. "If I train it right, it'll track down rare materials. It'll make me rich."

I had a thousand questions—but Rojer held up a hand. "Later. You two'll be seeing plenty of each other. And since you're both about to build something that'll scare the pants off the guild, let's get you set up. You brought your crawler?"

I pointed to my pack. "Right here."

"Good," Rojer grinned. "Then let's get you a bench."

Spindle's eyes narrowed. "Wait. Which bench?"

Rojer motioned to the only empty table near the door. "Axel's old spot."

Spindle recoiled like Rojer had just suggested necromancy. "You're putting him at *that* bench?"

"What?" I asked, suddenly wary.

She leaned in, voice low and ominous. "That bench is cursed. Axel blew his arm off right there."

Rojer held up a finger. "Only because he *ignored* safety protocols."

"Okay," said Spindle. "Then how do you explain Glinda? Took a chunk to the *head*. Now she can only speak in words that start with 'P.' Poor pretty princess."

Rojer barked a laugh. "I'm stealing that one."

What was the matter with these people? Starting with Dain, every engineer I'd met seemed to be dementedly dedicated to pulling the perfect prank.

I frowned. "So...what really happened?"

"Eh, Axel graduated last quarter," she said. "Joined an engineering corps in the Veil."

"Then why not just *say* that?"

Spindle winked. "Where's the fun in that?"

Before I could reply, she nodded toward my pack. "Well? Let's see what you've got, Grounder."

I unlatched the case and gently set Rach on the bench. Two flicks of her belly switches, and she came to life—scuttling in a neat circle around the tabletop like a wind-up soldier.

Spindle gave a low whistle. "You built this in *how* long?"

"Most of a day," I said.

"You're hilarious," she said. "Seriously."

"I had help."

Rojer raised a bushy brow. "Dain's good. But not *this* good. That's solid work. What's your end goal with it? What are you turning this crawler into?"

Well, what would you call what we're trying to make? I asked Aubrey.

An evo-mechanica, she said, *but you can call it an evo-mech.*

"An evo-mech," I answered.

They both looked at me as if trying to figure out if I was playing a prank on them. Rojer finally said,

"What in the wards is an evo-mech?"

Oh no. *Thanks a lot, Rhee! I near shouted into my mind. Exactly what is an evo-mech? The way you said it made it sound like it was a common term down here!*

I felt a strange, warm rush in my brain. Moist. Emotional.

You called me Rhee, Aubrey whispered. It finally happened...It's been weeks, months! And you finally—

NOW IS NOT THE TIME FOR FEELS, I snapped.

She sniffed. *Fine. Evo-mech: an AD that evolves.*

You mean like it gets smarter with training?

No, she replied. It grows stronger. Adapts to problems. Changes itself. Learns and reconfigures. An evolving machine.

That...is brakkin...amazing. Or insane.

You're welcome.

I didn't know that was possible, I said.

She sniffed. *If I were to list the number of things you didn't know were possible, it would take approximately six hundred eighteen years, four months, three days and one and a half hours.*

"You alright, lad?" Rojer asked, eyeing me like I'd started speaking goblin.

Spindle put a hand to her chest. "The curse of the bench must already have him."

I took a breath. Then faced them. "An evo-mech is an autonomous device that grows and evolves. It learns from experience, adapts, and upgrades itself based on the situations it faces."

They stared.

Then they both laughed.

"I *have* to steal that," Rojer wheezed. "That's rich."

I felt my face start to heat. *Thanks a lot, Rhee.*

Oh, I see, you only use my nickname when you're angry at me. That's just mean.

My face went hot. "I'm not joking."

Spindle doubled over. "Okay! *Okay!* Sure, Grounder. Next, you'll tell me it talks to you in your head."

I gritted my teeth and started rifling through the drawers at my bench to hide the color blooming in my cheeks.

Rojer finally noticed. The laughter drained from his face. "Wait... you're serious?"

I nodded.

"I've never heard of such a thing," said Rojer. "Are they common on the surface? I've never heard our people who've gone up there talk about them before."

Spindle shrugged. "Maybe it's like how the king makes foreigners sign a contract about not talking about the beauties of Alyndor." She looked at me. "Is it something like that?"

I shook my head. "No. They're not common up there. I saw something out there—during my pilgrimage—that stuck with me. Lit a fire I couldn't put out. Ever since then, I've been chasing this idea. I think I can make one."

Rojer narrowed his eyes. "And the materials? They actually... change?"

Aubrey?

If they're the right materials and they've got the correct Core.

And in the meantime? I asked.

In the meantime, there's a fair amount of manual work. Repeat after me.

I echoed her word for word. "While I'm training the AD, I'll have to facilitate most evolutions manually—build-outs, upgrades, the works. But once I lock in the proper Core and materials...the sky's the limit."

Spindle's eyes glittered. "How do you *know* all this?"

170

I hesitated. "I don't. Not for sure. It's a working theory, based on what I saw up top."

Her curiosity sharpened. "What *did* you see?"

I paused. "That...I can't talk about."

"Typical," she muttered. "But is it true what they say? That Ancient tech is just...scattered across the desert?"

I nodded. "It is. But so are the Ignavari. You don't want to run into them. Trust me."

Spindle scoffed. "You couldn't pay me my weight in gold to live on the surface."

"Smart," Rojer said with a grunt, then glanced at the wall clock. "Alright, I'm off to lecture. But I'm excited to see what you can do, lad."

He rapped his knuckles on my bench. "This is yours until you present a final project to the board. You're free to jump into any class, grad or undergrad—ask me or Spin what's worth your time. I'd start with advanced circuitry or control chips."

As we talked, more students filtered into the lab—glancing curiously my way but without the sneers and whispers I'd grown used to at G&L. There was no resentment in their eyes—just interest.

"Thanks, Professor," I said. "Really. I'm ready to get to work. Quick question though—can I use the supplies here, or...?"

Rojer chuckled. "The crown's footing the bill for you. You've got full access to anything in this lab—just not from someone else's bench. Need something special? Spin can help you submit a requisition."

He waved once and turned for the door. "Don't blow anything up, but if you do, make it impressive!"

As soon as the door shut, Spindle clapped me on the shoulder. "Alright, Grounder. Let's get to work. Ready?"

I grinned. "Beyond ready."

I could *feel* Aubrey's anticipation fluttering through my skull. The sooner we upgraded Rach, the sooner she could truly come into her own.

I spent some time browsing through the materials until I found a circuit board, I turned—and froze.

Spindle was hunched over her bench, goggles on, a bright white flame cutting through metal like sunlight through snow.

But the flame wasn't what made my breath catch.

It was the source of it.

A creature—twelve inches tall—balanced on three legs, with a single arm ending in a luminous bulb of white fire. Its body looked like it had been sculpted from molten rock, glowing from within with pulsing veins of red-hot energy.

The flame streamed from the sphere in its arm, cutting with perfect precision.

I stood transfixed.

Spindle glanced up and raised her goggles. "What?" she asked, brow arched. "Never seen someone summon a magmatite before?"

I shook my head, jaw slightly slack.

She grinned. "Ah right. You're a Grounder. Makes sense. The church gets all gripey about core crafting in front of outsiders. Personally, I think it's a steaming pile of rot."

"Aren't you afraid you're going to get in trouble?" I asked, eyes still locked on the little creature.

She snorted. "What am I gonna do? *Not* work when you're around? If the church wants to make a fuss, they can take it up with the crown."

I nodded, slowly. "Can...all Duskers summon things like *that*?"

"Most crafters, yeah. We specialize. Engineers tend to lean magmancy." She gestured to the creature. "This is Sparky. Makes welding a breeze."

"I can see that," I murmured.

Curious, I extended my perception. Sparky wasn't alive—not in the biological sense—but its presence was electric. It radiated power, its body tethered to Spindle like a blazing extension of her will. The energy pulsed down through her and into the stone floor beneath her boots.

I followed the line of energy with my mind's eye.

She's drawing power from the ground. I had no idea how she gathered the energy, but then again, I couldn't see the nova-field either. It was probably a similar form of energy.

"When you say 'core crafting'..." I began carefully. "Do you mean energy from a Master Synth-Core? Like the ones we use topside?"

Spindle winced. "Answering that *will* get me in hot water. Sorry."

I held up a hand. "Understood. Even the princess won't answer my questions about core crafting."

As I made my way toward the materials wall, I glanced around—and realized *almost every other bench* had its own magmatite helper. Some small, others hulking. Each shaped to its crafter's needs—some wielded hammers, others pincers, others threading spools of wiring through complex harnesses.

It was like walking through a symphony of stone and fire. I sighed.

"I wish I had something like that," I muttered under my breath. Then, I realized I had something far more powerful than a simple magmatite and she was hardwired into my mind.

Aw, first you call me Rhee, then you pay me a compliment? Best day ever, said Aubrey.

I snorted, but the corners of my mouth tilted up. *Let's get to work.*

22

Ribald's Junction

B y the end of the day, my hands were slick with machine grease, my brain buzzing with half-formed schematics, and my heart full in a way it hadn't been since leaving the surface. I'd managed just two upgrades to Rach—small ones on paper, but they changed everything. A signal receiver and an optical sensor.

For the first time, Aubrey could pilot Rach without my help.

I'm still practically blind. I have barely a two hundred degree view of grainy garbage, she complained. *This sensor is an insult to optics everywhere.*

I sighed. *Apologies, your brilliance. Would you prefer I shut it off?*

She blew a psychic raspberry that made my ears vibrate like someone had shaken my skull. I groaned, rubbing them furiously to get the horrible sensation to stop.

It didn't work.

I sprinted back to the castle, the bells already chiming a quarter to five. I couldn't be late to meet with the princess for our trip to the junction. My boots skidded on the polished stone as I ducked into the kitchen's side door. One of the prep cooks tossed me a knowing grin and pointed toward the cooling hatch.

"Still got some meat pies left. Don't say I never loved you."

I grabbed one, snagged a fistful of grapes, and bolted down the corridor, devouring them as I ran. In my room, I scrambled to gear up—mail shirt back on, twin daggers at my side, sword belt secure, canteen filled, and Rach safely tucked into my pack.

As the final bells rang out, I burst from my room and dashed toward the bridge, heart thundering. I wasn't about to show up late—not again. I arrived just in time to catch the fourth toll.

Amara caught my eye immediately—and she did *not* look pleased.

"What?" I gasped. "I'm right on time!"

I exchanged masculine nods with Draven and Val who stood flanking her. Val wore a dark gray jacket which clashed with his silvery hair. The hilt of a short sword peaked out from beneath the hem of the jacket. Draven wore his regular black leather armor. He appeared unarmed, but I knew he had weapons stashed all around his body.

Amara, dressed in near-black violet leathers and leaning against a steel-capped quarterstaff, looked every inch a royal war-bringer.

"Now that our *esteemed Grounder* has deigned to join us," she said icily, "we can proceed to the stables."

Esteemed Grounder? Oof. I winced. "I still don't understand—I'm here. On time."

Val clapped me on the back. "Quick tip. When it comes to royalty, you're only on time if you get there *before* them. I'd recommend at least five minutes early."

Amara's scowl deepened, but she didn't correct him.

Draven's lips twitched in what might have been a smile.

"I had Jolly prepare our mounts," Amara said as we walked.

My stomach dropped. "Mounts?" The word came out squeaky and cracked.

Her smile turned devilish. "Second time's always easier. You'd be a confident rider by now if you hadn't weaseled out every time I suggested it."

Definitely still mad.

At the stables, Jolly greeted me with a snort. "You'll be fine. Swallow's gentle. Loves company. Just let her follow Stormcrown."

Swallow, a black-maned mare with a tawny coat, whickered and nuzzled my shoulder. I felt slightly better—until I saw Amara vault onto her massive gray charger without so much as a stirrup.

"Missed me, didn't you, Storm?" she cooed, stroking his neck. "Blame Finn. He's the reason it's been so long."

Stormcrown tossed his head and *glared* at me.

I groaned, clambering into Swallow's saddle like a sack of potatoes. She snorted patiently.

We set off at a steady clip, hooves clacking over cobblestone as the city walls gave way to the wild edges of the Nightbriar. Draven edged his mount closer to Amara, Val sidled up beside me.

"I held my tongue through the city as requested, Princess," Draven said, voice low and sharp. "But would you care to explain why we're walking into a trap like lambs to the slaughter?"

Val raised a brow. Even *he* wanted to hear this.

Amara chuckled. "This is why I brought you, Lord Stonepath. Sir Michael's better with a blade, but he'd never challenge me to my face." Her tone was both amused and faintly patronizing.

I caught the flicker of emotion that passed through Draven's eyes— surprise, irritation, then...amusement. He was impressed.

Amara had checkmated him in a single move.

"Apologies, Your Highness," Draven said stiffly, dipping his head in acknowledgment. "But the question stands. Why are we walking into an obvious ambush?"

Amara's expression hardened. "Because the crown is worth the risk. And yes—we'll spring the trap. But I'm not walking into it alone. I've got a Watcher who can sniff out a lie in the wind, a Nyxian who loves the drama, and *you*—the fastest blades in the realm."

Her words were steel and fire.

"Besides," she added, "if Drake wanted to harm me, he could have done so in Cheapside last night."

Draven scowled, turning back to Amara. "I'm not worried about the petty gangster. "What if word of this meeting got out to Thal'Naris, or any of your family's other countless enemies? You're a prize target. Ransom, assassination, leverage. I'm going to insist that Finn and I scout ahead before you so much as cross a clearing."

Her jaw clenched. The regal princess mask slid into place, but I saw the fury simmering beneath it—tight knuckles, rigid spine.

She took a long breath. Then another.

"Very well," she said, voice clipped. "There's more Sir Michael in you than I gave credit for."

She jabbed her heels into Stormcrown's flanks and the stallion launched into a canter.

I hung on to the reins with one hand and the horn of the saddle with the other as Swallow increased her pace to keep up. My heart raced as we tore into the forest.

I'd always enjoyed our hikes into the Nightbriar. There was something very peaceful about walking under the branches of the large trees as birds and insects chittered and squawked around us.

Not this afternoon. There was an undercurrent of menace beneath the branches as the sun's light began to dampen. The clatter of our hoofbeats stilled the gentle sounds of the forest.

Even the animals in my perception were tense—rabbits frozen in burrows, birds huddled high and silent. Whatever peace this place once offered had curdled into something wary, waiting.

Draven was tense, too. And *that* unsettled me more than anything. I'd seen the weapons master wade through chaos with ice in his veins.

Seeing *him* worried sent a chill through my ribs.

We'd been cantering maybe thirty minutes when Amara pulled Stormcrown up short with a sharp tug on the reins. The stallion snorted and stamped.

"The Junction's about a mile ahead," she said, voice low but steady.

Draven's eyes scanned the trees like he expected them to come alive. He pointed toward a sparse clearing ahead. "You and Valdrath wait there. Finn and I will scout."

"I'm not sensing any threats yet," I offered, dismounting. "Just birds, squirrels, and nerves."

Draven misunderstood my movement. "We'll have more maneuverability on horseback if things go sideways."

"Yeah," I said, digging through my pack. "I'm not getting off permanently. Just posting eyes."

I pulled out Rach's case, popped it open, and placed the crawler at the base of a nearby tree.

"I added a new sensor earlier. Enhances my Watcher perception. She'll keep eyes on Amara from the canopy."

You will *let me know if you see anything unusual, right?*

Of course, said Aubrey. *I'll keep an eye on the princess, you focus on you.*

All three of them twitched when Rach activated and skittered up the tree trunk on clicking claws. I bit down a grin. The crawler settled into position on a high branch, her body blending almost too well into bark and shadow.

I remounted, awkward as ever, then checked my twin daggers. My palms were sweating.

"They'll be listening as we ride in," Draven said quietly. "I want you to tell me how many extra men are waiting by talking about your lunch. What'd you have?"

"Grapes and a meat pie."

"Grapes are the number of men over what Drake said he'd bring, meat pies are—"

"Too complex," I interrupted. "We're not digging through the striations. I already know."

Draven's gaze sharpened.

"He brought eight," I said. "Not three. I'll let you know via 'grape' if something new comes up."

He didn't smile. Just urged his horse into a trot. Swallow followed grudgingly, jarring every bone in my spine.

Ahead, the Junction emerged from the trees like a secret kept too long—quiet, eerie, the kind of crossroads where dirty deals were made.

A weathered signpost leaned like a drunk, pointing in every direction. A low well-house squatted at one corner like it was trying to disappear into the dirt.

Drake stepped out from behind it, shadow falling long behind him in the dying light.

"I appreciate the honor of Lord Stonepath's company," he called with a theatrical bow. "But no princess, no meeting."

Draven's voice was flint. "We're here to see just how badly you broke the terms of our agreement."

Drake cleared his throat and three men stepped out from the trees, shadows made flesh.

"I'm a man of my word," he said smoothly.

"Then where are the other five?" Draven asked, sighing like a disappointed father. "I've dealt with enough petty gangsters to know this dance. Either send them away—or this meeting's done. A mile. No closer."

I caught the flicker in Drake's eyes. He hadn't expected us to know.

He covered the slip quickly, glaring at Draven, who didn't blink.

Finally, Drake whistled and spun a finger over his head. "One mile," he barked.

I wheeled Swallow around, a little less gracefully than I would have liked, and galloped back to the clearing.

Amara and Val were already mounted, watching the tree line. I slowed Swallow and called out, "No ambushes. But he brought five more men than promised."

Val scratched at the silver stubble on his chin. "That's not enough muscle to take us down. So why lie? Why risk breaking the terms for a tiny advantage?"

"Maybe they're for *his* protection," Amara muttered.

Above us, Rach crept farther out on a branch, her body sagging the limb under her weight. Swallow shied and stepped back nervously.

"Easy," I murmured, patting her neck. "She's on our side."

I dismounted and held out my arms. Rach dropped into them like a cat and immediately wrapped around my neck at Aubrey's silent instruction.

We rode in silence, each of us turning inward—tuning out the birds, the wind, the rhythm of hooves. Something nagged at me.

"Val," I said, keeping my voice low. "Where exactly did you find the dead unicorns?"

He pointed north, eyes narrowing. "About half a mile that way. Edge of the Hollows."

I reached out with my perception, extending it like a web. Nothing. Just forest and old quiet. But the memory of Val's story of that slaughtered majesty crawled up my spine.

Then I spotted Draven, waiting.

We dismounted at the well-house. Val and Draven stood shoulder-to-shoulder, glaring at Drake's muscle like they were weighing their bones. I stayed back, eyes on Amara.

Amara was as calm as afternoon tea. "So, what information is so secretly valuable that it can only be passed on in the middle of the forest at dusk?"

23

Boglings

Rach crawled off my shoulders in a blur of skittering limbs, her claws clicking against the shingles of the well-house. She leapt to a nearby branch and vanished into the canopy.

"You call me out for extra men and you bring a golem to the meet?" Drake snarled.

"The terms didn't mention ADs," said Amara. "What's next, will you protest our horses? They're deadlier than that crawler."

"Fine," said Drake. "Let's get this over with."

"Let's," Amara said. "In your letter, you mentioned the church. How sure are you?"

"That they're behind the goblin attacks?" Drake asked.

Amara nodded.

"Ninety five percent. But it's far from simple. The church is working with Thal'Naris."

The princess' gaze hardened. "And? The church works with all the kingdoms."

"How often does the church mobilize a kingdom towards war?" Drake asked.

Amara held the gangster's gaze for an uncomfortable span. "Our intelligence uncovered no evidence that Thal'Naris is readying itself for war."

"They're always readying for war with somebody," drawled Val. "The sunblind grublickers can't get enough of rattling their armor. Nine times out of ten it's meaningless posturing."

Drake's jaw tightened. "This is the tenth time then." The gangster looked at Draven. "We *petty gangsters* don't have elaborate spy networks, but we do communicate between kingdoms. We always have an ear to the ground and we always know when our way of life is under threat. Jawbone runs the Thal'Naris enterprising underworld and his entire crew, and most of the less fortunates in the Southie neighborhood are running scared."

"From the military?" asked Amara.

"From the church," corrected Drake. "People of little consequence are disappearing on the regular. It started when the church offered protection ceremonies from goblin attacks—divine core crafted wards. Most of those who attended came out changed—over-zealous, almost rabid."

"What does that have to do with pushing Thal'Naris towards war?" asked Draven.

"The church calls their new group of over-zealous followers the Righteous Few. They're dragging others, especially non-believers, to these church led rituals. Once someone joins a ritual they become believers right quick. Now, the Righteous Few are pushing for a cleansing war. They want the rest of the kingdoms to fall in line."

"I overheard Renaux talking about something like that, how our kingdom could use a good cleansing of its foreign influences," said Val. "I thought it was just one of his regular digs at me and Finn."

"Renaux takes cues from his father, my dear uncle Drennic," said Amara. "The Duke has always supported the church's more...extreme views. But these Righteous Few sound too extreme, even for him."

"That's not even the worst of it," said Drake. "One of Jawbone's men was relieving one of the church's cathedrals of some valuables it no longer needed when he saw their Potentate meeting with a man and two smaller green-skinned allies in the wee hours of the morning. The man had a...frightful complexion."

Even as I listened to the conversation, something tickled my perception. A bunch of somethings—a ways to the north but moving our direction. Fast.

"Uh," I said. "I've got a dozen grapes and one meat pie coming from the north."

Everyone gave me an odd look but Draven. "How far out?" he asked.

Amara talked over Draven. "What do you mean by frightful complexion?"

Drake's eyes flicked from Draven to me, then back to Amara. "What are they talking about?"

"Drake! Focus. What did you mean by a frightful complexion?" Amara asked again.

Drake scanned the horizon then turned his attention back to the princess. "I mean that his face was—"

Thwap.

The sound was sickeningly soft. A dart appeared in Drake's neck like a magician's trick. His eyes bulged, fingers fumbling toward the feathered shaft, knocking it free from his neck. He dropped to one knee, then collapsed, limbs spasming.

Everyone froze. My heart slammed into my ribs.

The dart was fired by the same person who attacked me at the G&L guild—I felt the familiarity of their presence. What worried me was my perception didn't pick them up until the same moment the dart struck Drake. This person was able to mask themselves from my perception.

Which meant they knew about my skill.

I caught a blur running north—right toward the others I'd sensed earlier. The assassin had left a residue of power behind, a mark like scorched ozone in the air. My focus locked onto the trail.

"Protect the princess!" Draven barked, already stepping in front of her like a drawn sword.

Val snapped into action beside him, yanking his seax free.

"Call your men!" Val yelled to the three thugs surrounding the convulsing Drake.

The largest of them gave a shrill whistle.

"It'll take em at least five minutes to get here," said another.

Drake convulsed on the ground, foam flecking his lips. One of his men knelt beside him and lifted the dart. Even in the fading light, the green glitter of poison shimmered like something alive.

"How far out?" Draven demanded, eyes locked on me.

"Too close—three, four minutes," I said.

"Do you know what they are?" Draven asked.

I shook my head. "No, but they're running hot. Almost as hot as goblins. The meat pie is running even hotter, almost like a waxer."

Amara smacked her hands together. "*What* are you talking about?"

"We're about to be attacked," said Draven. "Valdrath, get her out of here. Mount the horses and ride!"

Draven looked at me. "You too, Finn. I'll buy you some time."

A horrible screech ricocheted through the forest, so high and shrill it felt like knives in my ears. The trees shook. Swallow shrieked and tore down the road in blind panic, the other horses fleeing behind.

I didn't move. I drew my sword.

"I'm staying."

Amara didn't hesitate. She dropped her staff and rubbed her palms together like she was warming up for a duel. "Then I'm staying too."

Draven's jaw clenched. "Your father is going to *kill* me."

Amara ignored him. She murmured something under her breath, her voice low and steady. I felt it, energy flaring to life around her hands.

Two crystalline teardrops formed above her open palms, pulsing with light. She flicked her wrists and they shot upward like twin comets. They exploded overhead—two miniature suns burning through the dusk.

Everything lit up. Every shadow. Every movement.

A dozen shapes burst from the trees, hunched, fast, howling.

Val's voice cracked. "Are those...*boglings?*"

Two creatures exploded from the underbrush, crashing through the ferns like battering rams. Their squat, muscular forms were covered in rust-colored shells—natural armor that clanked and scraped with every movement. Their dark gray skin, rough as gravel, flexed beneath the plating, studded with pebble-like growths. Clawed, three-fingered hands gripped brutal weapons, stone clubs, jagged axes, glinting with malice.

Amara sucked in a breath. "That can't be," she whispered, voice trembling. "Boglings are...gentle creatures."

Not these. There was nothing gentle about them.

Draven was already moving. The steel in his hands caught the light as he slipped under the wild swing of the first bogling and drove both blades into its neck in a flash of ruthless precision. It snarled and stumbled backward, black blood gushing, but not before ripping one dagger free as it fell, crashing down atop it with a wet thud.

Valdrath moved in like a shadow, lips moving in a low chant. A cloud of green vapor hissed into being above his head and zipped forward, curling around the second bogling's face. The creature reeled, letting out a birdlike screech that rattled my bones. Val slashed its throat, once, twice—the second hit driving deeper into its thick hide until the blade found purchase and bit.

The bogling collapsed in a heap, twitching.

Then the trees split wide open.

Five more boglings barreled toward us, their beaked mouths clicking, screeching their rage. Another five thundered in from the west, claws flashing in the golden light of Amara's conjured suns.

And still no sign of the meat pie.

A second shriek—sharper, darker—cut the air like a whip. One of the crystal suns above shattered, raining shards of glowing dust. The battlefield dimmed in a heartbeat, shadows crawling back in like predators.

Two of Drake's men panicked and bolted.

Three boglings dropped to all fours and gave chase, galloping like hounds let off the leash. The thugs didn't make it far. Claws sank deep. The screams were short-lived—crunch, rip, gurgle. Blood painted the leaves in scarlet arcs. The air stank of iron and rot.

The other five thugs, late arrivals from the one mile probation, charged headlong into the fray.

The gory, hooked beaks of the boglings crowed in challenge.

The street toughs' battle cries were raw with fear. They slammed into the trio of gore-drenched boglings with a clash of steel on bone.

Draven and Val were already carving through more of the enemy, blades flashing, parrying, cutting. Two boglings slipped past.

They came straight for me and Amara.

My heart pounded in my chest as I took a ready stance, sword in my right hand, dagger in my left.

You're a defender, Finn. A protector. Aubrey's words echoed in my mind. Calm. Steady. The world *slowed*.

I watched their stubby legs pound, watched how their low shells made the charge awkward—like when Jay pantsed Arken and the boy waddled about, red-faced and furious.

Why that memory? Now? Maybe it was a way of holding on to something human in a moment that felt anything but. I hoped they were safe. Even Jay.

The bogling raised its stone axe, telegraphing the blow. I waited.

Timing. Angles. Let the energy flow *past* you. *The null field is all about the counter.*

I'd spent forty-three hours training with shields, but the defensive pyramid Draven taught me wasn't quite the same—the blades had to act together to protect each other and me. Similar to a shield, but fluid.

At the last moment, I stepped right and angled my weapons, not to block, but to redirect. The heavy axe glanced off with a shriek of stone on steel, its momentum throwing the beast off balance. I shoved the creature's shell, using its own power to *flip* it.

It toppled like a boulder—legs flailing, shell rocking.

A furious, muffled shriek came from within.

I spun, heart still pounding, eyes searching for Amara.

I shouldn't have worried.

Her bogling was already blind, twin crystals jammed into its eye sockets, smoke curling from the wounds. She danced around it like a dervish, blades singing through the air, opening bloody lines across its throat until it collapsed in a final, shuddering groan.

There's a soft spot at the back of their necks, Aubrey said. *Draven easily severed one's spinal cord. Aim just above the shell.*

How'd she get that info?

Rach, I realized. She was feeding Aubrey the battlefield through her optical sensors. I glanced up just in time to see my bogling right itself, hissing.

"Go for the back of their necks, right above the shell!" I shouted at the top of my lungs, hoping it would help.

I struck without further hesitation. My sword sank *deep* into the sweet spot, sliding between vertebrae until I felt it strike bone. The creature's eyes went dull. It dropped.

The last thug still standing was barely holding his own, blood streaking down his chest from a gaping wound. Two boglings pressed him hard, claws slashing.

Amara was already moving.

She closed the gap in two blinks, her dagger opening the back of the first bogling's neck like a butcher cleaving a roast. Blood fountained, hot and bright.

The second turned—too slow.

I lunged, sword biting deep into pebbled flesh. The bogling turned directly into Amara's waiting blade.

The creature howled once and died.

We froze, breathing hard.

Amara wiped a streak of orange-black blood from her cheek and looked at me. Her eyes shone, wild and alive. The regal princess mask shattered. What stood before me now was raw fire, a woman burning with power and purpose.

She saw me seeing her. And didn't flinch.

My heart hammered. For a breathless second, I couldn't look away. I wanted to memorize those freckles, trace the constellations they made around her nose.

But her eyes went wide. The light in them turned to horror.

"By the core-wards," she breathed, looking over my shoulder. "What is *that*?"

24

Cinderfen Hag

I spun, every muscle locking in shock.

Hovering above the ground—six feet, seven inches in the air—was something out of a nightmare. A twisted crone, hunched and withered, her form no longer flesh but coal-black peat and scorched ash. Her seared root limbs writhed, her charred twig fingers tipped in burning embers.

But it was the mask that turned my breath to ice.

A cracked kiln mask, streaked with flaking glaze and glowing from within. Familiar, terrifying embers stared out through the hollow sockets—sentient, seething.

The creature tilted its head back and screamed.

It wasn't a sound. It was a sonic blade. My hands flew to my ears as the very air rippled, threatening to shatter my skull. Behind me, leaves shivered, and birds dropped from the trees.

The five surviving boglings immediately disengaged from battle. Their behavior changed in a heartbeat—animal fury replaced with obedience. They dropped to all fours and galloped, positioning themselves in a tight, armored arc around the floating fiend like loyal sentries.

Amara's voice was ragged with disbelief. "It looks like a bog witch, but—"

Val and Draven retreated to stand at our sides. "Bog witches are creatures of water and mud, not fire," said Draven.

Val's face was pale. "We have children's tales in Nyxia of a witch of fire and ash. Cinderfen hags, we call them. Stories meant to scare children."

My heart hammered. "And in those stories, how did they kill one?"

"They didn't," he muttered. "That was the lesson. If you see a cottage in the forest with a kiln outside, you run. The other way. Fast."

Great.

Rhee, I thought desperately, *do you see a weakness? Anything?*

Of the magical floating hag? Are you kidding me? How is she even floating? Her energy field makes no sense.

I pulsed my perception. She burned hot, like a waxer in full flame, but beneath the conflagration, something pulsed. She wasn't pure energy, not like a magmatite, there was something still clinging to life at her core. Twisted, corrupted, but alive. Which meant...

"She can die," I breathed.

We stood frozen in a hellish tableau, tension strung tighter than wire. Eight seconds passed, an eternity.

The hag's kiln mask turned, ember-eyes flaring as she studied each of us.

Then they locked onto a thug and she pointed.

The man convulsed.

A blur—Draven's throwing knife flew like a streak of silver lightning, slamming directly into her ashen chest.

Perfect shot, a direct hit.

The hag didn't flinch.

She extended her other hand, fingers twitching.

"You're afraid," she rasped, voice crackling like burning leaves.

"And your fear is...delicious."

The wiry gangster screamed as frost exploded across his skin. His lips turned blue. Ice webbed over his brows. A companion tried to drag him back, only to leap away as he saw the man's feet had frozen solid to the forest floor.

"She's pulling the heat from him!" the thug shouted in horror.

The hag's hands ignited, absorbing the man's essence. Her kiln mask glowed brighter, fed by his life. With a simple twist of her fingers, the man dropped, limbs lifeless. The glow of the mask faded into her peaty body and Draven's knife melted and dripped to the forest floor in a pool of molten slag.

She turned toward Amara.

"No," Draven muttered. "We have to cool her down, now! Val, aeromancy—"

"Already on it!"

Two pale blue clouds shimmered into existence above the hag. They drifted down like ghostly fists. The moment they touched her singed hair, she screamed—this time in pain.

I gritted my teeth and forced my perception deeper, even as the scream sliced at my mind like razors. The soundwaves were too tight, too dense, like a swarm of knives in the air.

I couldn't block it. But maybe...

The null field is about the counter. The auditory shield—like when we were training with Robert and his squad. How do I create one of those things, Rhee?

You can't. You need a series of emitters which overlap and amplify until the waves buzz so rapidly they can stop something physical.

An idea struck. *Rhee, magnify my focus, help me take in every single variable and process it. A calculation. Focus on her frequency. Show me the waveform. Help me match it.*

The waves snapped into clarity—like lines on a graph—streaming across our shared vision. We learned. Then instead of pulsing my perception I *pushed* at it.

A perfect counter-frequency.

Then, silence. It wasn't an auditory shield, but it *worked*.

I opened my eyes. My friends still clutched their heads, faces contorted in pain. I could see the soundwaves hammering them like fists. They looked dazed, like drunkards on the edge of collapse.

The hag paused, then removed her mask. By the stars.

Tentacles. Dozens of fire-wreathed, writhing tendrils burst from her molten face. In the center: a jagged, circular maw, leaking thick black tar.

Val staggered as the hag's radiance evaporated his vapors. He dropped to a knee, tusked mouth bleeding from clenched teeth as his core essence burned.

He growled, wiped away the blood, and found his feet.

The hag exhaled a cone of fire toward the boglings at her feet. They curled into their shells, absorbing the inferno like coal taking flame. Their carapaces changed hue from green to glowing orange-white.

They rose, stony limbs reemerging.

Their beaked mouths screamed a gurgling war cry and they charged.

Weapons forgotten, claws outstretched, they ran at us like meteors. Heat radiated from them in shimmering waves. Their intent was clear: melt us, or crush us against their blazing shells.

The hag lowered her mask, obscuring those awful tentacles and pointed her twiggy fingers at Val. Val summoned a thin blue mist as a counter, but his face was pale and strained.

Why did she lower the mask? Could her tentacled face be a vulnerability?

Too late, the boglings were upon us.

Amara fired a crystal shard at the closest bogling, aiming with surgical precision. It clinked harmlessly off the creature's beak. But when it dipped its head to charge, the second shard slammed straight into its exposed eye.

The bogling howled but didn't slow.

We moved as one, Amara veering left, me right. The bogling lunged, and its molten shell scorched the air around me. The heat was unbearable, like standing too close to a forge. I gritted my teeth and slashed for its throat.

The creature twisted, and my blade barely carved a shallow line into its neck.

Then Amara struck.

She was a blur—graceful, precise, terrifying. Her daggers flashed once, twice, three times. Each cut landed with practiced intent. The bogling shrieked, spasmed, and dropped, its arms curling in as its superheated shell sizzled against its own corpse.

We had no time to celebrate. The hag floated higher, shifting her focus to the wounded gangsters. Val must have been too annoying a challenge, for now she turned her fiery malice on easier prey. Two of the thugs were already smoldering. The third screamed as the hag drained him, pulling heat straight from his bones.

Draven was in trouble. He faced two boglings alone, blades flying in precise arcs—but each time he struck, the second beast rotated in, using its blazing shell like a living shield.

I lunged forward. I'd seen the pattern.

The moment the bogling spun to block Draven's strike, it exposed its soft, scaled neck. I darted in, eyes narrowed, heart thundering. My blade sliced upward at a perfect angle—three degrees above horizontal—cutting clean through the sinewy throat. Before it could collapse, I followed with a dagger strike, twelve degrees down, exactly where the spine would shift. I *felt* the pop.

The beast dropped.

Draven didn't break stride, barely grunting acknowledgment before pivoting to the next.

Then, Amara cried out.

The crone had chosen a new target.

Val knelt, spent, arms trembling as he summoned the last wisps of his icy mist to protect her. But the barrier faltered, flickering like a dying lantern. Amara stood her ground, refusing to retreat.

Rhee! The mask—can we get it off her? Is Rach close?

She will be, Aubrey responded. *Good idea. I need thirteen seconds.*

Amara wasn't waiting.

She hurled four crystalline shards with explosive force. The first embedded in the hag's chest. The second snapped off a blackened twig finger. The third pierced the hag's root-like arm. The fourth struck the mask—and shattered.

No reaction. No pain. No pause.

The hag was untouchable...as long as the mask remained.

Draven finished his foe with a sweep of his twin blades, then whirled and threw two daggers at the last bogling harassing the thugs. One blade hit its throat, the other its jaw. The beast collapsed in a heap.

Only two gangsters remained—barely standing, bleeding and burned.

Draven pulled two more throwing daggers from the seemingly inexhaustible supply in the sheaths wrapped around his body, but didn't throw them immediately. He paused, holding both blades in the weak mist of vapor Val barely kept active in front of Amara.

Draven threw a chilled dagger at the hag. It sunk deep into the creature's chest and this time it reacted with a shriek which forced us to cover our ears.

The cinderfen turned and directed her shriek into the forest. If she was calling for more allies we were going to be in serious trouble very quickly.

Rhee, where is Rach, we're running out of time!

Seven more seconds.

Draven pulled his hand back to throw the second dagger.

"Wait!" I yelled. "Draven—give me six seconds!"

His eyes flicked to me, confusion clear. But he held his throw.

The hag turned, preparing to strike again. Her ember-lit mask turned toward the thug with the cauterized chest. She stretched out her hand.

The thug screamed as his body iced over, his breath frosting in his throat. The wound in the hag's chest pushed out the chilled dagger—the gash was healing.

"Finn," Draven growled.

"Three seconds," I whispered, heart hammering.

Rach dropped from above in a streak of steel and sparks. She landed on the hag's head, eight legs locking down. Her front four jammed beneath the kiln mask, and with a metallic groan and a wet squelch, she ripped it off.

The hag's true face exploded into view.

Her nest of flaming tentacles writhed furiously about, scoring carbon sears against Rach's metal carapace.

Draven threw.

The dagger soared through the smoke-choked air and slammed into the center of that hideous, tar covered maw. The impact echoed like a drumbeat of finality. The creature jerked mid-air. No scream this time.

Only silence.

Then, as it sunk to the ground, both gnarled arms snapped forward. Pointing directly at *me.*

I saw the energy build, a final death throe. A torrent of searing malice, not just heat, but concentrated hatred, aimed directly at my heart.

I pushed my perception outward, trying to match the wavelength like I had before.

Too many layers. Too fast.

I tried to dodge, but I was too late.

The blast hit.

It struck my chest like a hammer. Light engulfed me, searing white, then choking black.

I sunk into darkness.

25

Waxer

2.5 Years Before Finn's Pilgrimage To Iron Mountain

"You're ready now," said Malik. "I can feel it. Nothing tethers you to the weaknesses of humanity anymore."

Carl nodded. Those ties were gone. Amber made sure of that.

Malik's head tilted. "Don't give her the credit," he snapped, like he'd torn the thought straight from Carl's mind. "She didn't make you. You *chose* this. You burned your old life to ash."

They stood at the base of the Droughtspire Range, just outside the tunnel that led into the world of fire. Malik handed Carl a breather mask. Carl strapped it on, inhaling the stale chemical air. The visor filtered the world into a sickly yellow hue, just like the first time.

"This should be the last time you ever need that," Malik said.

Carl didn't flinch. Let it be the last. He was ready.

Malik's skin shimmered—and then ignited, hair becoming flame, eyes glowing like forge-coals. The transformation happened in a breath. No hesitation.

They walked past the magma pool. The Ignavari lounging in the molten heat turned their ember-eyed gazes toward Carl. There were more this time. Double, at least. Their stares weren't curious. They were hungry.

Carl didn't look away. Let them watch.

He slid down into the prime Igni's chamber, the spherical room glowing with eerie stillness. His eyes roved over the stasis-locked curios, covering every inch of the room. The air throbbed with unspoken knowledge and memory.

The prime floated down, alabaster tendrils trailing in threads of living fire. Malik raised his arms and the white flame surged forward, touching his skin.

Carl flinched as Malik convulsed, his eyes rolling back, mouth stretching open unnaturally wide.

It reminded Carl of Marsha Slug's reaction when she used the control bar of the LeadSled. Was the Igni's communication similar to Melding? Carl had never melded before so had nothing to compare it to.

Malik's skin bubbled at the hinges of his jaw. For minutes they stood, joined in silent communion—language beyond words.

Finally, Malik pulled away, mouth trembling. He cracked his jaw back into place and turned to Carl.

"Your turn," he said, voice hoarse but resolute. "Don't move. Speak only the truth. This is going to hurt, but it's worth it."

Carl nodded. He realized he wasn't the slightest bit nervous. Not anymore.

The tendrils reached for him. And then came the *pain*.

Where they touched, his neck, his hands, it felt like white-hot wire was being dragged through his nerves. The agony rippled, growing and multiplying, filling every vein. Carl embraced the pain. Relished it.

Images poured out of him—his meeting with Amber, his vengeance. The Igni drank it in, it reacted to Carl's assault of his dead wife with satisfaction. The fire demon stopped on the image of Carl walking confidently from the Dead Crow's camp.

Power surged into Carl, flooded into the invincible version of the man who walked so confidently away from his past. *This. This is who you are now,* the power seemed to whisper into his mind.

New images flooded into Carl. He saw himself Melding with a large crawler and knew he now had that power—the power to Meld. Then came scenes of pirates—gathering, swarming toward Dawnford, driven by Malik and the Igni's human allies.

But Carl wasn't to help them.

He would *take* from them. Take a crawler. Take the future.

He saw images of himself driving the big rig crawler, operating the control bar. He was to act as transport for the candidates of this year's pilgrimage. The pilgrimage which had Camlock's annoying son Finn in it.

The prime ordered Carl to enter the Iron Mountain. Within the ancient ruin lay a secret, a shard of tech lost to the Ignavari for centuries. And now, it would be *his* to find. To bring back to the Ignavari. The images showed him where.

The Igni shared its plans for the Dead Crow camp. They were awful. Gloriously terrible. Carl saw himself wielding the power of a god as he visited vengeance on the pirates.

Carl smiled through his pain.

After the images stopped, light filled his vision. The power flooded him again with white searing pain.

A single question lingered in his consciousness. *DO YOU SUBMIT?*
Submit? I will not.

The pain intensified. It burned from within. Carl let the pain infuse him. He didn't want to submit to anyone. Never again.

NOT TO THE WHIMS OF PETTY HUMANS. The power looked at his past submission with the same contempt and disdain that Carl did.

The pain grew until there was nothing but pain.

BUT YOU WILL SUBMIT TO **ME!**

Carl knew. Deny this, and he would *die*—his body turned to ash before it hit the floor. But if he *accepted*...

He would become *something else*.

I submit, he whispered into the void, *but only to you.*

The prime accepted.

And Carl's body began to break.

The breather mask melted into his skin, fusing like molten iron. He tore it free with a scream and toxic air rushed into his lungs.

And then, his skin began to *boil*.

Blisters swelled and popped, blood and fluid running in rivulets. Heat licked through every pore. Then came the eyes.

One burst with a wet pop. Then the other.

He howled as the world went black.

A moment later—*fire.*

Two burning marbles ignited inside his skull, where his eyes had been. He gasped and the world snapped back into view, but now it looked different.

The Ignavari in front of him became more defined, the fluid fire telling a story of a leader amongst demons having to flee a dying world. The immense pain it carried was quantified. Carl knew in that moment that the flaming historian in front of him was the largest receptacle of pain of all the Ignavari on the planet.

Glowing red-white threads connected the prime to Malik who lay nearby—a conduit of shared agony. Carl looked down and saw his own thread.

And others. Hundreds. Thousands. Flowing through the rock and magma, webbing the world.

A network of pain.

Carl's ember eyes swept about the room. The curios, locked in each of the tiny shelves, looked different now. Each lit in a rainbow of colors of the visible spectrum as well as some new reds, deep and dark, he'd never seen before.

The embers burning in his sockets brought knowledge. He *knew* now.

The fire didn't just destroy. When these materials were consumed by the Igni, the absorption would enhance them into a new form of being. Not power, but a possibility, a chance for the Igni to imbue themselves with significance native to this world.

The prime called it pyrochromancy.

The significance seared into him from the pain link. When burned, the trace materials infused the Igni with understanding and power. Burn the material, earn the power of the burned. Metals burned for the longest, so they proved most useful, but knowledge could be gained from materials which burned fast too.

The deeper he reached, the more secrets unfurled. And then, the link snapped.

The prime severed the connection, withholding the answers Carl wasn't ready for yet.

A taste was all he'd get.

Malik steadied Carl when the searing link severed. Their ember eyes locked.

"You have your orders?" Malik asked.

Carl nodded. The answer was etched in fire behind his eyes.

He resisted the urge to reach for the flames now burning atop his head—flames that rose in defiance of wind or motion, dancing vertically no matter which way he turned. His scalp still screamed from the molten transformation, but the agony had settled into something deeper. Familiar. Constant pain was just another form of clarity.

Malik bent down and plucked up the remnants of Carl's melted breather mask, letting it drip between his fingers like tar. Then he turned and led the way out.

Carl followed, but said nothing until they emerged into the shade of the Droughtspire peaks. The air was dry and stung like guilt. "How do

I turn back to human form?" Carl asked.

Malik's laugh crackled like a campfire receiving a new log. "Always the first question. Come."

They hiked a jagged trail to a rocky bluff where a penned enclosure waited, holding a half-dozen desert goats. The animals shifted uneasily at their approach.

Without a word, Malik opened the gate and dragged one out—a black-horned buck that bleated in protest, trembling with instinctive dread.

Carl watched, breath shallow, as Malik pulled the goat into a secluded corner. He dropped to his knees, gripped the goat's horns, and locked eyes with the animal. A low growl vibrated in his throat, and suddenly the air shimmered.

The goat bucked and screamed, hooves gouging the dirt. But Malik didn't let go. The goat's screams turned pleading.

The heat rippled outward.

The goat's hide blackened and cracked. Its eyes bulged, shimmered, popped with a sickening squelch. When Malik stood, releasing the goat's ashen skull, he was human again.

The wiry man turned to Carl. "Your turn."

Carl caught and easily restrained another goat with his new strength. He led it bodily to the smaller enclosure. He knelt like Malik, holding the goat's head in his hands.

"You have to consume the essence of the goat. Send your fire into it, but also your pain," Malik coached. "And not just *your* pain, but the prime's pain."

Carl felt the goat heat up under his hands. It began to scream so he consumed its mouth first.

"Wait!" Malik cautioned. "Leave the eyes intact. You have to look into its eyes as you consume it. Keep a clear image of them. As the remnants of your flame consumes the goat, you *have* to reimagine those eyes back in your head."

Carl felt the goat burn to cinders with the last of his flame. He stood and the desert took on its regular, khaki hues again. He turned to Malik. "How'd I do."

Malik laughed. "You'll get better at it, I promise. It's a lot easier when you consume a human."

Carl frowned. He thought he did pretty well. He looked at his arms. They were covered in a layer of white fur—was that wool? He felt an odd sensation on his head and reached up to find the small nubbins of horns growing from his skull.

"When we take a life, we take on some of the properties of what we consume. When you get better at it you'll be able to differentiate and choose which qualities you take from your target. By consuming the goat, you'll notice you have greater balance and stamina than before."

"What do I do with the furry arms and the stupid horns?" Carl asked, slightly frantic.

Malik's eyes lit up with humor. "They will fade completely in a day or two, but so will the positive qualities of endurance and agility. The enhancements we gain from consumption are temporary. You're welcome to take your waxer form again and consume another goat, but I wouldn't recommend it."

"Why not?" Carl asked.

"Each transition takes a lot of energy," said Malik. "You gain most of it back from the living creature you consume, but not all. Transform to waxer and back and I doubt you'll be able to travel for at least a day, even with the goat's stamina enhancement."

"And you're sure I'll be free of the fur and horns by the time I get back to Dawnford?"

"It won't take that long," said Malik. "Since you weren't selective about the goat's enhancements, you got a tiny bit of all of them. When you're more selective, you'll be able to choose the ones you want and they will last a lot longer. I only accepted the goat's stamina, which should be with me for about a week. Since you took all of them, they'll start disappearing in a couple of hours."

Carl scowled at the man. "I'm going to hold you to that."

Malik smirked before his face turned serious. "Be ready for the next phase of our master's plan."

He turned and walked away.

Weeks turned to months.

Carl honed his new life in secret—testing his waxer form whenever he could escape the compound. Always in the desert, always in the burning daylight, where no one would see him embracing the pain, surrendering to the hate, letting the prime Igni's anguish ignite his body into something *more*.

Turning *back*? That was the hard part.

Malik hadn't mentioned the cost. The transition required a life force of equal power to anchor Carl's humanity. Bugs, lizards, rodents— they weren't enough. The smallest form he could use was a desert coyote and those were hard to catch even with his increased speed and strength as a waxer. Each shift was a gamble.

When the pirates attacked, Camlock's little brat, Finn, ruined the surprise. Less compounders lost their lives than should have.

In the aftermath of the attack, Carl made sure to stumble across the Warhog.

He reached out tentatively to the core of the large crawler. He expected a complicated interface or that he'd have to break through some defenses, but the Meld was surprisingly easy.

After communing with the prime Igni any connection was easy, Carl supposed.

He accepted the surprised praise of Ronin Tyre and Marsha Slug, and several other minor Melders in the compound. He also accepted their training. Ronin taught him the basics of using the control bar, while Marsha took him through the specifics of running a crawler.

Ronin was too busy to be suspicious and was thrilled to have another crawler driver become part of the compound. Marsha however seemed leery of his new power to Meld. Anytime she thought he wasn't looking, she would stare at him, calculating, like she was trying to understand what made this revitalized Carl Stinz tick.

Something he did *not* want her to find out.

He disabled the other crawler, the Badmash, right after the pirate attack. It was a simple sabotage of two of the wheel hubs, easy to blame on the pirates. His sabotage won him the chance to drive the candidates out to the Iron Mountain on their pilgrimage.

He accepted a final lesson from Marsha who insisted after the Leadsled failed an inspection.

Once Carl had the basics, he steered well clear of the perceptive Marsha Slug—something which would burn him badly in the days to come—especially after the horrible drive back to the compound in the midst of the nova-storm.

Thanks to the frustratingly handy Camlock whelp, the plan to have the entire pilgrimage die in the nova-storm failed. On top of that failure, Carl could not find the device the Igni were looking for in the depths of the Iron Mountain.

He had to think fast to discredit Finn's accomplishments and create a smear campaign against the little spit to get him kicked out of the compound.

He was forced to lure old man Crankhelm out of the compound one night to consume him. The man was deep in the throes of the flux sickness so no one would be surprised if he wandered off to die in the sands. Luckily, the man's forty years of politicking made him an incredible fount of persuasion and knowledge of everyone in the compound.

Carl greedily sucked up the essences of the old man, careful not to touch anything else when he morphed back to human. He put that knowledge and skill to immediate use in creating divisions within the compound.

Content with the chaos he created, he eagerly looked forward to the next step in his plan which would take place during Finn's trial.

Dealing with the Dead Crows and his erstwhile wife once and for all.

26

Bloommother

"Is he going to be okay?" Amara's voice was laced with panic. "Our healers couldn't find anything wrong with him, but he's still so cold. He's not...warming up."

"He remains dangerously chilled," came a voice—female, calm and melodic. I didn't recognize it. "And there's something else. Something...missing." A pause. "Lord Draven, please hand me the king's wort and the blood nettle."

I heard the soft clink of ceramic pots, the shuffle of hurried hands.

"Not that one—yes, *that* one," the woman corrected, still gently.

"I'm so relieved you were still here, Bloommother," Amara said, her voice stretched thin with exhaustion. "I thought you'd already returned to the Veil. We've all been so worried."

I wanted to know who Amara was talking about. Whoever it was clearly mattered to her. My heart twisted in dread.

Valdrath?

I tried to move—lift my head, twitch a finger, anything. But my body remained locked in stillness. My limbs were iron. My eyes sealed.

Then it hit me.

She wasn't talking about someone else. She was talking about *me*.

Panic surged.

I tried to scream, to reach outward with my perception, but the pulse faded into emptiness like shouting into a cavern. No echo. No reply.

Rhee! I shouted into the void of my mind. *Tell me what is going on!*

No answer.

Helplessness closed around me like a vice.

I heard the grind of pestle and mortar, the murmur of words in an ancient tongue that echoed with strange harmony. Then something hot touched my lips. I couldn't feel the cup—just the warmth. A moment later, liquid poured into my mouth, flooding my throat as a hand gently massaged my neck.

Heat burst in my belly. Then the fire came.

It raged through me, tearing through frozen veins and brittle muscles. The pain was unbearable. A thousand needles stabbing from the inside out. I wanted to thrash, to scream, but I was a prisoner in my own body.

And yet...it was something. After the numbness, the pain was proof that I still existed. That I wasn't gone.

But it burned. Stars, it burned.

The pain shifted, tingled, until it felt like my entire body was waking up wrong, like when a limb goes numb and then surges back with static. Except this was my entire self. Every twitching nerve drained me further, every pulse of sensation like a toll paid in strength.

It was too much. Voices blurred. The world receded into shadows.

Darkness took me again.

A slam. A door opening.

I hovered at the edge of waking.

"Princess!" the woman's gentle voice returned—closer now, scented with lilacs. "Have you been here all night? Sitting vigil won't help the Grounder."

"His *name* is Finn!" Amara snapped, then faltered. "I—I'm sorry, Healer Moonsong. Bloommother. I'm just...I'm not myself."

"I understand," Moonsong said, her voice dipping even softer. "There's nothing more wrenching than watching someone you care about suffer."

Amara's breath hitched. "I can't lose him. Not now. Not after Calder." Her voice wavered. "As much as we fought...losing my brother...ripped something out of me. All those memories from when we were children—happy, bright—now they feel broken...splintered. And now with Finn, lying there like this..."

She trailed off, broken.

I felt like I was intruding on a private conversation. A conversation about *me*. I wanted to speak up, to say, "I'm here. Stop, before you say something you'll be embarrassed by later!"

But I couldn't.

"I can't," Amara whispered. "I *can't* lose him too."

"He means a great deal to you," Moonsong said softly.

Silence stretched.

"Yes," Amara finally breathed. "He does. We've grown...close."

She let out a long sigh. "A princess isn't allowed friends. Not really. Sure, I mingle with the other noble children but every one of them has an agenda. Not Finn. He's...genuine. You can look at his face and know what he is thinking. He's never been taught to hide his emotion behind a mask. It's..." She paused searching for the word.

"Refreshing? Endearing? Tantalizingly different?" Healer Moonsong offered. "Have you ever told him how you felt about him?"

"Of course not," said Amara. "It wouldn't be proper. It also wouldn't be fair...to him...or to me."

I had no idea she felt this way. I tried desperately to squirm, to make some sort of movement so they knew I was here. Listening in on something like this felt so wrong.

"Why?" asked the Bloommother.

"You mean outside of the obvious? Because I'm a princess who's supposed to marry for station and advantage?"

"Yes, besides the obvious. Because who knows, the Grounder may very well be the equivalent of a prince of one of their compounds. We need strong alliances with those on the surface and I'd be shocked if this extraordinary young man didn't have parents in some position of power."

"Besides the obvious then. I don't *want* anything...more with him."

That hurt. I never really thought I had a chance with the princess anyway, but to hear her say it so bluntly was the death knell to the slim hope something might happen between us.

"Are you sure?" asked the Bloommother.

"I'm sure. He couldn't handle the world of the court. All the infighting, the backbiting, the political machinations, the jockeying for power. It's awful."

"I don't know about that. He seems like a capable young man."

"I didn't mean it like that. I mean it would change him. The thing I love about Finn is his open curiosity, his childlike wonder. He hasn't grown jaded like the other prats in the court. I won't be the one to crush that."

"We all change, princess," said Healer Moonsong. "And it's not always for the worst."

There was no answer. Just a soft sigh—and the sound of fabric shifting as Amara moved.

"Enough about me," Amara said, her voice regaining its strength. "How is he? Will he recover?"

Fingers brushed my forehead, warm. Gentle. I felt them now. A whisper of touch on my neck.

It was the first *real* thing I'd felt.

"His color is good," Moonsong said. "And his temperature's

improving. Promising signs. But...if young Valdrath Marsten is right, that creature you fought didn't just damage his body—it *took* something."

"Took what?"

"Something vital," the Bloommother said carefully. "I don't know if you're a believer, but the Church would call it 'core essence.' The nugget of truth which makes us...*us.*"

"Do you believe that?"

"I believe we each have a life thread—unique, and delicate. There's a reason why no two flowers are exactly alike. Some are stretched. Some are knotted. Some are fraying. But they are ours alone."

Amara was silent. Then: "Can someone live without it?"

There was a pause. Then a soft hand rested on my chest.

"Not for long."

"And if it's damaged?" Her voice dropped to a whisper. "Shattered?" Another pause. "Can it be healed?"

"I don't really know," the Bloommother said softly. "Over the years, I've seen a few things help. The first is *purpose*. A reason to pour the last ember of your essence into fixing what's broken. The second..." She hesitated. "Is a reminder of what makes that person unique. What makes them *them.*"

Purpose? I had it in spades. I had to stop the waxers. I had to bring down the Igni. Aubrey believed I could. I was training, learning, improving. The world of Ashara *needed* me.

I focused everything I had into that truth. I poured myself into it.

I tried to move. Nothing happened.

"So what do we do now?" Amara asked, voice ragged.

"Now," the Bloommother said, "we wait. His body's willing. But it's not enough. He needs to find that missing spark himself. In the meantime, Princess, you need rest. The kingdom needs you strong."

"Thank you, Bloommother," Amara replied. "But I'm not ready to leave him. Not yet."

"As you will, Your Highness." Footsteps softened. The door clicked shut.

Silence.

Then a hand wrapped around mine. Not tentative. Not gentle. A firm, desperate grip.

I wanted to scream—yes! I feel that!—but my body refused.

I felt her breath, warm and shaky, brush against my cheek. "Finn," she whispered, "if you're still in there, I want you to know..."

Her lips brushed my ear—so light, so real it ached.

"I love your curiosity. The way you care even when it makes no sense. I love that you *fight* to understand. That nothing is ever 'a few feet away' to you—it's always 'two feet, three inches.' I love your determination, the way you get up no matter how many times you're knocked down. I love the way you look at me. *See* me."

Her voice caught. "I love how you listen—really listen. How you don't treat me like royalty, but just like...*me*."

Something lit in my chest.

A spark.

"I don't want you back just to stop the waxers. Or to save the kingdom. I want you back because...I'm better when you're with me. And I don't want to face this world without you."

Her hand found my cheek, callused fingers brushing away what I couldn't shed.

The spark became a flame.

Her breath slid across my face, stopping *just* shy of my lips.

I gave everything—*everything*—to close that tiny gap.

And then her lips met mine.

The flame in my belly turned to a bonfire.

My finger twitched—*moved*—and brushed her chest. I felt the hammering of her heart, in time with my own.

My eyes fluttered. Light. Movement. *Her.*

She leaned in, and the kiss deepened, burning through the numbness, lighting up every nerve in my body like dawn setting fire to the horizon.

And then my hand moved—truly moved—threading behind her neck. I pulled her closer as our lips danced with everything left unsaid.

I didn't know how it was possible for a kiss to last an eternity and no time at all. This one did.

And then it broke, reluctantly.

I opened my eyes. Her amethyst gaze hit me like gravity.

I tried to speak. My voice came out like rust scraped from metal. "Thank you. For bringing me back. I would have been lost without you."

She kissed me again.

This one was sunshine.

She touched my lips with her fingertips—tiny sparks leapt from her skin to mine.

"Thank *you,*" she said. "The world's brighter with you in it."

I shifted—and winced. My limbs still wouldn't obey.

"I can't move most of me," I croaked.

She smiled—*that* smile—and brushed my brow. "You were a breath from death, Finn. Four days you've been like this. One twitch is a miracle. We'll take it."

I tried to laugh. A dry wheeze came out. "That kiss was more than a...twitch."

"Sleep," she whispered, voice like velvet.

I pointed at her with my one good finger on my one good arm. "Only if you sleep too."

She kissed me once more. "I'll be back in the morning."

Darkness took me—but this time it was gentle.

Well, well, look who's up, came the voice in my head.

Rhee! I shouted into my mind. *I thought you were dead.*

I'm not that easy to kill, she said.

What happened?

Long story, Rhee said. *That cinderfen hag was one nasty piece of work. Whatever death curse she sent your way was meant to steal your life force to replace her own.*

Was she successful? I asked. *I kind of missed the last part of the fight. I thought we'd killed her.*

Only partly. Quick thinking on that auditory shield you made. Draven lopped her nasty, tentacled head off right as I killed her connection to your life force, said Rhee.

What do you mean? I said.

I had to divert the last spark of your life force into my memory banks, said Aubrey. *When I did that, it put me into hibernation. I put a failsafe in place to transfer the life force back to your nervous system but it needed a spark to jumpstart it.*

Like what? I asked.

500 volts would do it, but a powerful emotion could do the job too. And since I don't see any 'lectric power around here, what was it?

What was what? I asked, playing as dumb as I knew how.

The strong emotion that brought you back.

Nothing you need know about, I said.

Her laugh filled my head. *Oh Finn, the whole kingdom has been waiting for the two of you to kiss. Do you think I wouldn't have felt that? It's about time by the way.*

Hey, I can feel my other hand now, I said as way of changing the subject. *I must be getting better.*

Keep taking whatever that healer lady is giving you and I'll continue repairing stuff from in here. We'll get you tip top in no time.

I smiled when the Bloommother entered, her expression tight with hope and surprise.

"Thank you for saving my life," I said, lifting myself with my good arm.

She checked my vitals with swift, practiced hands. "You did the hard part."

Her touch found my neck, chest, underarms. She gave a small, satisfied hum.

"Drink this," she said, holding out a vial. "If the rest of you responds as well as that arm, we might even get you out of here by tomorrow."

27

The Song

I took *two brutal weeks* before I could stand on my own. Two weeks of aching muscles, bone-deep fatigue, and relying on Val or Amara just to shuffle across the room. While I was still trapped in that brakking bed, Val brought me three more packets from Professor Cloud.

"And tell him," Val said in a passable imitation of the professor's voice, "that he will be tested *immediately* upon return. We *cannot* have him falling behind."

It earned a weak laugh from me. Val grinned like he'd won a prize.

Spin and Rojer sent some design ideas for Rach. Spin included her seeker golem schematics and, to my surprise, asked for my input. I was touched. I scrawled notes in the margins, and Val—perhaps a little *too* eager—snatched them up to deliver.

Amara watched him go, a knowing glint in her eye. "I think he's a little smitten with Miss Korra Jex."

It took me a beat to remember that was Spin's real name. Of course, *Amara* would use it. Formality clung to her like a royal cloak she didn't know how to take off.

That same formality was a kingdom-sized impediment to advancing whatever there was between us.

The moment I could stand without help, I waited and picked the right time.

I stumbled into a small alcove not too far from the healer's quarters in the castle. When she followed me with concern, I regained my bearings and looked her directly in the eyes. I swept a stray piece of hair from her face and went in for a kiss, backing her against the stone wall.

She responded hungrily—for one point three seconds.

Then she pushed me away.

"Finn, I can't," she said, her voice tight. "I have a duty. A kingdom. Princesses don't get to have...dalliances."

"I know," I said softly. "I've been trying to find the right time to tell you something, but we haven't had a moment alone since...since that last kiss."

She nodded, and I watched the princess mask slide into place like armor. "That was intentional."

She took a breath, then pointed from herself to me and back. "This, we, can't work. So don't say something clever or rakish to change my mind."

"You find me rakish?" I smirked, forcing it even as my heart cracked a little.

Her mask faltered for half a heartbeat. Then returned.

"I'm serious, Finn. Those kisses were a mistake. I care for you, but I don't think of you that way."

I shook my head. "I'm sorry, princess, but it's only fair that you know I heard everything you told the Bloommother."

Her eyes widened. "That was very private stuff!"

I nodded. "I know, but it's not like I could do anything about it. I couldn't move, couldn't see, couldn't even feel. All I could do was hear. Even when you guys were talking I tried to yell, 'stop! Don't share in front of me,' but I was stuck."

She took a couple of deep breaths as she tried to patch together her regal princess mask. "My feelings on this, on you, are irrelevant in the face of my duty to the kingdom."

"And if I'm actually a Grounder prince?" I asked.

The corner of her mouth twitched. "Are you?"

"Of course. My lineage goes back fourteen generations to King Camlock the First."

She snorted. "Right. And your people banish their princes?"

"Only the really exceptional ones," I said. "It's part of the princely trials."

That earned me a playful shove. It was better than the awkwardness between us since the kisses on the Bloommother's table.

"Why tell me?" she asked. "Why not keep that knowledge and use it?"

"Because I heard the rest too, the part about the court," I said. "That's not me. Not telling you wouldn't have been fair."

She studied me for a long, quiet moment, then threaded her fingers through mine.

"Are you okay just being friends?" She gave my hand a squeeze and grinned. "At least until your patents of nobility clear the censors?"

I smiled. "I'll take what I can get. As long as it's *close* friends."

It hurt, but at least I understood where she was coming from. I knew she had feelings for me and that would have to be enough for now.

Besides, we were both too busy to dedicate any time pursuing something further right now.

Keep telling yourself that and maybe it will come true, Aubrey piped in.

It's the only thing keeping me from banging my head against the wall right now, okay? Let me have this.

Aubrey began to whistle—a piercing melody, a dirge—which made me feel worse while also making we want to sneeze, like something stuck in my sinuses.

Rhee!

Fine, but this isn't over, she said.

I arrived at the G&L guild two hours before class started to take the qualifying exam. We met in Professor Cloud's personal lab.

The professor had nearly as many optical tables set up as in our practice lab. Strewn amongst them were a series of mirrors, lenses, shades, prisms, slit boards, and light sources. My gaze took in all of it and I wished I understood more about what she was researching.

I smiled when I saw the professor.

The smile died on my lips when guildmaster Farsmith stood from a crouching position behind one of the lab tables where he analyzed Cloud's research.

"Do you mind if I stay for the exam?" Farsmith asked.

To her credit, Cloud looked to me before answering.

I shrugged. "Sure, it would be nice to have another body in the room in case I get attacked again."

Farsmith's lips curled into something like a snarl. "And thank you for running straight to the king after I asked you not to."

I didn't blink. "Thirty-six hours, twelve minutes, eighteen seconds *after*, to be precise. Precision matters, right? Or has the guild forgotten its own motto?"

Cloud's mouth *almost* twitched into a smile. Almost.

Farsmith's sneer deepened. "Shame Grounders never learned the concept of respect."

"Oh, we've got respect. We just don't hand it out to anyone with a fancy title."

"Gentlemen," interrupted Cloud. "We are cutting into valuable test time."

Cloud led me over to a table which had all the optical equipment a budding G&L student would ever need. On the table in front of me were several barriers of different heights which had been erected into something which resembled a maze.

"Finn, your job is to move light from that light source," she pointed to a light box on one side of the table which led into the first "hallway" of the maze. "All the way to this light sensitive paper. You have to use the tools in front of you to demonstrate you understand the concept of refraction and reflection. Extra credit will be given if you can also demonstrate some form of diffraction and interference. Is the task understood?"

I nodded. It sounded like fun.

"With one caveat," Farsmith added, voice oily. "You must score the paper with a luminosity no less than seventy percent of the starting light source."

Professor Cloud's brow pinched in disapproval. "This is my class and my test, guildmaster. That condition was not applied to the others."

Farsmith's smile was all venom. "Well, I'm sure our young prodigy," the man spat the word, "can handle it. Can't you, Master Camlock?"

I looked at the maze, then the equipment in front of me. Oh yeah, I can do this.

Of course we can, said Rhee.

"I'll do my best," I said, refusing to give the guildmaster the satisfaction of a firm, "challenge accepted."

I went to work. I pulsed my perception outward. I hit the initial light source first. Light energy was different than sound. It had the potential to act in a wave-like manner, but it didn't always act that way which is what made it so interesting to follow.

The maze wasn't the challenge, not really.

The layout came together in my mind. A series of mirrors with a single lens to refract the light, focusing it up the small incline the professor set. I knew the correct angles in my head, though Rhee helped me get the placements exact. I sketched the pattern down quickly, adding a little math to make sure the luminosity wouldn't drop too much in the dispersion section of the maze.

I wasn't sure why this was so easy for me to do in my head, but the combination of my perception and Rhee's help with the precision of the angles made the problem trivial.

Then I flipped the light on, and everything changed.

A deep, resonant *thrum* filled the air. It wasn't loud. Not exactly. It felt like sound inside my bones. Inside my blood.

"What is that?" I asked, squinting toward the humming box. "That *sound*."

Professor Cloud tilted her head, puzzled. "What sound?"

I turned it off. Silence. Turned it on. *Thrum.*

"From the light source," I said.

"I'm sorry Master Camlock, I can't hear anything," said Professor Cloud.

Odd. I glanced at Farsmith out of the corner of my eye. He looked puzzled too. Could they really not hear it?

Whatever you're sensing is not within the auditory range, Rhee said into my head.

You can't hear it either?

Not yet, but I should be able to hear anything you do. Still tweaking some sensors, Aubrey said.

Most light sources were based on heat. The flame from a torch was an obvious one, but if you heated up a small metal filament, it also emitted light along with heat energy.

I turned the light on again and held my hand over it. I could barely feel any heat. "What's this light source, Professor?"

She furrowed her brow. "Core energy."

"Meaning it has been core crafted to create light?"

She shook her head. "No, it has a static link to the core."

I frowned. "To what core?"

"The core of the planet," she said, surprised by the question, as if the answer should be obvious.

No one had ever told me that. Core crafting didn't just draw on magical fuel—it was *tethered* to something deeper. Older.

My heart hammered. I erased my initial plan. I needed to know more. Time to improvise.

I diverted the beam with a mirror, redirected it into an open section of the table. Then I added a concave lens. The thrum rose in pitch.

Switched it for a convex. It dropped like a moan. So strange.

Rhee?

It's singing, I said. *You're hearing the light sing.*

I needed more.

"Can I use a prism?" I asked Professor Cloud.

She hesitated. "That's not part of the test."

"Please."

She handed one over, and I placed it with shaking hands.

The beam split. And so did the sound.

Eight distinct tones rang out in perfect harmony, like a choir of crystals singing in color. Each spectrum sang its own note, higher or lower depending on refraction, and the deeper reds resonated in my chest like memory.

My fingers flew, driven by instinct. I layered filters, focused lenses, and mirrors—some splitting waves, others merging them. As I manipulated the light, the melody twisted, deepened, soared into something alien and ancient and beautiful.

You only have ten minutes left, Rhee said into my mind. *Finish it.*

I snapped out of the trance. The song faded as I reassembled the beams, funneling the combined light down the maze's final corridor.

The light struck the paper.

And in a flash—not bright, but felt—something moved through me. A pulse of power that made my skin prickle and my breath hitch.

I stepped back and stared.

On the paper was a symbol. A sphere cracked in the center, light bursting from the crack.

I flipped the light source off.

The pulse vanished.

Turned it back on.

The energy returned, stronger. Buzzing beneath my skin like lightning with no storm.

Then I looked up, and *saw*.

Around Professor Cloud was a blue aura, glowing faint but steady, like starlight through fog. Her mouth was parted in awe.

Farsmith had one too, twisted and sickly, a vortex of muddy red and swamp-green coiling like an infection around his shoulders.

"What...is this?" I whispered.

I stepped away from my creation and looked down at the table. The work I'd been doing in the engineering guild must have been lingering in my mind because what I saw as the result of my experimentation looked just like a—

"Master Camlock, did you create an optical circuit?" Professor Cloud asked, looking down at the table.

I nodded numbly. "I think it was influenced by my work in engineering."

"Fascinating," she said. "What does it do?"

"Still working that out, professor," I mumbled. "For the moment it just creates the symbol at the end."

"Pointless grandstanding," muttered Farsmith. He stormed out of the room.

"Very impressive, young man," Cloud said. That aura around her pulsed, the blue more defined.

I zoned out the praise and stared down at the circuit. It *was* impressive. Did this mean I could harness the power from the core even if I couldn't summon it like core crafters could?

I wish I could show it to Dain to get his take. I'd ask Rojer later. No, who I really wanted to ask was Ravic. Because, the instant that deep, soul-echoing *thrum* hit me, I thought of Ravic. Of his obsession with the First Song.

Could it be?

If the First Song which lay at Ravic's core belief was rooted in sound, was it possible the Last Song was created by light?

I need answers, I whispered into my mind.

Then let's start asking questions, said Rhee.

28

The Report

I pushed through the rest of lab that afternoon like a man possessed, laser-focused, every motion driven by the need to build. I had to recreate the phenomenon from Cloud's test table before the memory of it faded into dream. My hands moved with purpose, assembling lenses, mirrors, focusing mounts, and filters with a speed and precision that made even the apprentices slow down to watch.

Snide laughter trickled through the air like rot.

Renaux and his noble lapdogs were at it again, voices oozing contempt as I passed.

"Still limping, are we?"

"Careful, he might smear that mongrel blood all over the optics."

"Unpure coy-dog."

I didn't even flinch.

If anything, they were *less* creative than the stuff Jay and Arken used to cook up. And that was saying something. These idiots were amateurs.

I'd grown a very thick skin growing up in Dawnford.

Still, a few of their jabs hit Valdrath harder than they did me.

"As if any of them could last five minutes against a cinderfen hag," Val growled, jaw tight, fists clenched.

"Let it go," I said, placing a calming hand on his forearm. "Bullies hate being ignored. It drives them nuts."

His nostrils flared. "I could take a stroll into the Murkmire tonight. Find a snake. Maybe drop it in Renaux's bath."

I laughed. "I can't believe I missed that prank growing up."

But the laughter faded quickly. The pressure building in my chest was more than annoyance. It was urgency—like something unseen was coiling closer. Whatever that light circuit was, whatever I'd stumbled on in Cloud's lab...it wasn't just science. It was important.

And we were running out of time.

Val slammed a fist on the table, optics jumping from the vibration. "I think I'm gonna call it early. Don't know why this crap's getting to me so much. Maybe because the ones who talk the loudest are always the ones who've risked the least."

"Don't forget," I said, lowering my voice, "we've got that meeting later. We need our heads clear." I raised a brow. The king had invited Val to our next strategy session. The smug nobles didn't need to know we were meeting with the king though.

"Got it." Val nodded. "I'll be there."

"Val! Good to see you, lad," the king said. A genuine smile broke through the haggard expression he wore anytime we met these days.

I didn't envy the weight on his shoulders—goblins, waxers, looming war with Thal'Naris—and tonight, we were about to add a church conspiracy on to his lap

Val bowed—not his usual lazy dip, but a full, respectful gesture. That alone spoke volumes. "Your Majesty. Your Highness," he added with a nod to the queen.

Her eyes, sharp and royal, softened. "Our daughter tells us you saved her life on the Murkmire's edge. We owe you thanks, Earl Marsten."

"Only after she saved mine," Val said with a small smile. "That night was....difficult."

The king glanced between us with warmth that quickly cooled into royal command. "You three make a formidable team," he said. "And I'm grateful for it. But I'm afraid we must get on to business. Amara, your mother says you've been sitting on dangerous intelligence since before I returned from the Veil. Out with it."

Amara shared everything Drake told us before dying in the Nightbriar.

"That is...concerning," said the king. He leaned forward in his chair and pinned Amara with a stare. "And you believe this Drake? The gangster? That the Potentate of Thal'Naris was meeting with goblins and a...waxer?"

Amara's jaw was set. Controlled. "I do. I can't think of a reason why Drake would lie about such a thing. He seemed genuinely spooked by the idea of these Righteous Few, these cultists, coming to Alyndor. His contact in Thal'Naris convinced him it wasn't a matter of whether they would make their way here, but when."

The king frowned. "What did he gain from telling *you*?"

"A debt," Amara said. "We saved his sister in Drumsorrow. That matters in his world. He wasn't being noble. He was being smart. If this cult Drake was talking about, these Righteous Few, spreads? It'll start with his people—the poor, the invisible. He wanted a chance to survive."

"And why *you*?" the king pressed. "Why not come to the crown himself?"

Amara inhaled deeply. "He was having Finn followed."

I tensed, caught off guard.

"I thought Drake might be part of the conspiracy," she continued. "Trying to manipulate Finn, maybe use him against us. But now I believe he meant to pass the information through him. To me. I just happened to be in the right place at the right time."

I stared at Amara, wide-eyed. Not just from surprise, from awe.

The depth of her thinking, the clarity with which she laid it bare under pressure, it shook me a little. She'd dropped hints before, sure. Told me to assume I was always being followed. But I'd never really believed it. Not until now.

She'd *known* I was being tailed.

All that talk about transparency between us? It only went one way— *hers*. That stung. A part of me wanted to be furious. But if she *had* told me, would Drake have approached at all?

She was right about one thing: I was out of my depth when it came to the court. Whatever game she was playing, she was ten steps ahead.

The king's gaze narrowed as he studied his daughter—measured, calculating. Then he slowly nodded.

"We heard whispers of these cultists while I was in the Veil," he said, his voice low and heavy. "I don't know the Potentate personally, but I find it hard to believe the Church would stoop so low as to ally with waxers. A man can fall to corruption, yes—but an entire *institution*? That takes decades. I can't believe the Oracle would turn against us."

"You could ask her," said the queen quietly. There was something pointed in her voice.

The king's eyes flickered with an emotion I couldn't quite place. Regret? Hesitation?

"We've known each other a long time," he admitted, gravely. "Perhaps I should."

He shifted his gaze to Amara again. "And what of your brother's warning—*beware the melt*? Did Drake say anything about that?"

Amara shook her head, lips pursed.

The king's jaw tightened. "I can't shake the feeling we're missing a piece of the puzzle. Maybe it's just a warning about the waxers. But with all this talk of cleansing...I fear it goes deeper."

A grim look passed between king and queen. Silent, loaded. Whatever it meant, we weren't invited into it.

Then his tone turned brisk. "Tell me about these Murkmire beasts."

Amara stood taller. "It started when Val found two dead unicorns on the edge of the swamp. Brutally dissected. Experimented on. Burned from the inside."

The king's face darkened. "It takes a foul heart to harm such noble creatures."

"And the ones you fought?"

"They weren't normal Murkmire beasts," Amara said. Then she turned to me.

I stepped forward. "They ran hot, your majesty. You know I have some skill to perceive life forms and their temperatures. The boglings, they ran as hot as goblins. But the cinderfen hag? She radiated like a waxer."

The king's expression didn't change, but the tension in the room coiled tighter. "And what do you think it means, Master Camlock?"

I swallowed. "Nothing good, sir. I don't know anything for certain, but if I had to guess, I would say these beasts are being changed by the waxers, or something else allied with the Igni. Add the dead unicorns and...?"

The words hung heavy in the air.

"And there's more," Amara added, almost reluctantly. "Before the ambush... Finn believes he saw an essentia vapor in the trees. One that looked exactly like my cousin Renaux's."

The queen's eyes widened. "Renaux? Drennic's boy?"

Amara nodded. "I tried to convince Finn all core constructs look alike but—"

"But I know what I saw," I interrupted. "Your majesty, I've seen enough core constructs by now to know that while they might look alike, they have very distinct energy signatures. I've only seen Renaux's vapor twice, but I'm convinced what I saw in the wood was the same construct."

The king leaned forward, eyes narrowing. "How sure?"

"Ninety-five percent," I said.

The weight of that number settled on the room like a tombstone.

"That's not enough to shackle a duke's heir," the king said, voice like a drawn blade. "Not yet."

He hesitated, then turned to Val. "What do you know of this?"

Val cleared his throat. "Renaux's been saying things in class, your majesty. About purity. About cleansing. A lot of the same twisted rhetoric we're hearing out of Thal'Naris. I thought he was just being a smug prat, but lately...it's gotten darker."

The king's eyes narrowed, burning with intensity. "That *is* concerning."

He stood, slowly. "Keep an eye on him. Both of you. Don't confront him. Don't warn his father. If something's festering under the duke's roof, I'll root it out myself."

He paced to the door, the weight of his decision pressing on every step. His hand touched the handle—then paused.

He looked back at us.

"Thank you. All of you. This is no longer a matter of suspicion—it's war in slow motion. And it's already begun."

He opened the door, then turned back one last time, voice iron and fire.

"Watch each other's backs."

29

Light Training

I slipped into bed that night exhausted. I was healing well but everything took more energy than normal and my schedule hadn't let up even a little. I closed my eyes and—

We've been too lax with training while you've healed. It's time.

I didn't argue. She was right. The threats around us were too numerous, too strong, and I knew they weren't about to take a break.

I'm ready.

I opened my eyes to the familiar sight of the North Bailey in Dawnford. A wave of homesickness rippled through me, hitting much harder than I expected. I spun and took it in. It was the North Bailey but it wasn't really the place I trained in so many months ago. The walls were empty of soldiers and I couldn't hear the steady murmur of the community around me.

This was different from previous training where I was plopped into one of Robert Cross's memories. This felt staged, more of a simulation.

That's because it is, Rhee said. *If we are going to train with light, who better to train against than a heliurgist?*

A familiar figure stepped into the ring: the Jackal. The same wily trader I'd befriended before everything spiraled during our trip down to the Dusker kingdom. He looked just like I remembered, down to the crooked grin and that annoying sparkle in his eyes.

"Young Camlock," he said. "I'll be your trainer tonight."

My trainer? The Jackal performed admirably in the fight against the goblins, but he isn't the most talented heliurgist in the compound. Not even close.

This version of him is, said Rhee. *I scraped your memories of all the heliurgy you've ever seen and squeezed them into this representation of the Jackal.*

I pulsed my perception across him—flawless. From his energy signature to the way he shifted his weight.

I looked down and realized I was dressed in Robert Cross's old sparring gear. The same worn training vest, even the same sweat-wicking fabric around my wrists.

This is your show, Finn, Rhee said. *Imagine whatever weapons or armor you want to carry, and they will appear.*

I imagined my nova-blade and dagger and felt the hilts snap into my hands with satisfying weight. I imagined a training vest and felt its weight on my shoulders. I flipped on the nova-blade and the vest with a thought and they hummed to life. I hadn't felt the hum of my blade since I left the upper caverns of the Wickwater Hills.

I spun my nova-blade in a tight arc and smiled at the familiar *zimm-zumm* it made cutting through the air. Stars, I missed the sound. For a second, I glanced around, searching for Shea. Or even Jay. Or Arken.

Focus, Finn, said Rhee. *We can't afford distractions.*

I centered myself and locked eyes with the Jackal. He held only a dagger, but his confidence screamed experience. He nodded.

"Begin."

I darted forward, a feint. His hand snapped up. A burst of raw light, searing with a radiant flare. Another memory of Arken using the same move against me during one of our sparring sessions.

This time I was ready.

I closed my eyes and leaned on my perception. I could sense the Jackal, the energy he emitted bright in my awareness. Two steps forward and five different attacks flitted through my mind which could easily lay my opponent low.

The Jackal wasn't half the bladesman I was now.

But that wasn't the point of this exercise. *The null field is about the counter.* Okay, how do I counter a radiant flare?

I summoned a wide bladed dagger to my left hand, similar to Val's seax, but with a high polish. I held it in front of my eyes at a reflection angle of one point five degrees south of horizontal.

The radiant flare reflected off the blade as if it had hit a mirror and shot directly into the Jackal's eyes.

The man staggered back, and the radiant flare died.

Good, said Rhee. *Now imagine you didn't have a blade.*

Right, I needed to be more versatile. I replaced the seax-like blade with my regular dagger.

Round two. The Jackal charged. Dagger high. A second flare incoming. I summoned welding-dark goggles just in time. The world dimmed and the pain vanished.

It worked, but so what? This was *simulation-only* stuff. Useless in the real world unless I could find a way to adapt. I needed a real counter, something I could rely on. More than a trick, I needed understanding.

We lined up again. *Rhee, can you magnify my focus again, like what we did against the cinderfen hag?*

I sprang into action and the Jackal reacted. Another flare. I focused on the light waves, like I did with the sound emitted by the cinderfen. I reached, tried to *push.*

Nothing.

The light came too fast. Too wild. Even with Rhee backing me up. Even when I got the briefest glimpse of a light wave, it changed to something else—like a stream of dust particles. I couldn't find anything constant, except the burn in my eyes.

Light was trickier than sound. By a lot.

What about the science of Robert's time, Rhee? Is there a frequency of sound which can shield from light.

Rhee responded by showing me the wave. *We call the frequency ultrasound,* she said.

I pushed out a sound pulse as the Jackal attacked again. It met the flare, and scattered it. The light dispersed like mist catching wind. Dazzling, but no longer blinding.

Better. I needed to take it further.

What if instead of diffracting the light, I could create some sort of sound based prism? Could I capture the light, manipulate it like I did in the exam this morning?

The science isn't there, Rhee said. *Sound can split like light with an auditory prism, but sound can't split light that way. Try something else.*

The next round came fast. The Jackal didn't waste time, a concentrated pulse of pure light shot from his open palm, hammering my nova-vest. I staggered back.

No delay. No wind-up. Just pain. This wasn't a flare—it was a *gunshot.*

I tried to counter, but it was like reacting to lightning. Unless I predicted the moment—read it perfectly—I couldn't stop it.

I preemptively raised an ultrasound field, and that worked—sort of. The pulse was diminished, but not diffused. It still hurt.

There had to be another way. Just like I had to push with my perception to counter sound, why couldn't I figure out how to do the same thing with light?

It escaped me.

I lined up against the Jackal again. Then he switched tactics.

A flare hit the ground, boom, and suddenly three Jackals stood before me, flickering and real.

Illusions. *Real* illusions of the Jackal, all taking different stances in front of me.

I blinked. "This can't be real."

There had always been rumors of great heliurgists of the past creating detailed illusions. I'd written them off as fanciful stories.

It's technically plausible, said Rhee. *Think of the image you created this morning.*

Yes, but I had a piece of paper to project onto, what is this?

I threw three throwing knives, one at each version of the Jackal. Two passed through illusions while the third was parried by a quick reaction from the trader.

Another flash of light from the Jackal and the images moved again.

He was kicking up dust. The flares were staged to create projection surfaces.

That's brilliant.

Thank you, said Aubrey. *I thought so.*

This is all you? I asked.

Of course, but it's still an extrapolation from your memories.

You could have just told me how it worked, I said.

And robbed you of the epiphany? Do you really think telling you would have stuck?

We went again.

I threw knives—one for each image. Two passed through smoke. The third clanged steel.

I grinned. Found you.

More flares. More illusions. My simulated muscles ached. My mind throbbed. Aubrey had told me to stop an hour ago, but I *couldn't*. I was chasing something. A pattern. A rhythm.

Each burst of light—each flare and pulse—carried something deeper. A tune, almost. Like the hum of a nova-blade, or the cadence of a voice just before it breaks.

It hovered at the edge of my awareness, a song I knew but couldn't remember.

Frustration burned in my gut. So close. The answer was *right there.*

The Jackal raised a hand.

I squared up again. Breathing hard. Drenched in sweat, even in the simulation.

What am I missing? What am I not seeing?

No answer came.

Only the lingering echo of a melody I couldn't hum, but somehow knew by heart.

I didn't even remember drifting off to sleep.

30

Core Switch

"bvi," Spindle said. "Creating core lights is kinda my gem, if you catch my sparkle."

I had no idea what she meant, but it sounded positive. "So...can you make me one?"

"I don't know," she said. "The real question is what can you do for me?"

I frowned. I could never tell when Spindle was joking. "What do you need?"

She bit at her bottom lip. "How well do you know Val Marsten?"

That was unexpected. "He's my only real friend in the kingdom. Why?"

She held a hand to her heart. "You wound me, Grounder. What does that make me, sliced grubs?"

I took a second to parse her words. "You're...a friend?" It came out as a question. I didn't want to presume.

She rolled her eyes. "Oh, thank you, you're too kind." She paused for a second and I noticed a tinge of...uncertainty on her face. Something I'd never seen before on Spindle. She was always certain of everything, even when she was wrong.

"How open do you think he'd be to grabbing a...meal with me?" she asked.

I smirked. "I could ask him."

Whap. She smacked me hard on the shoulder.

"Don't *ask* him, you sun-blind grublicker. I just want to know if you think he'd be open to it."

"I'm pretty clueless about such things," I said. "But the princess believes he's got a crush on you."

Her face lit up like a forge. "Now *that's* useful information. I trust her take on people a lot more than yours."

"Appreciate the vote of confidence."

"I'm just saying, your vibe's more 'accidental mushroom eater,' hers is 'reads three books before breakfast, before manipulating the court to her bidding.'"

"Thanks, *friend*," I said. "I was going to meet him after we're done here. Want to tag along?"

She smoothed down her leather apron, then looked at the grease on her hands and a smudge on her shirt. "Ah, I don't know, I'm not really dressed for that," she said. Another new look on Spindle—self-consciousness.

"You look great. If I know Val, I think he likes you because you don't care about that kind of stuff."

She shook her head. "That is just about the dumbest thing you can say to a woman."

"What part?" I asked, confused.

"That I don't care about my looks...are you kidding me?"

I gulped. "I meant it as a...compliment?"

"I'm just messing with you, Grounder." She shook her head again. "But seriously, don't ever say that to another woman again."

I nodded at her serious tone. And I filed away her advice.

She pointed at me, holding my eyes in her steely gaze. "Ever." Her face split in a grin. "Now, let's make you that core light."

"It starts with summoning an earth shard." She raised her hands and murmured something in High Cellarian. A jagged chunk of obsidian appeared in her hands.

She tossed it to Sparky, her magmatite, who caught it with a clank. His third leg *shifted* up into a new arm and he cradled the shard between both glowing hands. The heat rippling off him made the shard blush from black to red to white-hot.

I watched, transfixed, as he shaped it with his three fingered hands into a perfect sphere, like it was clay.

Spindle's brow was slick with sweat. "Now the interesting part."

Sparky slowly sank into the sphere—first his fingers, then his legs, until his whole body disappeared into the molten core.

"And now for the finishing touch," Spindle's voice strained at the effort. She mumbled a whole bunch of High Cellarian. The core sphere blazed with light then went dark.

"What just happened?" I asked, taking a step back in surprise.

"He's fine," Spindle said between breaths. "I sent him back to the core so he could anchor the bind. I'll summon him again in an hour."

She handed me the glowing orb. It pulsed once, then went dim. "What do you need it for?"

"You'll see when it's ready. How do I turn it on?"

Her eyes sparkled. "I'll show you—*when* you're done."

I dove into the build. It was brutal. I was trying to jam a lab's worth of optics into a space the size of my hand.

The protoboard wasn't built for this. Lenses wobbled. Mirrors popped loose. My soldering iron fought me the whole way.

I kept glancing at the magmatites around the room, all gliding around with perfect fluidity, assisting other students.

Would've been nice to have some help, but I wasn't used to nice. I was used to hard work.

On the third try, I got something functional. Not pretty, but functional. It was hard to capture and manipulate the eight different colors of light post-prism, but I finally got something working with a standard light source.

I called Spindle over.

"It's called a core switch," she said, tossing me a copper tab from a nearby drawer. "We have a whole drawer-full of em on the back wall."

Her eyes roved over the mess of my board. "I've never seen lenses and mirrors on a—wait, is that a prism?"

I nodded.

She kept talking without looking at me, eyes glued to my creation. "On a protoboard. It almost looks like a circuit." She turned to me. "Is that what it is, an optical circuit? How did you get those things to stay on the board without a magmatite?"

I snorted. "A lot of rage," I said, doing my best not to clench my teeth.

"What does it do?" she asked.

"Not much in its current state. Let me hook up the core switch and I'll show you."

Hooking up the switch was the easiest part of the entire project. It fit nicely onto the board and it only need proximity to the core for it to function.

I asked how that worked, and Spindle shook her head. There were some things I wasn't ever going to get to know about core crafting.

I flipped the switch and the vibrant thrum began. It didn't have quite the same pulse of what I created earlier in Cloud's lab, but the minute I switched it on, an aura appeared around Spindle.

The aura wasn't as strong as the ones around Professor Cloud and Farsmith, but it was there, and it was a mix between yellow and blue. When the colors of the auras transposed a bit of green shone through.

It flickered quite a bit. After a moment or two, the blue of Spindle's aura slowly shifted to yellow.

I flushed with excitement. It felt almost like when I first got the hang of skiing during my very first simulation. Still a ton to learn, but I could see the possibility. There was something satisfying about earning a new skill.

I wish I knew what the colors meant. Hmmm...maybe someone who was good at signals could figure that out for me.

Working on it, Rhee muttered. She sounded distracted.

"What does it do?" Spindle asked again.

I put a small metal housing over the board, leaving one side open. I put a piece of paper in front of it and the same pattern of light, the sphere with a light burst exploding from its center appeared. It wasn't as clean as the one I created earlier but it could clearly be made out.

"All that to make a pretty picture?" Spindle asked, her aura now completely yellow.

"For now," I said. "I promise it will be more impressive when I'm done."

"Right," said Spindle, drawing out the word. "I'm not going to hold my breath until then, okay?"

"You just wait," I said.

"Give me a ten-minute heads up before we go meet Val, okay?"

I looked to the clock. Brak! I only had a half hour left and I still wanted to cut a circular hole in a metal sheet to complete the housing.

You think we can add it to Rach as is? I posed into my head.

And what exactly is it?

Imagine this device with a circular hole on one end where the light comes out. But not only that, there's a receiver one either side of the emitter.

I pulled Rach out of her case and set her back on my bench right next to the new optical circuit board.

You mean like an...ohhhhhh, Aubrey said. *Like an eye. I already*

*enhanced those garbage optical sensors you gave her with my own sensors,
and with her chip I can pretty much pick up anything she can. What else do
you expect her to see?*

You can't pick up these auras, I said.

Only because I haven't figured out what *you're seeing yet. It won't take
long once I do.*

Right, I said drawing out the word just like Spindle just did with me.
*Humor me. We'll install it now and I'll make improvements to it as we go.
I know these auras are going to be important, it's all a bigger part of the
light experiment and the Songs.*

We don't even know what the auras mean yet, Aubrey complained.

I popped the small plate off Rach's head segment and carefully fit
the new device inside. It was still too big.

I'd have to figure out how to cut it by half if I was going to fit two of
these circuits in there. The two brackets fit the circuit snugly into her
head cavity, but Rach might be slightly unbalanced until I got a second
version of it in there.

*If we have it running constantly for the next couple of days, it should get
you enough data to work out what the auras are telling us, right?* I asked.

Silence. I didn't know if Rhee was pouting or hard at work. Probably
a little of both.

Finn! Rhee's voice broke through with an urgency I'd only heard
from her once before, when we were fighting the cinderfen. *My sensors
are picking up a bell pattern I've never heard before. And a lot of people
are running for the castle.*

I strained to listen, but didn't hear any bells. I opened the door and
walked out of the lab into the hallway.

Still no bells.

But I did hear the screams.

242

31

Toads & Turtles

"Hey," Spindle snapped. "I told you to give me a ten minute heads up before you left."

I held a finger to my lips, cutting her off. Her glare darkened into a snarl, but I just bared my teeth and pointed to my ear.

She froze. Her mouth opened, then closed.

She tilted her head. "Is that...screaming?"

I nodded.

Her face drained of color.

I turned on my heel and *ran*—the limp forgotten, adrenaline devouring the pain. Back inside the lab, I yanked my mail shirt from my pack and shoved it over my head, the links clinking like warning bells. My nova-blade locked into place on one hip, a long dagger on the other.

Rhee, we need intel. Now. I said.

Snap the top plate back on Rach's head. Her voice cracked like a whip.

I cursed under my breath—*brakking stupid!*—and latched the plate into place. It gave a sharp *click* as it sealed.

Rach jolted to life, sprang from the table like a coyote from a trap, and zipped through the door without another word.

A couple of benches away, loud crashes echoed—shouts, the metallic ring of tools slamming into gear.

I looked up as Spindle tore open drawers and cabinets, barking orders like a commander in battle. "Arm yourselves! I don't care if it's a hammer or a hot plate. Find something lethal!"

One journeyman hesitated. "Spindle, how do we even know if it's—"

"Oh, I don't know, Craig," she snapped, artfully blending outrage and sarcasm. "Maybe go outside and ask the things causing the screaming if this is serious?"

She turned to me, wild-eyed but focused. "Finn! Help!"

Spindle held out an arm. A compact wrist-mounted crossbow was strapped to her forearm, but the auto-loader was jamming against her elbow.

It didn't take long to understand how the contraption worked. Once I understood it, I loosened the strap, slid it down and spun it eight degrees around her arm. I cinched it tight and clapped her on the shoulder.

Other engineers scrambled around us, slapping together combat-ready golems with whatever they had. Some were crude and half-formed—barely functional—but armed with hammers, pipes, and even dismantled boiler rods.

Rojer Varn burst into the lab.

He looked like a warrior dragged out of legend—shoulders broad, warhammer dripping with greenish-black blood. His face was streaked with soot, his eyes electric.

A trail of terrified apprentices streamed behind him.

"To the back wall!" he barked. "Move!"

The apprentices didn't argue. They ran like their lives depended on it. Maybe they did.

"Craig! Lenore! You're holding this room." Rojer's voice cracked like thunder. "Use your golems, use the tools, use your bare hands if you have to. *Nothing gets past that door.* Do you understand?"

They nodded.

"I said—*do you understand?*"

"We understand!" they shouted in unison, then spun into motion.

"For the rest of you," Rojer said, turning toward us with fire in his eyes, "we're reinforcing the town wall. The castle's under siege. The city guard and the army are defending the keep. That leaves the militia, and us, to hold the line out here."

Spindle's voice rang across the lab. "What are we up against, Chief?"

"Don't know yet," Rojer growled. "Reports are chaos. But I *saw* things—things from the Murkmire."

A skinny student with trembling hands raised his arm. "I—I don't have any combat training, sir."

Rojer nodded. "I know. Most of you don't. But we fight now—or we fight in the streets, scattered, bleeding, running. We make our stand at the wall, with numbers. With strategy."

Spindle clambered up onto a bench, holding a hammer like a battle standard. "So grab a hammer and a spanner, and let's do this!"

A nervous laugh echoed. It was Rojer who brought it home.

He looked around the room, locking eyes with each of us. "You made it into this guild because you've got grit. Brains. Fire. You've heard the saying—*Ware the engineer on the way to war.* Now let's make them remember *why.*"

"Hammer and spanner!" Spindle roared.

"Hammer and spanner!" the journeymen roared back, rushing to arm themselves.

It's total chaos outside, said Rhee. *But you should know something, Finn. The princess leads the militia on the wall.*

I felt my already elevated heart rate jump. *Why is she down here?*

I didn't talk to her, Rhee snapped. *But she's on the wall. Be careful—it's worse than we thought.*

I grabbed Rojer's shoulder. "I have to get to the wall. The princess is out there."

Rojer nodded. "I heard. Let her know I'm bringing reinforcements."

I sprinted for the door when a shriek of, "Wait for me!" stopped me in my tracks.

"Seriously," Spindle huffed, catching up. "Quit trying to ditch me. You're better off with someone watching your back."

I gave her a nod. "Thanks."

I bolted again. She grabbed my arm.

"Spin, we don't have time—"

"Shut up. There's a loading dock exit on the north side—cuts our route in half."

She didn't wait for me to reply. She took off.

We darted through the guild, past loading platforms stacked with war machines and gear. Crews scrambled to douse spreading fires with sand and foam, smoke stinging our eyes.

We skidded to a stop in front of a squat iron door.

Spindle yanked at the handle.

Locked.

"Brak!" I cursed.

"Hold on." She reached into her apron and pulled out a tangle of keys. She sorted through, then slid a deep red one into the lock.

Click.

We burst outside—and the world was burning.

The loading docks were ablaze. Smoke coiled through the air like grasping hands. Engineers shouted over the roar of fire, loading weapons onto flatbeds and vehicles—some four-wheeled, some six, one massive ten-wheeler belching steam like a charging beast.

We dashed through the chaos.

I almost tripped.

A frog—no, a toad—squatted in the middle of the street. A foot long.

Covered in gray-brown warts that suddenly began to glow.

Oh, that's not good.

The warts pulsed—then *swelled.*

Instinct took over. I spun and kicked the thing toward a deserted corner of the street.

It *exploded* in a fiery burst of gunk and flame. The air filled with a sizzle and stink of something half-cooked, half-alive.

From the docks, someone screamed, "No, you fool! You need *sand* for blistertoads! That stuff spreads!"

I turned back to the carnage. The flames licked toward the building. A trail of burning goo oozed from the blast.

And we had no time.

"Let's move!" I shouted. Spindle and I sprinted into the burning streets, toward the wall, toward the fight, toward Amara.

I barely got ten more strides before I saw it—another blistertoad, skin pulsing with that telltale infernal heat.

"They're everywhere," I spat.

It sprang at Spindle with a hiss, rubbery limbs coiled mid-air. Without breaking stride, she spun and smashed it out of the sky with her hammer. The thing detonated midair—flames splashed across a flowerpot outside a shuttered shop. Purple-yellow blossoms withered into black sludge as the fiery goo consumed them.

We didn't stop.

People stumbled through the streets in a fog of panic—eyes wide, lungs heaving, some bleeding, others screaming. We darted down an alley. I didn't even need to ask why. I'd just seen a toad land in a young woman's hair and erupt into flame.

The smell. Stars, the *smell.* Burnt flesh. Scorched hair. It clawed up my sinuses and coiled in the back of my throat like smoke-drenched death. I coughed, gagged. That stench would haunt me for weeks.

We pushed past a pair of shops, dodging a rolling cart that had been abandoned mid-flee, until—

The town wall rose ahead like a promise. Not towering like the castle's, but solid—sturdy cut stone, fifteen feet thick and ten feet high. A squat, unpolished bulwark of defense, patched together with mortar and prayer.

We hit the sand and ash, an intentional firebreak, scorched clean to prevent more of those monsters from leaping straight in, and powered up the stairs.

"Huh," Spindle panted beside me. "Somebody up there's got a brain."

That *somebody* was Amara.

The princess stood atop the wall like a storm-forged pylon, her deep violet leathers catching the last rays of the artificial sun. Chaos swirled around her—militia scrambling, bows firing, crossbows reloading—but within a few feet of her presence, people calmed. Steadied. Waited for instruction like planets orbiting their star.

She didn't shout. She didn't panic. She radiated command.

Beside her, Val Marsten moved like silver lightning—barking orders, demonstrating grips, rerouting traffic with a clarity that cut through the noise like a nova-blade. He wasn't yelling; he guided, and somehow every soldier he touched left sharper, faster, more sure.

Spindle exhaled beside me, breathless. "By the wards...he's *beautiful.*"

Now wasn't the time to tease her—but she wasn't wrong. In this moment, Val and Amara looked like Dusker demi-gods carved out of myth, holding the line between order and annihilation.

I shoved through the crowd, twice forced to throw an elbow just to break into the circle around them.

Amara's eyes lit up when she saw me—then *narrowed.*

"Finn, what in the core's name are you doing here?" she snapped. "You're barely cleared to spar. You can't be—"

"And you *brought* Korra with you?" Val added, his silver brows nearly leaping off his face. "Are you out of your mind?"

Spindle didn't hesitate. She pointed her hammer at Val and stormed toward him.

"Hey! You shut that *beautiful* face of yours!" she barked. "Me being here? *My choice.* Not Finn's."

Val froze, clearly stunned by both her words and the fire behind them. His hand drifted up to his cheek as if feeling it for the first time.

I could've sworn he whispered, "Beautiful?" to himself.

Spindle reached up, grabbed the back of his neck, and *kissed* him. Quick, fierce, and entirely her.

"Just in case one of us doesn't make it," she said, breath hot against his lips. "Now tell me what I *can* do."

Val stared for a beat, dazed, then nodded.

I turned to Amara, dropping my voice low. "How bad is it?"

Her face darkened. "Bad. No help's coming from the castle, at least for a while yet. We're on our own."

Rhee had told me as much during the sprint here. But I needed to hear it from her. The gravity of it.

"Go," she said, pointing toward the edge of the wall. "See for yourself. Then come back. We need a plan to win this thing."

I jogged to the battlements, every step heavier than the last.

Rhee had given me the numbers. *Numbers* were easy. Numbers didn't scream or bleed or eat your face.

Then I looked out, and my breath caught.

The blistertoads kept coming—dozens of them—skittering over rooftops, leaping onto the walls. Sticky feet clung to stone as they crawled toward the top.

A militia soldier next to me swung a broad metal paddle and *launched* one into the sky like a flaming discus. It exploded midair, showering the army below with a rain of molten death.

But the real horror was what waited beyond the firebreak on the other side of the wall.

A field of nightmares.

Hundreds of boglings swarmed the eastern edge—mud-caked, twitchy, and nervous. Not nervous because of *us*, but of the monstrous shapes to the west.

They were reptiles the size of wagons. Gleaming scales. Jaws packed with teeth like knives. I'd read about crocodiles, never seen one.

Now I'd seen, sixty-six or was it sixty-seven. Too many.

Behind them...I blinked, rubbed my eyes. Floating orbs of green light flickered among the trees—almost like wisps from legend. But not the gentle, lucky signs from old stories. These throbbed with menace.

"What *are* those?" I muttered.

"W-will-o'-wisps," the soldier beside me stammered. "Saw one once and thought it meant good luck. Saw *three* today and thought I'd win the lottery." His voice cracked. "That was before one turned red and shot a bolt of something through poor Clem Goldman. Lit him up like a funeral pyre, it did."

He shuddered.

"And those things?" I asked, pointing at the crocodiles.

"Them crocs you mean?"

"Yeah, do they have some form of fire too?"

"Scorchjaws," he muttered. "Rumor is they breathe fire. Haven't seen it myself. Don't want to."

I exhaled. "That's fair."

I clapped his shoulder and turned back to the horde. The creatures were restless—snapping at one another, crowding the line, scales grinding against shells, all motion and chaos.

And then, like a shadow slipping loose from a nightmare, she *floated* out of the forest.

A cinderfen hag.

Tall. Thin. Masked. Her kiln mask jutted with twisted metal, spikes radiating from jagged slashes that gave the illusion of a screaming mouth.

Another emerged.

Then a third.

They moved like smoke across a still pond, arms outstretched.

And then—they *shrieked.*

Unholy, piercing, and full of wrath.

The forest *answered.*

The Murkmire horde surged forward—hopping, slithering, crashing, charging.

And the battle for the wall began.

32

Revenge

1 Week Before Finn's Banishment from Dawnford

Carl met Malik in the same place he'd first crossed paths with the waxer mentor who changed everything—a remote bluff, half an hour's speeder ride from the scorched metal shanties of the Dead Crow camp.

"I told you," Malik said, brushing a crimson lock from his sweat-slicked brow, "revenge tastes better aged."

Carl didn't smile. His eyes stayed fixed on the camp below, where fires crackled and lights pulsed with stolen power. "I've waited nearly fifteen years. Spent most of that time not even knowing *who* I was supposed to hate."

Malik's eyes burned with that strange, patient fire. "Ready to change the world?"

Carl nodded. He swung a leg over the speeder and barely blinked when Malik climbed on behind him. He still had no idea how the man moved so quickly between kingdoms—waxer tricks he couldn't yet grasp. Magic wrapped in mystery.

They didn't wait for nightfall.

They didn't bother to hide.

Carl parked the speeder just beyond bow range. He left his shotgun strapped to the seat. He wouldn't need it—not for what he was about to do.

He raised his hands and walked straight into the lion's maw.

Shouts rang out. Bows raised. Sentries sprinted to intercept. Carl felt the ropes tighten around his wrists as they were bound, Malik's hands similarly tied. He barely flinched.

They were marched through the camp under buzzing lectric lights— no more flickering generators or fire barrels. The pirates had finished the theft of Dawnford's lectric. Good. That meant everything was in place.

They were shoved through the squat stone building nestled beneath the gaping skull that loomed over the Dead Crow camp like a god of death.

And there she was.

Amber.

She stood in the shadows, her expression pale and pulled tight like old leather. Her eyes widened as she took them in. "Carl...I *told* you not to come back. I told you what would happen."

Her voice wavered, pity, fear, regret all tangled together.

Then he arrived.

A man carved from muscle and sun and arrogance. Jalil. Amber's pirate beau.

Amber must have been lying about liking awkward men too. Once a pirate, always a pirate. Stealing hearts and stealing lectric. It sounded like a *Dune Striders* song.

Jalil strode into the room like he owned gravity, sweat glistening across taut cords of strength. His smile was the smug kind of confident that begged for a fist.

"This him?" Jalil asked without even looking at Carl. "The mark?"

Amber nodded, sadness swirling like stormclouds behind her eyes.

Carl met her gaze—cold and flat. The love he once had was gone, buried in a grave she helped dig.

Jalil turned to face him. "So. Why come back? Wasn't it enough, knowing she lied to you? Lied every day she wore your name?"

Carl shrugged, voice like splintered glass. "I've had time to reflect." He looked Jalil up and down—noticed how the others lingered near the walls, silent, waiting. He's the king here.

"Let me ask *you* something," Carl said. "What's it like knowing someone else was sleeping with your wife?"

Jalil didn't even blink—just *kicked* Carl in the face.

Stars exploded behind Carl's eyes. Blood spattered across the stone floor as he hit it hard. Amber gasped, a hand covering her mouth.

Carl spat a tooth, rolled onto his side, grinning through the pain. "You'd think the chief of a pirate camp wouldn't have to pimp his own wife for power. Or is that common here?"

"I wasn't chief then," Jalil growled.

"So, you were just taking orders?" Carl coughed a laugh. "Good little pirate. You really know how to pick em, Amber."

Jalil drove his boot into Carl's gut, folding him in half. The air fled his lungs in a violent *whoosh*, but Carl didn't scream. He lay there, shuddering, smiling.

"That's all you needed," Malik murmured behind him. "Confirmation."

Carl's eyes flashed at his mentor. "Don't you *dare* ruin this for me."

Jalil grabbed his shirt, hauled him upright. "Ruin what?" Jalil asked. "Death by jealous husband? You came back after holding a gun on Amber, then braining her across the head. What'd you think was going to happen? There's only one way this ends, mark."

That brought a bloody smile to Carl's face. "You're right, and it's not going to be the way you think."

Jalil punched him full in the face. "You really thought you could come here and...what? Change her mind about you?"

Joy filled Carl. "I'll change her mind alright, but I'm not going to stop there."

Jalil punched him again.

Carl laughed.

It started low.

But it grew—*mad*, wild, howling laughter that made the sentries shift uncomfortably.

"I'm not here to fix *anything*," he gasped. "I'm here to burn it all down."

Another punch cracked against his jaw. His laughter *only grew*.

"Just take him outside," Amber said coldly, "and finish it."

That did it.

It unlocked something deep, primal, in Carl's core.

The rage, the *betrayal*, the endless nights of grinding silence.

He let go.

He *gave in.*

The heat burst from him like a dam breaking. Fire bled through his pores, turning his skin slick and waxen. His hands, still bound, ignited.

He relished the shock in Amber's eyes when he transformed.

Jalil stepped back, but it was too late.

Carl's flaming hand plunged into his stomach.

The man howled, but he fed on *her* scream.

Malik was already moving, having taken his own form. He waved his hand, melting the lock on the door. *No one in. No one out.*

"See it," Malik coached. "The image the prime Igni burned into your mind. Slow, steady. Control the flame."

Carl obeyed.

He imagined it: green skin, orange hair, twisted limbs and cruel, goblin eyes. He fed a thread of silver fire up through Jalil's gut, into his lungs, his blood, his heart.

Where it touched, skin rippled, color draining, then shifting—yellow, then *green*. Muscles bloated, then sagged. Jaw unhinged, teeth sharpening.

The pirate who ruled this camp became *nothing*—just another twisted goblin husk.

And Carl smiled as he watched the man collapse in a groaning heap of mutated flesh.

Amber trembled. Her lips quivered as he approached.

"Please," she whispered. "For what we once had, don't do this."

Carl knelt in front of her, the flames whispering around his hands. "You just told your husband to kill me, Amber. For what we once had?"

"I have children," she choked. "Please, Carl."

"Like the ones *we* were supposed to have?" His voice was quiet now—quieter than flame. "Don't worry. I'll try to find them. Convert them first. Before your goblin husband gets hungry."

Her eyes filled with horror.

"Goblins," he said, "have very unique ideas about parenting."

And then, with only a flicker of hesitation, Carl pressed his fingers into her belly.

She screamed.

He felt the heat surge through him—controlled, focused. Just like Malik taught.

"I can't believe you became this," she sobbed. "This *monster*."

He looked into her eyes, letting her see the truth. The fury. The finality.

"You *made* me this, Amber," he said, voice crackling like a forge. "So be proud. Be *very* proud."

Then he lit the fire.

And the world changed.

By the end of the first day, Carl was running on fumes.

His breath came ragged. His hands trembled. The last two conversions had nearly hollowed him out. Each new goblin he'd created pulled something from him—a piece of pain, a spark of fury—and left him just a little colder, a little more numb. The raw anger that had once roared inside him, the fury at Amber, at Dawnford, at the world that broke him, it was starting to...fade.

Malik noticed. Of course he did.

"Pick it up," the red-haired waxer snapped, wiping gore off his hands with the edge of his coat. "I've converted three times what you have in the last hour. Worse, you see that?" He jabbed a finger at Carl's flickering head flame. "Your fire's guttering like a tavern candle."

Carl didn't lift his head. "The hate's dying," he said hoarsely. "Every conversion, it burns a little more out of me. I don't think I can keep this pace."

Malik discarded the child he was converting—a boy, no older than ten—like he weighed nothing. In a blur, he closed the space between them and *slapped* Carl across the face.

The crack echoed across the clearing.

Carl staggered but didn't flinch. A weak chuckle escaped his lips. "Appreciate the effort, but pain alone won't do it anymore."

"That wasn't to wake you up, you Grounder-bred fool." Malik's molten eyes bored into his. "It was because you're doing it wrong."

Carl blinked. "Wrong?"

"You're pouring *yourself* into them. Feeding them your own hate, your pain. That worked in the beginning, but now? You'll burn out. I taught you this! When that fire fades, you don't draw from your own essence. You pull from the prime. The Igni gladly bear the weight."

Carl stared at him, a pit forming in his gut. Malik was right. He'd gotten drunk on the first rush of vengeance, on watching Amber's world collapse. But now the high was gone, and in its place: Emptiness. Fatigue. Temptation. The thought of a drink—just one—crept into his mind like a snake.

No. He burned it out. He was not that man anymore. Not the lost drunk stumbling through Dawnford's alleys. He was fire now. Flame. A *hand* of the prime.

Carl reached deeper. Deeper than he ever had. Into the churning white heart of the Igni. He pulled.

Energy coursed through him. For the first time, he felt a sense of...relief from the Igni prime. Approval. Like the prime itself acknowledged his pull. No longer a servant. A vessel.

The conversions resumed.

It took nearly three more days to finish the job.

By the end, the Dead Crow camp was unrecognizable—an infernal cradle from which six hundred goblins had been born.

Some had died in the fight. A few resisted to the bitter end. Most had fallen quickly, broken not just by wax and flame, but by the hopeless inevitability of their transformation.

And some had been...experiments.

Malik, ever the artist, grew bolder as the days went on. He reshaped his goblins—twisting their forms, morphing limbs into weapons, grafting smoldering iron into muscle. One experiment attempted to bind a desert sidewinder as a tail to a goblin's spine. Both creature and host screamed until the fires silenced them for good.

But not all experiments failed.

Soon, the camp filled with blade-arm and hammer-foot goblins with claws of obsidian and skin fused with smelted metal. Carl didn't experiment himself, but he watched. He learned. He remembered.

When the final goblin fell into line, Malik raised his hands and addressed their monstrous army. "Keep doing what you do best— raid, steal, spread chaos. But now, you answer to us. When we call, you come."

Jalil—the pirate Carl had twisted into the first of them—remained in charge, his bloated green form slinking into command with twisted pride.

Carl tried to issue orders, but Jalil didn't understand. Words weren't enough.

Malik sighed. "Think, Carl. How did the prime speak to *you*?"

Carl's frown deepened. Then it clicked. Not words. Images. Emotions. The bond they shared, the sliver of his soul he'd poured into every goblin—it was still there. Waiting. He reached out with his mind and *felt* the tether.

And when he *pulled*, it snapped to attention.

He grinned. "Jalil. Hit him." Carl pointed his chin at a nearby goblin.

The goblin didn't hesitate. He spun and struck the subordinate with a meaty, spiked fist. The creature crumpled.

Carl laughed. It was a low, hungry sound.

"Good," Malik said. "Now, finish your work here. And when the Camlock brat's trial is done, I'll need you in the kingdoms. Alyndor's royal family has become...*inconvenient*. Their faith, their pride—they need to be shaken."

Carl's grin faded into something darker. "The trial ends next week. I'll be clear of the compound after that. Patrice Splitter's already after me. I'll enjoy turning her into a goblin someday."

"Then embrace it," Malik said, voice like molten glass. "Experiment. Expand your power. What I need...is for you to break the princess. Use the goblins to isolate her while I work on the rest of the royal family."

Carl's eyes narrowed. The flame on his head pulsed brighter.

"Tell me everything," he said.

259

33

The Charge

The three cinderfen hags raised their twisted arms in eerie unison—and shrieked.

Not a cry of warning.

A command—soaked in hate. A sound ripped from the torments of the dead, so unnatural and resonant it vibrated the stone beneath our boots.

The horde surged forward in a wave of snapping jaws and slithering limbs—a stampede of nightmares. Crocodilian scorchjaws bellowed and lashed out, biting at boglings even as the will-o'-wisps flared, searing chunks of scale and flesh indiscriminately. There was no coordination, only chaos, and that chaos made them even more terrifying.

My heart jumped when I heard the fanfare of bugles from the castle wall.

Hope surged through me.

Reinforcements! The army!

I turned, along with dozens of others, only to feel that hope snap like dry tinder.

Dust and smoke roiled from the castle's edge. The trumpet cry wasn't meant for us. The keep was under attack. Defenders scrambled, fighting for their own walls.

We'd get no help from the castle. We were alone.

It's mostly goblins at the castle, Rhee whispered in my head, tone grim. *A lot of goblins.*

The timing. The tactics. This wasn't random. It was a coordinated assault. And we'd failed to uncover the hand directing it.

I pushed the thought away. There would be time for blame if we survived.

"Make the first volley count, Commander," Amara called from her command position, voice sharp and composed.

The gray-mustached militia leader raised his arm with solemn precision. The man looked like he hadn't slept in years, and tonight wasn't about to help.

"ARCHERS...*LOOSE!*"

The twang of bowstrings snapped like whip cracks. Arrows and bolts screamed down from the wall in a deadly rain.

I reached out with my perception. Dozens hit, but most bounced harmlessly off thick scales, carapaces, or passed uselessly through the intangible bogpyres. *Only sixteen* of the beasts dropped. Sixteen, out of a thousand and eighty-two. Against our four hundred seventeen.

Amara's voice boomed again. This time the sound waves of command came from *everywhere*, echoing along the battlements.

"FOCUS FIRE—EYES AND EARS! STRIKE WHERE THEY ARE WEAK!"

The effect was instantaneous. Militia troops straightened. Their hands steadied. Their aim focused. Her voice didn't just command, it anchored.

"ARCHERS...*LOOSE!*"

More screams. This time from the enemy. I felt forty-three creatures fall. Better.

Still not enough. Not even close.

The hags shrieked again.

I prepared to push back against the attack, like I'd done in the woods. Maybe I could extend my pushback to cover more—to protect my friends.

This shriek wasn't directed at us, but towards their own forces.

Then something *shifted.*

The charge turned into a frenzy.

Boglings shrieked as their bodies began to glow, shells shimmering like heated iron. The will-o'-wisps morphed from placid green to scarlet rage, bobbing like angry hornets.

The shrieks went on and on. So much power. Where did it come from?

The scorchjaws changed most of all.

Their dark green scales split, veins of lava coursing through them, transforming their hides into obsidian armor. Molten drool hissed as it fell, and their tails left smoking trenches in the earth.

The horde had become a wave of malevolent fire.

A third volley loosed, forty-eight kills. The enemy was closer now. Easier to hit. Then the bogpyres—twisting orbs of infernal energy—bobbed into range.

They fired.

Focused beams lanced out like celestial punishment. Where they struck, defenders ignited—men and women turned to living torches.

Screams tore through the air. The smell—stars, that horrible smell—of burnt flesh and scorched bone clawed into my throat.

Thirty-seven died instantly. A dozen more collapsed, writhing, their bodies too broken to fight.

The next wave of bogpyres attacked. This time the militia was ready. They ducked behind stone and shield. Only two died.

The bogpyres, their rage spent, faded back to green and floated lazily upward, as if the killing had lightened them.

The archers kept firing, but I couldn't see the enemy faltering.

They swarmed at the base of the wall.

Then the next surprise: boglings *stacking* themselves. They formed hideous pyramids of blistering shells to climb.

They burned each other to do it. But they climbed.

The defenders countered with halberds, spears, pipes. Anything long enough to knock the piles down.

But still, boglings cleared the wall. And soldiers fell to searing claws and blistering shells.

One crested the top near the command post, its claws already mid-swipe at a militia fighter—the same man who'd told me about the wisps.

I drew my nova-blade and leapt, slashing through its spine with a searing hiss of energy.

The man looked up, eyes wide with gratitude.

"Back of the neck!" I yelled. "*Go for the neck!*"

Amara's voice echoed my command in every direction. The tide turned—slightly. The boglings already on the wall began to fall, their hot shells tumbling and creating dangerous gaps in our lines. But we held...until the scorchjaws struck.

Their massive tails hammered the wall, each strike a tremor. Mortar cracked. Stone groaned.

They bit at the rock itself—gnawing through like molten termites.

And then the boglings got creative.

I watched in horror as one leapt onto a scorchjaw's back and jabbed it with a claw.

The beast whipped its tail, launching the bogling into the air.

A primitive catapult—and it worked.

The creature landed atop the wall, claws tearing into defenders. Others followed, flung skyward like burning stones. Some even soared over the wall, landing in the streets below.

Moments later, the screams began again—this time from *inside* the town.

And then the wall...broke.

A section no thicker than seven feet, weakened from the pounding, finally gave way beneath the relentless blows of two scorchjaws working in unison.

It crumbled.

The enemy poured through.

We were no longer holding the line.

We were being overrun.

The boglings on the wall were closing in—slow and inevitable—creeping toward the command post like death on blistered claws. More flew overhead, launched by their monstrous croc-apult kin. We were being pincered from the sky and the stone.

A glance at the field made my stomach lurch. The green wisps, no longer bogpyres, were drifting back toward the forest, lazily orbiting the cinderfen hags like fireflies returning home. The hags hovered just above the loam of the forest, low and still, but I could *feel* the power building. Whether they were drawing energy from the land or bleeding it into the ground, I couldn't tell. But their cracked, blackened kiln-masks had begun to glow again, burning with renewed fury.

If they recharged the wisps...we wouldn't survive the next wave.

Another deafening boom ripped through the night.

A second section of wall crumbled like stale bread. Militia poured down to the streets below, desperate to seal the breaches. Already, half were gone from the battlements.

I turned, back-to-back with Spindle as three more boglings stalked toward us. Her breath hitched. It was the first time I'd heard real fear from her.

And then a fourth creature—its claws slick with the blood of the militia man who'd told me about the wisps—spotted us and charged.

I didn't have time to grieve the man.

I'd never faced more than one of these things at a time, and the battlement didn't leave much room to maneuver. I threw myself into the space between them, forcing one to block the other with its bulk. My only priority was keeping Spindle at my back.

The pair rushed, their grotesque shells slamming together. One hissed and flinched as the other's burning armor grazed it. That was all I needed.

I surged forward, caught the claws of the left bogling with my dagger long enough to trap them, then pivoted hard. The one on the right overcommitted, and I used the leverage to drive its comrade's claws into its face. It shrieked in confusion, then rage, as I slipped behind and carved my nova-blade across the base of its neck. It dropped with a clattering, wet *thunk*.

The second bogling lashed out, and I caught the blow on my sword. Big mistake. I couldn't believe the strength of the turtle man. The force dragged my arm down, slamming my wrist into the still-searing shell of the first one. I screamed as my skin sizzled.

I gritted my teeth and twisted, using the sword's hilt against the shell for leverage. We spun—now its arm was forced down to the burning corpse.

Now, it screamed.

My dagger was at my feet. I hooked it with my boot, stretched, twisted down without letting my face touch the shell, and snatched it up.

With a final lunge, I jammed the blade into the back of its neck.

It collapsed in a heap of steam and gore.

That's when the hags shrieked again.

It was like standing beneath a cathedral bell during a thunder crack. My skull vibrated. My knees almost buckled. I looked up and saw defenders clutching their ears, staggering.

But the boglings? Completely unaffected.

One raised its claw to strike Spindle, who stood frozen in the blast of sound. I had to do something. No time to think.

I reached for my perception and *pushed*. Not toward the hags this time, but at the bogling.

The effect was immediate. It staggered, stunned.

I sprinted, drove my sword through its neck, spun around, and turned the push of my perception against the hags.

The pressure on my skull relented. My soundwaves met theirs and canceled out in a pulse of silence so sharp I heard the sighs of relief from the troops behind me.

But it wasn't over.

Only two of the hags continued screaming. The third had already begun funneling energy into the bogpyres. Their cores flared scarlet again.

This was about to get very bad.

The shrieks finally ceased. I let the push fade, panting.

And then—

Drums.

A deep, thunderous rhythm rolled through the chaos. Not from the forest. Not from the wall.

From *inside* the city.

I spun. My perception couldn't pinpoint the source. The noise was everywhere. Chaos layered upon chaos.

"Look!" Spindle cried, pointing not to the hags, but into the burning city behind us.

Through the thick smoke and flame, movement resolved.

Not more enemies. *Machines.*

Dozens of them—rolling, stomping, clanking—some piloted, others autonomous, all surging toward the wall like a fleet of mechanical titans.

The engineers marched to war.

And at their center, encased in the chest of a massive humanoid mech, stood Rojer Varn. I'd never seen anything so beautiful.

The chief engineer moved his limbs, and the giant mirrored him. An axe in one hand, a hammer in the other.

The hammer came down. *Boom.*

A bogling, just beyond the wall, was crushed so completely it ceased to exist.

Then came the beams of light.

One of the newly recharged bogpyres hovered up—and a *blue* lance of light speared it through. It popped like a bubble of plasma, scattering in glowing motes of red and blue.

Three more fell before I could blink.

From out of the smoke stepped Professor Cloud, flanked by Farsmith and the entire Glass & Light Guild. They were armed with glowing tubes of light and core-enhanced crafting tools. Every weapon fired focused beams or searing blasts. Mirrors and lenses refracted the energy—arcs of light danced from bogling to bogling, carving through shell and claw alike.

They weren't alone.

At their side marched Cheapside's roughest—brawlers with spanners, blades, clubs, chains—anything heavy enough to kill.

Alyntown. *All* of Alyntown had rallied.

Amara stood atop the command post, surveying the reinforcements like a goddess of war. Hands on hips. A defiant smile on her face.

"You're late," she said.

Rojer crushed another bogling beneath his hammer. "Apologies, Princess. We ran into a traffic jam of angry amphibians. Where do you want us?"

She nodded. "Glad to have you." Her gaze shifted to the guild. "You too, Uncy Sheldon."

Farsmith allowed the barest flicker of a smile. Barely.

Amara's voice rang out, crisp and commanding.

"Engineers, shore up the wall! Lenscrafters, hold the line and burn every wisp you see. Everyone else, grab a weapon and fight for your lives!"

She raised her sword, and her voice became thunder.

"THIS IS OUR CITY. THIS IS OUR WALL. AND THIS...IS WHERE WE MAKE OUR STAND!"

The battle wasn't over.

But for the first time in hours, it felt like we had a chance.

34

Goblins

The timbre of the battle changed in an instant—from chaos and desperation to sudden, electrified purpose. The engineers roared like a forge brought to life. Massive front loaders barreled forward, heaving boulders and debris into the two gaping breaches in the wall. The sound of their engines was like thunder, gritty and relentless.

Catapults behind the wall hurled jagged wall rubble over the top, raining ruin on the remaining scorchjaws and boglings clawing to climb. The impact of each shot echoed like distant avalanches, followed by inhuman shrieks and the crunch of shattered bone and scale.

Then the gates slammed open.

Through them poured a battalion of golems—brass-plated behemoths and advanced constructs—joined by ADs of every size and shape. They flooded the battlefield like a river of metal fury, smashing into the morphed crocs and boglings with bladed limbs, spiked fists, and hydraulic precision. The ground itself trembled beneath their march.

Rojer Varn stood at eye-level with the top of the wall, still embedded in the cockpit of his humanoid war-machine. Too large to fit through the gates, he didn't hesitate. He detached with practiced ease, extracting two massive weapons from inside the mech's ribcage-like core. In one hand, he gripped a hammer shaped like a thunderbolt. In the other, a pair of heavily modified iron tongs—sleek, angular, deadly.

And he wasn't done.

He kept the controller arms of the mech strapped to his shoulders, suspiciously similar to the device he'd created to manage his club foot— the arms an extension of himself now, too. His augmented arm whirred as he turned toward a charging bogling.

The creature leapt for him, shrieking, an overheated shell gleaming like molten tar.

Rojer calmly opened the tongs.

Clang.

He caught the bogling mid-air. It snarled, claws swiping, furious— until Rojer flipped a switch. Spring-loaded blades snapped shut from within the tongs, piercing shell, muscle, and marrow. The creature's shriek choked off instantly as its body went limp.

Rojer shook it off the blades like trash from a shovel.

He strode forward, the air behind him humming with the aftershock of his calm brutality.

Farsmith, Cloud, and Alyntown's latest underworld chief joined the gathering at the wall. Their faces bore soot, blood, and exhaustion, but their eyes blazed with resolve.

"We end this," Amara said, voice flint-hard. "The hags are the source. If they rise again—if they charge those wisps—we're in trouble."

"Any chance they'll retreat?" asked professor Cloud.

"Doubt it," said the princess. "They don't seem to have the will for self-preservation. All that's left is fire and madness."

"How do we kill them?" Rojer asked, hammer resting across his shoulder.

"Rip the mask off," said Amara. "Then drive something frozen straight into the center of their maw. If you can. Bring earplugs. And don't stick around when they die."

"Why?" Farsmith asked, frowning.

"Because they curse the air with their last breath," I said. "And it kills. Quickly."

The G&L guild unleashed another wave of focused beams—blinding flashes, colored bursts, and streaks of purified energy. Bogpyres died in showers of brilliant light.

But the hags weren't done yet. They shrieked again.

Not a sound, but a detonation of hate. Their cry ripped across the field and surged through the ranks of beasts. The enemy howled in unison, a crescendo of madness. One final push.

I gritted my teeth, drew my blades, and opened my perception wide.

Then the world turned upside down.

An explosion, massive and shuddering, ripped through the cavern. Everything stopped. Even the beasts froze—waiting, sensing.

A second of anticipatory silence. Would the explosion bring the cavern down on our heads?

Then screaming ululations began again, rolling down from the castle. I turned to look.

Smoke. Dust. A plume rising from somewhere deep beneath it.

New ululations answered the ones from the castle, louder this time, *closer.*

The ground split in front of us, a long jagged crack cutting across the field like a fresh wound.

From that wound...goblins erupted.

Hundreds. Maybe thousands. Pouring from the earth like ants from a shattered nest. And more raced down the road from the castle, screams harmonizing with those streaming from the crack.

This fight was nowhere near over.

* * *

Inside the castle, he grinned as goblins rushed past him, shrieking through the halls like gleeful demons. None dared touch him. Not one.

His orders were clear—kill the soldiers, leave the servants. They would need bodies to bolster the next wave. And every beast here knew who had given the order.

He avoided the hallways where he could see or hear fighting.

He didn't want to ruin the surprise.

To get to the royal wing, he had to use his new trick a couple of times to sneak past the two knights still standing guard. He'd grown in confidence with the trick, and this was good practice. And if he got caught...so be it, he'd fall back on...conventional methods.

When he reached the elaborately carved door of the royal guest suite, his heart thudded—not with fear, but satisfaction. He'd memorized this door the moment he agreed to help the prime. Now it opened at his touch.

Inside, Malik didn't even glance up.

"You can leave the tea on the side table, Maria," he said, scribbling.

He stepped in and shut the door. Quickly surveyed the room, two other doors to separate bedrooms. He chuckled. These royals lived well.

Malik froze. Slowly looked up.

"Carl," he growled. "What in the core-blighted wards are you doing here? They *know* you down here after that Drumsorrow debacle. You're going to brak this *entire* operation."

Carl chuckled inwardly at Malik's usage of Grounder slang, but he didn't show it on his melted face. "No, I'm not," said Carl. "No one saw me."

"You can't know that."

"I'm a heliurgist. Of course I can," said Carl.

He snapped his fingers, and his flame turned black. Not just dark, a complete absence of light. A void. Shadow incarnate.

"In some ways, I have surpassed even your skills, *teacher*." Carl tired of their one-sided power dynamic.

Malik stared at him, probably wondering how Carl was able to access the field from down here. Probably figuring out. Malik was a lot of things, stupid was not one of them.

"Using your bond to the prime to access the field," Malik said. "Clever."

Carl shrugged. It *was* clever.

"You know what wasn't clever—using an explosive in an *underground* cavern!" Malik said. "What in the holy wards were you thinking? You could have brought it all down."

Carl shrugged again. "A calculated risk. One your Dusker friends didn't expect."

"An unnecessary risk!" Malik snarled. "We *had* the upper hand without you tearing a hole in the castle with that explosive. Now, I'm going to have to fix the mess you created."

"Well," drawled Carl. "*You're* not going to fix it. You'll have your peons do it. You noble Duskers are all alike in that way."

From behind a door came a voice—soft and feminine.

"Dear? Everything alright out there?"

Malik pointed at Carl, then the door.

Carl smiled. Stayed put.

"I'm fine, darling," Malik said, voice syrup-thick.

"Are you sure, Drennic? I thought I heard—"

Carl's grin widened. Now he could leave.

He'd found out Malik's real name. Drennic. He'd heard of Drennic. He wasn't just a trusted ally to the king, he was family.

He gave his former mentor a mock bow and slipped silently from the room.

He had decisions to make.

Back to the surface? Or stay? The Dusker cities were beautiful, untouched, full of opportunities. He could easily take over the identity of someone in the castle. Nobility, if he wanted. Now that he had mastered retaking human form, the waxer side of him could assume another's identity for almost two weeks.

But with his prime-enhanced heliurgist power, he could keep up the illusion indefinitely.

Yes.

Carl walked calmly back into the smoke-choked halls.

It was time to check on his army.

* * *

The entire battlefield shifted again—violently.

With the fresh tide of goblins, the defenders were once more slammed against the edge of desperation. These weren't mindless Murkmire beasts. They were more organized. Intelligent.

They came like a plague.

Our few remaining archers fired furiously from the battlements, but the goblins surged forward with terrifying efficiency. They forced the boglings into shield formations, trudging backward, their blistered shells absorbing arrow and bolt alike. Projectiles ricocheted uselessly from their scorched backs, littering the ground with snapped shafts and broken hope.

Still, the volleys bought us precious time.

Behind us, the engineers wrestled their golems and machines back inside the gates, sweat and soot clinging to their brows. They knew—

we *all* knew—they were our last real hope of plugging the bleeding holes in our defenses.

Then came the engineer's catapults.

Massive stones whistled overhead and slammed into the enemy ranks with bone-crunching force. Where they landed, boglings were flattened or ricocheted into the goblin ranks like spinning destruction, snapping limbs and crushing skulls on impact.

One hundred and forty-one dead. In a single volley.

Not that it mattered.

More goblins spilled from the crack in the earth every second, endless as time.

The goblins redirected the slackjaws to batter our weakest wall segments. Their target: the catapults. They knew. They understood.

The top of the wall turned red with blood. It was barely seven feet high in places—easy for the goblins to scale. They used the corpses of boglings like grotesque stepping stones, clawing over crenellations and slashing down with fury.

Two G&L professors—men who had once judged my entrance exam— dropped in front of me, necks pierced by poisoned darts. I saw militia fall in droves. One moment alive, the next screaming, burning, dying.

I clenched my fists. I wanted to move. I *needed* to. But I had my orders.

Hold this section of the wall—no matter what.

Around me, the command circle was a tightly wound spring. Even Amara's jaw was clenched like iron. Farsmith roared with every shot he fired—"*Die, putrid scum!*"—his beams cleaving through goblins like the wrath of the core itself. Beside him, Professor Cloud moved with fluid elegance, unleashing precise blasts that dropped enemy after enemy.

I'd counted thirty-three kills between them.

Thirty-four.

I was glad they were on our side.

The engineers were just as lethal. Spindle's twin wrist crossbows sang with deadly rhythm, one bolt every three seconds, each one burying itself into a goblin's face with mechanical finality.

Amara, Val, and Renaux openly used core crafting to cover our flanks. The royal cousin, Renaux, had gained the wall in the wake of the other G&L guild members.

Amara's hands glowed with raw power. From her palms flew crystalline shards that found eyes, slid through necks, and dropped enemies mid-leap. Val's mist hardened into instant armor, deflecting arrows and throwing knives with glimmering elegance. Even Renaux—arrogant, smirking Renaux—was fighting like a man possessed, his essentia vapor dancing from elegant teardrop to spear of ice, impaling goblins like kebabs and melting back to mist.

He might be a noble ass, but tonight, he was our ass.

And me? I just stood there. Useless without a ranged weapon.

Until I remembered what Ravic told me once, voice warm with the embers of memory:

"The First Song isn't just a philosophy, boy. It's power—for those with purpose and the will to shape it."

Purpose, I had in spades. What I lacked was knowledge. Faith in that crazy Watcher creed.

I began to sing.

A *Dune Strider* tune—raw, aching, defiant. The first song I sang when I was stuck in those tunnels. The melody felt like scraping rust off my bones. The sound waves flickered to life, weak at first, scattered in the chaos. But when the goblins forced three injured boglings toward us like shields, something inside me snapped.

I sang louder. And this time—I *pushed.*

The wave surged forward.

Sound became force. A *blast* of pressure hurled the boglings and their handlers from the wall like toys tossed by a tantrum. They vanished into the screaming horde below.

My allies stopped fighting, staring at me in stunned silence.

But we didn't have time to be awed.

The goblins broke through on the other side.

I dove into the melee, ceasing my song for fear of knocking allies off the wall. Val flanked my left, his seax slicing across a goblin's face. It fell mid-scream.

A bone-club came down at me. I caught it with my sword and lunged forward, burying my dagger into the goblin's throat. It gurgled, staggered, died.

Another came—leaping, axe overhead.

I pivoted. Fourteen inches to the left. The goblin landed where I'd been, my sword waiting. The blade pierced its ribs and drove through its heart. It spasmed once, then crumpled.

Renaux flowed into the gap I left from killing the goblin. He struck like a duelist—quick, cold, and beautiful. A dagger to the eye. A spin. Another kill.

And then, he turned too far. His body caught my hip in exactly the wrong way.

The world tilted. I tumbled over the wall.

Air rushed past me. Time slowed.

I landed hard on something soft and angry—a goblin, staring up in surprise just as my blade punched through its sternum.

"Finn!" Amara and Val screamed in unison.

I rolled to my feet, heart pounding. Looked up. No way back to my perch. The wall here was deliberately smooth. A defensible command post, now a prison.

I cursed myself. Again. How many times would I underestimate the enemy?

No. Not the enemy. *Renaux.*

The way he'd turned. The force. Too perfect to be chance. I didn't even need Rhee to confirm it for me. And if he'd finally made his move— now, in the middle of battle—it meant he wasn't worried about dying with the rest of us.

He wasn't just a snake. He was *protected* somehow.

Working with the enemy? Had to be. The assassination attempt at the G&L entrance exam. Drake's murder. The way he always seemed one step ahead. I'd suspected it for weeks.

Now I was certain. Little good it did me. I was a fool.

I clenched my jaw. Rage surged through me, hot and clean. He'd pay. *But first...I had to survive.*

I turned, my back to the wall, my blades in hand.

I prepared to face the horde of goblins roaring toward me.

By myself.

35

Salvation

I sucked in a terrified breath and took stock. Nothing broken. Lucky. *Too* lucky.

A horde of hateful yellow eyes turned in my direction. I had only seconds. My back was to the wall, the corpse of the goblin I landed on still twitching at my feet. Only two directions to defend. I could work with that.

But the goblins were smart—*organized*. They came as a pack, not the chaotic wave I was used to. Without Rhee's brutal training, I'd have died in the first breath.

So I shut everything else down.

No thoughts. No fear.

Only survival.

I darted right, fast and low, brushing my dagger hilt against the nearest goblin's arm—indexing—*stab*. My sword punched through its face like paper. Before the corpse dropped, I ducked under a wild swing from another, sidestepped, yanked the attacker's arm forward—and buried my dagger into its eye without even looking.

Two down.

The rhythm took over. The world narrowed to heat, blood, breath, steel.

A sudden blast of heat. Too close. The goblin I'd killed first had masked the approach of a scorchjaw, slithering low like death incarnate. I jumped straight up, boots landing on its snout as its molten jaws snapped closed beneath me with a sickening *crack*. I could feel the heat through my soles—burning, alive.

I adjusted, ready to plunge my blade into its eye, but twin crystal shards struck first. The creature collapsed, lava bleeding from its ruined face. I whispered thanks—to the stars, to Amara, to anything that still gave a damn.

Then the bogling came. Fast. Claws out.

I tried to dodge, but space was gone. My shirt tore, the mail underneath caught. Pain flared across my ribs. I hissed, twisted, used its momentum, kicked up the wall, and brought my sword around in a brutal arc.

The head didn't come clean off, but the message to the goblins was clear.

I didn't plan to go down easy.

I sprinted at the wall, leapt onto the searing shell of a fallen bogling, and reached. Fingers found the ledge—salvation!—until something *latched* onto my ankle and *ripped* me back.

I slammed down hard. Looked up and saw it.

The biggest, ugliest goblin I've ever seen. Taller than the rest, rotted teeth grinning, breath like a corpse pit. My blades snapped into a defensive pyramid just in time. The brute sneered, raised his club, and summoned two friends to finish the job.

I was on my back. No leverage. No escape.

No time.

Then—CRACK.

The weight vanished from my leg.

I blinked and looked up.

Rojer Varn stood over the twitching corpse of the giant goblin, one mechanized leg jammed through its shattered skull. I'd never seen anything so brutal—or beautiful.

He grinned, splattered with orange blood. "I'd never be able to face Dain if I let you die down here, boy."

Together, we butchered everything that came at us—blade and hammer, steel and sweat. The corpses rose around us like a grotesque altar. And that was the problem.

The goblins used the corpses. Climbing. Scaling. A ramp to the wall.

I turned to warn Rojer—when I saw *her*—one of the cinderfen hags.

Her twisted shape floated toward us, mask glowing full of heat and madness.

"Rojer!" I screamed. "Earplugs!"

He reached for a pocket, momentarily taking his eyes from the battle.

The goblin spear came from the side, a blur of black steel. It struck Rojer through the neck. A gurgle. Shock. And then silence as he fell.

Dead. Just like that.

A hundred things I could've done raced through my head. A hundred what ifs. None of them changed the fact that the best man in this battle was lying dead beside me.

My chest went hollow. My brain silent.

Then the hag *screamed.*

I threw up a wall of perception just in time to block the pulse from breaking me. It didn't matter. The tide was too great. My strength was fractured.

Something in me had died with Rojer.

Hope.

Don't you do it, Finn. Rhee's voice echoed in my skull. *Don't you dare give up on me.*

I ignored her. I thought of home. I thought of my parents, of Dawnford. I reached into my pocket and my fingers brushed my grandfather's old watch. The magic inside was long spent, but the *memory* remained.

A time when I was twelve. Arken had just gotten access to his flux. Everyone was so happy for him. Nothing I did in school ever got me that kind of attention. It made me feel invisible.

My mother's voice echoed through time: "Sometimes I wish I was invisible. There's power in not being seen."

I hadn't understood it then. I didn't fully understand it now, but I caught a whiff of it, here at the end. Not being seen had *always* been a boon, as much as I hated it when I was little.

It let me form an identity unbiased by the expectations of others. All Finn.

I began to hum the lullaby she used to sing. Soft. Full of love and pain—as if her love could shield me.

A shield.

I couldn't manipulate light, couldn't push it like I could with sound, but that didn't mean I couldn't counter it. The lullaby I sang became inquisitive.

One last try.

I knew the very moment the light reflected off of me, because the world went dark. I could still hear the goblins racing towards me, but I could no longer see them.

From their yelps of surprise and confusion, they could no longer see me either.

Rhee, I need your eyes.

Dive left, now! Roll! Crawl to your left—feel the wall? Good. Burnt bogling shell on your right—duck under it! Take cover in the burnt out husk of that bogling pyramid.

I moved, singeing my hands on searing husks. Felt guts squelch beneath my palms. But no blade struck me. No claws tore into my back.

I was forced to rely on my other senses. On my perception.

From the energy of the sound waves I knew I had a slight reprieve. The sound waves got me wondering how Rhee could see.

I sang. Softer now. Still hidden in my own void.

Rach, of course. Rach's sensors.

If Rhee could use them, why couldn't I? The signal to her control chip was just energy, wasn't it?

It is, but it won't accept a true Meld, Rhee said. *It's not strong enough. Not yet.*

I'd just have to find that out on my own. I traced the signal to the autonomous device. Traced the chip which allowed her to function. I *linked* to the signal, then traced the current of control, mirrored its energy, enhanced it with my own. Rhee boosted me, and in a breath—I *saw* through Rach's eye.

Goblins blazed red with rage. Allies glowed blue and gold with courage and fear. And beneath the crack—a *rumble.*

Something big. Something...worse?

Then, a buzzing. Familiar. Sharp. *Mechanical.*

My heart skipped. I turned, still *seeing* through Rach's sensors.

A *drill* burst through the ground, pulverizing goblins to paste. Rocks shot from tubes I didn't recognize, spitting death. Mowing goblins down on all sides.

The *Core Drifter* had arrived.

36

Worlds Collide

I didn't recognize the tubes that were firing chunks of stone with terrifying speed. Dain, I realized. He must've followed through on those upgrades he mentioned. Somehow, he'd turned the rock and ore—pulled straight from the intake tubes—into artillery. It was genius. Brutal, beautiful genius. Exactly the kind of engineering Rojer would've loved.

I turned toward what was left of Rojer's body, crushed and twisted in the mud. My throat tightened. He should have seen this.

Dain was going to be shattered when he found out.

The Core Drifter belched out its last payload of stone before its hatch hissed open. Soldiers—fifty-eight by my count—poured from its belly in precise formation. Some wore tunneler gear, but these weren't the gritty, grease-covered types I remembered. Most of these soldiers looked like Grounders, of the trained and lethal sort.

And in the middle of them, like righteous fury wrapped in steel, was Patrice Splitter.

She looked entirely out of place in this madness, but she didn't hesitate. Didn't even blink. Her twin blades whirled as she cut down goblins with terrifying grace. She had gotten better. Much better.

Which probably meant bad things for Dawnford.

She was flanked by a monstrous man, massive, brutal, wielding twin axes with devastating force. I had no choice but to recognize him. It had to be Jay Torsion. He'd grown taller, broader, meaner. Like something out of one of the legends I'd heard of Iron Mike.

And between them, carving goblins with smooth, practiced arcs of her nova blade—*Shea.* My heart caught in my chest.

Their arrival was like lightning jump-starting the heart of our defense. The wall surged with renewed spirit. The gates opened again, and our golems and ADs stormed into the fray, engines roaring, steel limbs flailing.

Then the Drifter did something unexpected—it dove.

Retreating? No. A minute later, it surfaced like a great earthen whale, directly beneath another goblin cluster. Its drill turned them to goo, and the stone-shooters roared again, filled with fresh ammo from the dive.

I didn't hesitate. I jumped back into the chaos, blades flashing alongside the engineers. At one point, I found myself shoulder-to-shoulder with Jay. It felt...*right.* He had become a much better fighter. He didn't have my training, but his sheer strength made up for gaps in skill. We danced through the slaughter, unspoken understanding binding us.

And then, the cavalry truly arrived.

From the castle above, a warhorn bellowed—and a wedge of knights thundered down. At their front rode Draven, grim and gleaming alongside Duke Althar, the steel-clad Duke of the March. They slammed into the last pocket of goblin resistance like vengeance.

The tide broke.

The swamp beasts—slimy, scorched, and staggered—began to fall back, slinking into the darkened forest. I toggled between my perception and Rach's feed high above the canopy. The hags were leaving first. That surprised me. I expected them to drag this out until the last beast burned.

The goblins retreated into the chasm they'd emerged from. I scanned the striations of the stone and easily mapped their tunnels twisting deep below. But no one gave chase. We had nothing left to give.

We were alive. *Barely.*

Smoke and blood hung heavy in the air. I took a long pull from my canteen, then turned toward the Drifter. A shout from the wall made me pause. Amara and Val were scrambling down to meet me. I glanced back—no sign of Renaux. Spindle gave me a weak thumbs-up from where she lay, scorched and already wrapped in bandages from the healer standing over her.

We moved towards the Drifter. We didn't get far before we were intercepted.

"Finn Camlock," Patrice said, gripping my hand in a warrior's handshake, clapping my back hard enough to rattle my ribs. "Didn't think you'd still be breathing."

"Camlock," said Jay with a sharp nod. His eyes flicked toward Val, then landed on Draven. "You've learned to fight," he said, "Like *them.*"

"Where's Arken?" I asked.

Jay's expression darkened. His jaw tightened. "Dead. Like Ronin. Like Raven. Like my father."

The news rocked me back on my heels. My legs went weak. "And my—my father?"

Jay gave a grim nod. "He's chief now."

I staggered, as if the battlefield had tilted under my feet. *My dad... Chief.* A hundred what-ifs crashed into each other behind my eyes.

"And my mother? Dawnford?"

"She's alive," said Shea, stepping forward. "But injured." She wrapped me in a sudden, fierce hug. "We missed you up there. Your ideas, your stubbornness, your attitude." Her voice dropped to a whisper. "*I missed you.*"

She held on longer than she needed to. Her fingers brushed my arm when she let go.

I felt heat behind me and turned. Amara stood just a step away. Her gaze burned through Shea like a blade. For a heartbeat, her mask slipped, pure fury in her eyes. Then the regal princess mask returned, smooth and cold. She stepped closer until her shoulder pressed against mine.

"Thank you," she said to Patrice, giving her a small bow, her voice cool but formal. "Your aid saved this city."

Patrice nodded back. "Princess."

Amara stared at Shea, and the Grounder stared right back. There was no mistaking it this time. Regal fire met Grounder iron. I wasn't exactly sure what was happening, but I felt like I was in trouble for some reason.

Before I could say something incredibly stupid, the Drifters approached, Captain Marek at their lead.

"Seems we owe you our lives," said Amara, smiling brightly. "*Again.*"

Captain Marek winked. "Don't make a habit of it, princess. We were on our way to the kingdom to deliver these folks anyway." She pointed her chin at Patrice. "When Ravic insisted he *heard* something... interesting."

Ravic wrapped his arms around my waist in a firm hug, eyes sparkling. "I *knew* it was you, lad. The moment I heard it. A melody older than memory. A song only whispered about in myth. You and I—" his grip tightened, "—we have *much* to discuss."

Amara, ever alert, turned toward Patrice. "What brings you below, Captain?"

I blinked. *Captain?* I hadn't noticed the insignia stitched to Patrice's shoulder, but Amara had. Of course she had—trained to spot such details in the blood and chaos of war.

Patrice had been promoted. A congratulations sat on the edge of my tongue, but with the news of fallen comrades still fresh, I swallowed it.

Patrice exhaled, exhaustion bleeding from every word. "We came to beg for help. We've been under siege for months." She swept her gaze across the broken battlefield. "I didn't expect it to be this bad down here, too."

Amara's sigh matched hers. "It hasn't always been. But the goblin scourge and their waxer masters are digging in. We'll grant you audience, Captain. It's time to reinforce old alliances with our friends on the surface."

She pivoted sharply. "Lord Stonepath," she said to Draven. "Is the keep secure?"

"For now," he said with a firm nod. "We held, thanks to the efforts of my old crew, and to the timely return of the duke and his forces from the Marches."

"Then let's get off this cursed field. Everyone deserves a hot bath, a clean bed, and a feast fit for heroes."

Amara turned to me and offered her hand. "Finn. Walk with me. I need your counsel."

Part of me wanted to stay—to speak with the Drifters, to ask about *home*, to hear about Dawnford. My parents. Everything I'd been aching to know. But the urgency in her touch said this wasn't just about politics.

I joined her. Heat flared at my other side. I looked—*Shea*. Her glare tracked us like a drawn bowstring. This would be a problem—one I had no capacity to deal with now.

Val fell in behind us. Draven and his knights snapped around, an escort of steel.

Amara leaned close. "Fill me in on the power dynamics of the Grounders," she whispered. "We need to approach this alliance carefully."

I frowned. "We can't use my people as pieces on your game board, Amara. This alliance *has* to go both ways. We all bleed the same against goblins and waxers."

She gave a sideways glance, all steel. "Spoken like a true Grounder prince."

"I'm not a—" I stopped. My father *was* chief now. Which changed nothing. "It doesn't work that way. Not with us. My father being chief doesn't mean I hold power."

Amara stopped mid-step and whirled on me. "But you *do* hold power. Don't be blind to it, Finn. You're the only one with a foot in *both* worlds. That makes you more than a bridge—it makes you leverage. My people *will* see you as powerful, even if yours don't. And I *need* that."

She hesitated, visibly choosing her next words. "And your new status provides other... alliance opportunities."

I blinked. What was she talking about? Oh. Ohhhh. "You mean like...between us?" My voice cracked. It *cracked*. So smooth.

You are so brakking hopeless, Aubrey said.

Thank you for that. You're always there to prop me up.

Amara's tone softened, but her eyes remained sharp. "Yes. Between *us*. Unless you've changed your mind."

I swallowed hard. "No. I haven't. It's just...new. All of it."

She gave me a nod, but it wasn't just acknowledgment. It was a promise. This conversation wasn't over.

* * *

Before any of the political conversations took place, Ravic pulled me aside, practically vibrating with excitement.

"That *song*," he said. "The one you were singing in the battle—tell me more."

"I think I might have been drawing on the power of the First Song." I told him about the hags, learning to use sound to counter. "When I *pushed* out with my perception, the sound, responded. I didn't know it was even possible."

Ravic clapped his hands together like a child receiving a long-awaited gift. "Yes! It is possible! But no one's believed it for generations. They thought only the earth could sing the Great Songs. But *you*—you've done it! Just like the legends claimed about Master Hollowborn, the first Watcher."

He stepped back, gripping his mustache. "But that wasn't the song I heard."

I tilted my head. "What do you mean?"

"The one I heard when I turned the Drifter in your direction—it was something else. Something I've *never* heard. Not in all my years."

"Do you think it's the Last Song?" I asked. I told him about the experiments I had been doing with light, then called Rach over and showed him the optical image we'd recorded—the strange starburst symbol in the sphere which we couldn't decipher.

Ravic stared at the projection for a long time. Too long.

He went pale. "Oh no."

"What?" I demanded. "You think I got it wrong? It's not the Last Song?"

He shook his head again. "No, I think you were right. That's the problem. If the Last Song is showing us this, we might be in much bigger trouble than I imagined."

"And you're getting all of that from that one image? What are you seeing that I'm not."

Ravic gulped. "I believe the projection is an image of the core."

I frowned. "The core of what?"

"The core of the planet," he said. "And I believe the Last Song is telling us the core has been fractured. That's what the starbust from the center is."

"If the core is fractured, the planet is going to die—and kill all of us along with it."

This is the end of book 2

Exclusive Prequel Short Story

Didn't quite get your fill of the post-apocalyptic world of Ashara?

The prequel story dives into a tumultuous month in the life of Finn's father, Denis Camlock when he was Finn's age. Learn more about the nova-field, nova flux, and the grid which protects the Grounders of Dawnford. It's the same story shared in the first book, so if you already downloaded it, don't worry about getting it again.

Sign up for the newsletter, and I'll shoot you the exclusive short story ASAP!

Thanks for reading!
   -Sean

Thank you!

Thank you so much for diving into *The Embers Below*! I hope you enjoyed following Finn's adventures as much as I loved bringing them to life. If his journey sparked your imagination, I'd be thrilled if you could share your thoughts with a review on Amazon.

Your feedback isn't just fuel for future stories — it's the spark that keeps the adventure alive and growing. Reviews help me fine-tune what you love and make the next chapter even more exciting. It also makes writing a lot more fun when I know what people think of my work! Thank you for being part of the journey.

Newsletter and Facebook

If you would like me to notify you when the next book is released, or get some fun extras, please sign up for my newsletter or Facebook author page.

About the Author

Sean graduated with a bachelor's degree in physics and did absolutely nothing with it. He became a coder, an entrepreneur and now a writer. He lives in Colorado with his beautiful wife, a ski-racing, softball spin master of a younger daughter, an old rescue dog with a napoleon complex, and a neurotic German shepherd whose love language is ball. He misses having his older daughter filling the house with sax riffs and spanish soliloquies, but the siren's call of a California education proved too strong.

When Sean's not writing, you can find him outside wandering around looking for inspiration or tracking down the perfect scoop of ice cream.

You can connect with me on:

🌐 https://seanhkennedy.com

f https://www.facebook.com/profile.php?id=61552008412362

Subscribe to my newsletter:

✉ https://subscribepage.io/XlgsQy

Also by Sean Kennedy

The Evolution Trials:

Join Kavi Stonecrest and his band of misfits as they face down quests, gods, and even the powerful Ancients which shaped the world of Grendar. A rousing fantasy adventure with more mature themes and language than *The Fire Within*.

The Evolution Trials:
   Ghost Squad
   Heretic Squad
   First Wave
   Extinction

The Ashen Legacy:
   The Fire Within
   The Embers Below